Do Your Worst

GEMMA BROOKS

For the girl who never left the farm

AUTHOR'S NOTE

This series is, in many ways, a love letter to the kinds of Thoroughbred breeding and training farms that I lived and worked on growing up in Florida. I did, however, take many creative liberties throughout the book, ultimately developing my own alternate version of the region and related organizations rather than trying to match the setting to any specific real-world counterpart. If you are familiar with the industry, I hope you will forgive my tweaks for the sake of story.

Please note there is mention of off-page animal death and a brief depiction of potential animal injury; there is no animal abuse or illness in this book.

No one could say I didn't warn him.

The day Mark Aladyne steered his pickup truck down my driveway to take me on our first date, I was waiting on the front porch of the small cottage I rented on my parents' Thoroughbred farm. It was cold—nearly real cold, not just Florida cold—but the sharp air felt good against my flushed skin. My body seemed to have a lot of feelings about this life choice, and I couldn't say I blamed it.

Not even when Mark stepped out of his truck looking like a goddamn model. He had always known how to put an outfit together, and that day was no different. The simple dress shirt he wore had to have been tailored to hug his body that close, and I had no doubt his black jeans would make his ass look infuriatingly good whenever I got a chance to look. His hair was disheveled, but in a cute way that suggested he'd been messing with it on the drive over, and his coat just barely toed the right line of pretentiously fashionable.

It all worked on me to a genuinely annoying degree.

So when he stepped up onto the porch, that crooked smile of his practically dripping with smugness, I didn't settle for saying hi. "You're going to regret this," I said instead.

The smugness shifted into delighted amusement, like he was watching a puppy bark at its reflection for the first time. "I seriously doubt that," he said, his voice resonant with certainty. "There are a lot of things I regret, Songbird. Spending time with you has never been among them."

That fucking nickname. I let him call me that in a post-orgasmic haze one time and now I couldn't get rid of it.

I didn't scoff as he leaned in to brush a kiss against my lips, chaste and sweet despite my attempts to deepen it, and I didn't even swat his hand away as he pressed against my lower back to guide me to the truck, because I was a model of restraint. When I reached for the door, he pulled me back against his chest. "This is a date, Lark. Let me be a gentleman."

His words were a warm caress on my skin, and I pressed my hips to his with enough pressure to tease him. "I like you better when you aren't so worried about etiquette."

The hitch in his breath as he opened the door told me he wasn't immune to my advance. "Plenty of time for that later."

Settling myself in the passenger seat, I reached over to lightly run my fingers through his hair. He had the kind of natural highlights from working in the sun that most people paid hundreds of dollars to get, and I loved seeing the different shades catch the light. "Promise?"

That crooked grin was back, but it had a glint of mischief to it this time. "I guess it depends on if I'm the kind of guy who puts out on the first date."

I rolled my eyes and tried not to think too hard about the fact that I let him talk me into an honest-to-god date. I'd been fighting this for over a year, my breakup with Gabriel having proven to me that no one will put me and my career first except for me. I did a damn good job of steering clear of anything with even the slightest potential to become serious.

Until Mark.

He had a whole day planned, and the knot in the pit of my stomach pulled tighter as the hours passed. Mark remembered little things I let drop in the few scattered moments of conversation I allowed before and after our encounters, and he built the day around them. Lunch at my favorite pizza place. Meandering around Silver Springs because I was sick the day my class went there on a field trip in fourth grade. A visit to a museum exhibit I wanted to see—that one, I didn't know how he had figured out—followed by dinner in a restaurant owned by one of our mutual acquaintances.

It was all just so aggressively *pleasant.* His eyes lit up anytime he made me laugh, and they grew serious and thoughtful when I explained what I liked about the art. He gently corrected the waiter when my meal came out wrong, even though I would have eaten it anyway, and he deferred to me when it came to the wine selection. When I chose a red simply because I knew he preferred white, he just gave me that grin again and I swore I felt it in my freaking bone marrow.

I was buzzing a bit from the wine by the time dinner ended, and I leapt at the chance to go visit Aladyne Stud, Mark's parents' farm, when he offered. It was the first time I would be on the property without the excuse of one of his family's famous parties, because Mark came to me whenever we hooked up. It was simpler that way. But I liked seeing other farms at night, when all was quiet and still. It was when they felt safest.

Mark's truck rumbled happily through the dark as he drove past the main barns and deep into the back of the farm. I protested, because it was foaling season and I lived to coo over a baby horse, but Mark shushed me. "I want to show you something," he said.

He drove a little further, getting out once to open a gate, before stopping in the middle of a field, near a large oak tree. He cut the truck engine, plunging us into silence. I knew it wasn't true, but in the dark I could pretend we were miles from any other humans. All that was left were the crickets and the occasional huff of a horse grazing in the distance.

I let him help me out of the truck without protest. I wanted to be close to him, to feel the steady beat of his heart next to my own. This was the longest we had ever been around each other without orgasms involved, and my body was going through withdrawal.

Once he shut the door behind me, I leaned back, tugging on the lapels of his jacket. I stood on my tip-toes—he was just tall enough to make me do that, damn him—and moaned softly as I tasted his lips. I strained to bring our bodies even closer, but he took a half-step back, breaking the kiss. "You don't have to be a gentleman anymore," I pouted.

"Soon," he promised. He had more self-control than I expected, and it made me grumpy. "Come with me."

He wrapped his hand around mine and led me in the direction of the tree. The grass was dense, though it had been cut recently, and sticks and broken branches littered our path, but Mark was always there to catch me when my footing stumbled.

When he came to a halt, I glanced around, confused. He grinned. "Look up."

I lifted my eyes above me, a soft glow of light appearing overhead to supplement the dim moonlight, but it still took a long moment to parse what I was seeing. When I finally did, I laughed. "A treehouse?"

My delight delighted him. He motioned to the slats of wood nailed into the tree trunk. "After you."

"Is it safe?" I didn't exactly want to end the night by falling out of a tree. Or with a splinter.

He smacked my ass. "Just climb."

Well, okay then. I did as he said, taking my time with each step of the makeshift ladder. The structure was built into the strong, sloping limbs of the tree, and when I emerged onto the floor, I realized my worries about splinters were for naught. The floor was completely finished, and half the space had walls and a roof, while the other half was open. A pile of blankets sat on the enclosed side, while a lantern and a few other items sat on the other. It was tall enough for me to stand straight up, my head just skimming the roof, which left Mark to hunch a little when he came up to join me.

I shifted over toward the blankets, sitting down and stretching my legs out in front of me. "This is amazing."

He crouched in front of me, his gaze unexpectedly shy. "Yeah? You like it?"

I did. But I worried if I told him how much, it would send the wrong signal, so I went for a joke instead. "I bet this is where you bring all the girls."

The tilt of his head told me his answer before he spoke. "No. Just you, Lark."

"Well," I said, determined not to process that information, "shall we make you glad you brought me here?"

He might have wanted to hesitate longer, but I didn't give him the chance. Leaning forward, I kissed him, tugging his shirt free from his pants to slide my hands underneath and find his bare skin. This time, he was the one who moaned, parting my lips with his tongue and pushing me down onto my back.

I traced my fingernails up and down his back as our tongues danced together. Then his mouth left mine, his lips exploring my neck and my chest as his fingers found the hem of my dress and started crawling up my thighs. He moved slowly, deliberately, and for once, I decided not to rush.

He froze the moment his fingers slipped from stockings to skin. "What are you wearing under here?" he murmured.

I lifted my hips to let him take my dress all the way off. It has been too cold out to go bare-legged, but I was not above ensuring easy access, should he have been inclined. Thigh-highs and garters had been a fair compromise, and it was paying off now.

Lying there in just my underwear and tights, I grinned at him. "And here I thought you'd have taken a peek while I was climbing up the ladder."

Mark leaned down, kissing my thigh right at the lacy border of my tights. "I was still trying to behave. Clearly that was a mistake."

"Then maybe you should be making up for lost time."

He didn't make me wait any longer. We knew each other's bodies well by then, and his fingers teased me through the fabric of my panties as his mouth found the sensitive spot by my collarbone that always sent shivers running through me. I tugged my bra down, freeing my breasts so he could play with them, his tongue working over my already firm nipples.

I wrapped my legs around his waist and he sat up, leaving me to hiss in his ear as I straddled his lap, settling myself over the fullness of his erection. He groaned with pleasure when I began to grind against him, and I matched it with one of my own as he seized one of my nipples with his teeth, pulling gently.

We had done this enough I knew the next steps. He'd make me come, his fingers and mouth working my most sensitive areas, and I'd take him in my mouth until he was ready to burst. Then he'd fuck me until neither of us could stand it anymore. Sometimes the details varied—the order, the location, maybe a toy or two for some added fun—but that was how it worked with us.

And it worked damn well.

But he changed the routine on me. After the initial flurry of touches, it was like he remembered something important. He didn't meet my rough frenzy with his own. Each time I tried to speed things up, or throw in a little dirty talk, he slowed things down and spoke in soft, gentle tones.

I knew then, but I needed the release so badly I let my body get ahead of my brain. His kisses turned soft and romantic, his touch became a series of caresses, and even when he finally slid inside me, his strokes were steady and intentional.

The simple truth was: in the moment, it felt amazing. I had fucked my share of guys, and my ex had even gone so far as to look me in the eye mid-thrust and declare that he was making love to me once, but this was the first time I actually felt cherished and special. My orgasm was softer than I was used to, but I felt it down to the tips of my toes in long, wonderful waves.

I could have stayed in blissful, chosen ignorance of what it meant, but Mark had to go and ruin it. He embraced me afterward, his hand on my stomach, my body spooned inside his. His nose brushed against my cheek, my body warm every place he had touched despite the winter air.

"I love you, Lark."

Some ungodly large percentage of the population would have loved nothing more than to hear those words from a man like Mark Aladyne. For a few heartbeats, I wondered if I could be one of them. But I knew all too well what letting him love me would mean: he and I like this, every night. No more making my own decisions, based off of nothing other than what I need most. My choices would be *our* choices, and what I did would matter to him. Worse, what he did would matter to me.

I wasn't opposed to that in theory, but the business I never wanted to start was still in its infancy. For the first time, I had my own clients. I had horses in my care—*solely* in my care. I couldn't afford to get lost in someone else when I needed every ounce of myself to make it work.

When someone loved you, they expected you to love them back. And I wasn't in a place to give anyone that right now.

I sat up, immediately searching for my clothes. He watched as I pulled my dress back on, hurt already in his eyes, and I held out his pants. "Get dressed," I whispered. "I'd like you to take me home."

"Lark." My name was a plea. "Talk to me."

"Take me home. Please."

His face settled into a calm mask, the one he wore when speaking to clients he didn't really like, and I hated, *hated* that I had let myself get so careless with my boundaries that I knew that much about him. We were silent the entire drive, and I had the door open before he put the truck in park. I had to get inside before I started to cry, because Mark was as stubborn as they came.

If he thought I was anything other than a frigid bitch, he'd never let me go.

"Goddamnit, Lark. Wait!"

I fumbled getting the key into the lock on my front door, which gave him time to catch up to me. He reached out, but I jerked away before he could make contact. "I'm sorry, Mark. I did try to warn you."

"I don't need you to say it back, Lark. I just need you to *know*."

I finally got the lock open, but made the mistake of looking over at him. The mask was gone, his face full of pain and confusion. I crumbled inside, but knew I couldn't back down. "I don't—" I hurried to correct myself, knowing it was better to leave him without hope. "I *can't* love you. I can't. It was fine when it was just sex, and the date was sweet. But this...this isn't what I want. It's over, Mark." I looked away, choking on my own words, even if they were all true. "I really am sorry."

"I don't regret being honest with you." Mark's ragged voice pulled me back, his gaze a vivisection to the very heart of me. He reached past me, opening the door. Giving me one more chance.

When I stepped inside and out of his reach, he nodded. Heartache and acceptance and sheer determination all warred for dominance on his face. "I'll never regret tonight, Songbird. But one day, you'll wish you had let me in."

I waited to shut the door until he walked back down the driveway, started his truck, and drove away. I waited until I had fought back any tears that threatened to fall, any sobs that wanted to pull themselves from my chest. I waited until my mind was as numb as my body was from the cold.

And then I shut the door on any chance I'd ever regret saying goodbye to Mark Aladyne.

CHAPTER 1

LARK

There's something to be said for a day that tells you it's going to suck from the jump.

It's barely six in the morning, and I've already spilled my entire cup of coffee onto my favorite pair of jeans, jumped my truck because the freaking window motor drained the battery again, and absorbed a text from my most annoying—but most potentially lucrative—client declaring that he wants his best horse scratched from the sale.

I'm also pretty sure I hit a squirrel on the drive to the sales grounds, though I'm trying not to think too much about that one. Poor squirrel.

My small truck is practically a matchbox car in comparison to the massive duallies parked in the lot already, but with the way this day is going, it's just nice to know I have options if someone needs to tow my ass out of here later. I pull into a spot as close to my assigned barn as I can get, for what little good that does. It'll be a hike regardless.

I've done this dance before—I've been working the local Thoroughbred sales since I was in middle school. The sales grounds are as familiar to me as my own home, the peculiar combination of blue-collar workers and filthy-rich racehorse owners and gorgeous, marginally unhinged animals comforting despite my nerves. If it were any other year, I wouldn't be nervous.

But this year is different. This year, for the first time, I have my own consignment. My own horses in the sale. I'm not working for my parents. I am the boss.

It's not something I ever planned, and it's scary as hell.

I'm doing it anyway.

I grab my barn sign with one hand and tuck a stack of buckets under my other arm, then hurry off to the main office. The sales company insists on hanging the barn signs themselves, undoubtedly for insurance liability reasons, and I didn't have time to pick mine up from the painter until yesterday.

By the time I reach the office, I'm sweating enough to wonder once again why anyone thought doing this sale in August in Florida was a good idea. People fantasize about moving it to September or October, but so far, we've all been left to suffer. The air conditioning is a welcome respite when I step inside, even as I realize too late that I should have dropped the buckets by the barn first. Now I'm navigating narrow doorways with absolutely zero extra clearance, but I'm too committed to back down. As far as everyone in this office knows, these buckets belong right here and nowhere else.

My first lucky break of the day comes when I find Miss Betty settling in behind the counter. She beams as I walk up, her deep brown skin wrinkling far less than it should at her age as she greets me with a smile. "Lark Reynolds! If you aren't a ray of sunshine this early in the morning."

"I don't know if I'd go that far, but I'm glad to see you, too."

"What can I do you for, my dear?" She pulls a pair of

reading glasses out and sets them on the tip of her nose, completing her look as the all-knowing office manager she is. When I was a kid going through my shy phase, Miss Betty would always quietly sneak me a piece of candy while I hid behind my dad's legs. She never tried to make me talk, just said hello and made sure I had a treat. I haven't wavered in my loyalty to her since.

"I need to drop off my barn sign. I know I'm a little late, but I was hoping we could get it up soon?"

Miss Betty narrows her eyes. "Don't use that smile on me, child. You know I'll help if I can." She turns her attention to the computer in front of her. "Which barn is Landow in this time?"

"Oh." I suddenly long for the days when I could unwrap my candy and stay silent. I'm just now realizing that this will be an ongoing confusion, and wonder how many times I'll have this conversation over the next couple weeks. "I'm on my own this time, actually. Barn 32."

"Well, if that isn't the best news I've heard all day."

"It's 6:23 in the morning, Miss Betty."

"I never said it was a high bar, dear."

Damn. Burned by a grandmother. Add it to the day's tally.

"I also need to scratch hip 492," I say with a heavy sigh. "Owned by Jack Nugent." That colt would have paid my bills for the next six months if he sold for as much as he was supposed to, but his owner has the right to scratch him. My contract ensures I'll still get paid for my prep time, but I wanted to bring the colt here—not just for my percentage of the sale price, but so people can see that I know my way around a quality horse.

Miss Betty slides me a caramel. "You deserve that, if you're working with Mr. Nugent." I sign the form she hands me next, keeping my sigh inside. "The scratch will be entered by the end of the day. Hand over the sign, and I'll get

Darren to put yours up ASAP. He can't resist my feminine wiles."

"Who amongst us could?" I ask with a wink, setting the sign on the counter. I pop the candy in my mouth and hoist my buckets once more, stepping back out into the wall of humidity.

Barn 32 is tucked away in the back of the sales grounds, about as far from the front office as possible. I duck my head and settle in for the trek ahead, but I should have known better. Within the first thirty feet, I have to stop and chat with a groom who used to work for my parents back when I was a small child; he makes a big deal out of the fact that my hair is less curly than it used to be. Another forty feet brings me to one of the trainers who works locally; she brings up the time I tripped and fell directly into a mud puddle when I was twelve. Twenty feet after *that*, I am drawn into a one-armed hug by one of my mother's best friends; she tells me how proud she is that I am on my own this time.

I'd love to know how Mom handled *that* conversation.

This is the reality of having grown up in this business. I know everyone, and everyone knows me. When it comes to the locals, anyway—I don't have to worry about the teams from Saudi Arabia having embarrassing stories about me as a kid.

Mostly.

I hope that being known in the community will make transitioning into my own consignment easier. But everyone here knows me first and foremost as my parents' kid, and I'm not sure that's an association I'm going to be able to escape anytime soon.

Especially when, another few steps later, it's my mother who catches me. "There you are!" she calls, her voice disproportionately loud for the relative quiet of the morning.

"Hey, Mom." My mother is the type of person who could

be outside in the summer heat, surrounded by horses, and have neither a speck of dirt nor a hair out of place to show for it. Case in point: right now, her hair is pulled up into a fancy braid—that skill has definitely skipped a generation, because all I can manage is a ponytail I have to reset at least five times a day—and she's wearing a button-down in the royal purple of Landow Thoroughbreds that's tucked into pants that ride a perfect line between dress slacks and jeans. She looks immaculate, while I look barely human. "You're here early."

She scoffs. "Not all of us like to scurry in at the last moment."

The arm holding my buckets clenches so tight I'm worried for the integrity of the plastic, but I keep my expression calm. "I'm perfectly capable of keeping my own schedule."

"Mm." Mom won't go so far as to overtly insult me—not when there are so many people around—but the skepticism is evident in her little hum of acknowledgement. "Are you sure you're ready for this?"

It's a question that could be interpreted as supportive—a mother making sure her daughter has what she needs on a day that marks a major career milestone. But the only reason I'm wearing robin's egg blue instead of the colors of Landow is because my parents made it clear they think I'm not good enough to have any sort of leadership position on their farm.

"Yep." I keep my tone breezy, like the doubt in her voice doesn't sting. "It's not like I have a choice."

If I thought that might make her feel a hint of remorse, I am immediately proven wrong. "Just remember, don't pull Landow into your mess when things go wrong."

"I would never dream of it." Ever since my parents took over ownership of Landow Thoroughbreds from the farm's founders—the *actual* Landows, who have since retired to somewhere on the Italian coast—they have been fiercely protective of the farm's name and reputation. It was made very clear to me that my consignment could not expect any support from the Landow brand.

Which is fine by me. I intend to succeed or fail entirely on my own. No name-dropping required.

"I'll see you later, Mom."

"Be at the house for dinner next Saturday," she says, before effectively dismissing me. She cheerily greets an approaching acquaintance, and I speedwalk the rest of the way to my barn. I shake off the encounter as I step into the raked dirt of the barn aisle, my shoulders relaxing now that I'm inside. I have four stalls assigned to me at the northern end of the barn: three for the horses, one for my supplies. With ten horses in the sale—nine now, I suppose—I'll be swapping head in and out over the next two weeks. It's the only way the grounds can manage the sheer number of horses that need to be processed. Some of the bigger farms, like Landow, get closer to a one-to-one number, but my fledgling operation is a long way from meriting that kind of affordance.

I duck into the stall I've designated as my feed room, grateful to finally be setting the buckets down. My arm has basically become a glorified noodle, and the whole stack clatters to the floor as my strength gives out at long last. I cringe at the noise, murmuring apologies to no one under my breath. I haven't had time to research who has the stalls next to me, but I don't want them to start out hating me.

"You sound like you need this." Alicia steps into the stall, holding a coffee out to me. Her pink braids are a burst of joy in this wild day. "God knows it's too damn early to be at work."

Alicia Parks is short and sturdily built, the kind of woman who could stand firm in a hurricane. She's worked on horse farms and race tracks her whole life, bouncing from California to Kentucky to Florida as an exercise rider and farm hand. At the end of the month, she'll be heading up to New York to work Belmont's fall meet, but she agreed to serve as my backup during the sale.

God knows I'll need it. And the coffee she comes with.

"If you want to sleep in, you're in the wrong line of work entirely."

She sighs. "Yeah, you're right. Can I quit?"

"No."

"I was afraid of that. Shall we?"

We spend the morning getting my truck unloaded and readying the stalls for their occupants. My first three horses are scheduled to ship in at noon, so we have to get everything in place before then. We over-fill the stalls with shavings, because shavings have a tendency to magically evaporate, and deliver all the buckets I carried in to their proper homes. We attach fans and misters to the stall doors, and then set up some in the grass in front of our small section of barn, too, so that prospective buyers will have a break from the heat when they come by. The tent we put up nearly kills both of us on more than one occasion, but eventually I am reasonably convinced it's attached to the ground with some level of security.

The last thing I want is to be the person whose tent blows away during the inevitable afternoon thunderstorms.

By 11:30, our space has been transformed. It isn't as fancy as some of the other farms—not even close—but our area is comfortable and neat. That's enough.

"Lunch," I declare once we finish setting up a folding table under the tent. "We need to eat before the horses show up."

As Alicia and I scarf down sandwiches in the feed room, I scroll through my notifications to see what I missed while we were busy. For the most part, everything at the barn I work out of should be set to carry on without me. I got up before four this morning to bring the horses in, feed them their first meal, and make sure there had been no disasters overnight. Maria, the barn manager who charges me slightly less than the cost of a human soul for my barn and paddock space, has promised to keep an eye on them throughout the day. It's my farrier and friend Gideon, though, who is on track to be the biggest lifesaver. He's offered to swing by to feed and turn out in the evenings, which saves me from driving nearly an hour out of my way each night to do it myself.

I basically owe him my first born.

Luckily, the only new drama waiting for me on my phone is one I can handle.

DAPHNE

Remind me when the sale ends and I can be the one in crisis again?

I snort, knowing I brought this on myself.

ME

The sale hasn't even started yet, technically. You've got two weeks to be the capable one.

My best friend, Daphne, has solemnly sworn that she will have neither a personal nor professional crisis for the entirety of the sale so that I can spiral as much as I need to. It's her way of showing up for me even though she is currently living and working in Vancouver. But the truth is, Daphne has spent the years since she left this town in a perpetual state of low-grade existential crisis, so two drama-free weeks will be a challenge.

DAPHNE

Shit.

Okay. Never mind. Pretend I didn't say anything. I'm totally fine and definitely not in the middle of a romantic dilemma.

I check the time, then press the button to call my ridiculous friend. "You have five minutes," I inform her once she answers.

"Oh, thank goodness." Daphne's voice is a welcome sound today. I miss her, but made peace long ago with the fact that she isn't ever moving back. "That guy Stefan asked me out and I don't know what to do."

"Do you want to go out with him?"

"I don't know!"

"You're the one who told me anything less than yes is a no, Daffy."

"But he's so hot and so kind. And so rich. Like borderline unethical rich. But also hot. Stupid hot."

"So you like him."

"Not like that. I don't think."

"I don't know what to do with the words you're saying right now."

"Exactly!" Her voice peaks from exasperation before she sighs. "I know this doesn't make any sense. I should just say yes. A hot, rich, *good* man asked me out. I just don't feel anything when I think about him, you know? This guy is a freaking 1200 on a scale of 10, and all I felt when he asked me out was a general malaise."

"Then say no. You can't force yourself to like him. Give him my number instead."

"Absolutely not. You'd destroy him." I'd take offense, but she's not wrong. It's not safe for a man like Stefan to take a shot with me. The last one who tried learned that the hard way. "I'm sorry, I'm the worst," Daphne declares, changing the subject. "How are things going with you?"

Alicia puts what's left of our food in the cooler while I grab a couple lead ropes, and we head out. We have to get going if we want to meet the transporter when they arrive with the first set of horses. "This morning was a shit show, but the day is looking up."

I pause at the end of the barn when I see that the barn signs are going up. The signs for the southern half of the barn are familiar: KLS Consignment and Found Paradise Farms, both mid-sized operations with good reputations. I won't interact with them much, because these barns are built without a middle aisle, but I feel a flush of pleasure knowing they'll be nearby.

As I watch, a man who must be Darren moves his ladder and climbs to add another sign. I let myself revel in the moment as he hangs the sign for Lark Sales. The design is simple: wood carved into the shape of a flying bird, painted my chosen eggshell blue, with the company name scrawled in white script along the body. The fact that it's simple doesn't matter so much as the fact that it's *mine*, and a spark of begrudging pride burns inside my chest when I see it hang alongside the other, more established farms.

For the first time, this forced endeavor of mine feels utterly, terrifyingly real.

In my ear, Daphne is giving me an ongoing pep talk, telling me how amazing I am and that the sale is going to be great. Darren reaches for the last sign, and the blood begins to drain from my face before I even fully process what I'm seeing. "I've gotta go," I mutter absently, dropping my phone to my side as I recognize the sign going up next to mine—the sign for the farm it will be impossible to avoid for the next two weeks. The one I share an aisle with, the one whose stalls will be next to mine.

I blink, hoping maybe I'm hallucinating, but the name remains: Aladyne Stud.

Turns out the day could get worse after all.

My gaze falls from the sign, but it doesn't have far to go. He stands halfway down the aisle, his hands tucked into his jean pockets as he rests against a stall door, chatting casually with someone wearing an all-too-familiar shade of red.

The man I haven't seen in six months.

The man who told me he loved me before I slammed the door in his face.

The man I swore I'd never talk to again.

Mark fucking Aladyne.

As if he can tell I'm watching, he looks up, a knowing smirk crossing his face as we lock eyes. The familiar curve of his lips makes my stomach lurch, like my body doesn't understand why we're staying still when he's right there.

He's *right there*. And he will be for the next two weeks.

As I try to get a handle on the emotions that are threatening to drown me alive, my phone buzzes in my hand with what is undoubtedly a text from my transporter. It's a well-timed reminder that it doesn't actually matter if Mark's here or not. This sale has nothing to do with him and everything to do with my career.

But before I can tear myself away, Mark pulls one hand free and fucking *salutes* me before returning his attention to whoever he's talking to, breaking the eye contact that had kept me frozen in place. His nonchalance after the intensity of our last interaction spikes a fury I can barely control, but I force myself to use it as motivation instead. I spin on my heel and get back to work.

Mark Aladyne can get bent. I have horses to sell.

CHAPTER 2

MARK

I thought I had braced myself to see Lark again, but the moment I lay eyes on her, it feels like I'm an asteroid being pulled straight into the sun.

She's an utter mess. Small blonde hairs frizz in a halo around her forehead. A smear of dirt sits across her cheek. Her shirt is covered in sweat stains. I have no doubt there is horse shit on her boots. The expression on her face as she looks at me draws from a deep well of murderous intent.

And it takes every ounce of stubborn will I have to keep myself from storming over to kiss her.

I think she's going to pop a blood vessel when I salute her. Pulling my focus back to my conversation with Javier requires Herculean levels of strength, despite the fact that Javi has worked for Aladyne longer than I've been alive and I genuinely enjoy hearing about his family. But even as I laugh at a story about his granddaughter, I don't miss the way Lark stomps off with both her anger and her pink-haired employee in tow.

Fuck, but I missed her.

I've replayed our date in my mind every day for the past

six months, and I have arrived at the conclusion that Lark was, quite simply, wrong. I don't regret anything that happened that night. It was a perfect date. The sex was next-level good. Was I hurt and disappointed that she shut down the moment I told her how I felt? Yes. But she needed to hear it.

The one thing I'll never do is pretend not to be in love with Lark Reynolds.

And if the way her body went still as stone when she laid eyes on me just now was any indication, she's as wrapped up in all of this as I am. I have no doubt she continues to be in denial about having feelings for me, but she certainly isn't indifferent.

That's enough to start.

Assuming my sister doesn't kill me before I can make my move. The moment I finish chatting with Javi, Maddie appears at my side, her eyes narrow. "A word?"

I dutifully allow her to drag me to the end of the barn, because a lifetime with my twin has taught me it all works better if I just let her yell at me. We cross our arms and face off. "Out with it," I order.

"I'll take over the sale. You can run the farm."

I roll my eyes. "I'm not leaving."

"I'm not judging you, okay?" It sounds like she's judging me. "But we both know she's going to haunt your useless ass."

"I've been looking forward to being haunted," I admit.

Maddie's expression flips from protective to exasperated. "You *knew?*" When I raise a shoulder, she takes a slow breath. "If you tell me you arranged this, I will kick you in the nuts."

"I didn't arrange anything."

"I don't believe you."

The grin on my face isn't wise, because my sister's threats

of violence are always sincere, but I am damn pleased with the way things worked out. "So distrusting."

"This is a stupid idea, Mark."

She's not wrong. "You can say *I told you so* when it all blows up in my face."

"I absolutely will." My sister frowns, her frustration fading to concern. "She fucked you up once. I don't like the idea of it happening again."

"Mads." I wait for her to give me her full attention, because she needs to hear what I'm about to say. "I was the one who changed the rules. Not Lark. What happened between us is on me. Promise me you won't take it out on her. This sale matters too much for her to have to worry about hostility from our side of the barn." Off her doubtful frown, I repeat, "Promise me."

She gives me the look she's been specializing in our whole lives, the one that says she's older than me by a full twenty-one minutes and she plans to use every inch of authority it allows her, before finally relenting. "Fine. I promise. But I'm not helping with whatever stupid plan you have, either. I can't in good conscience support the constant rhyming."

The fact that our names rhyme is my favorite part, but I seem to be alone in that opinion. "Understood."

Maddie shakes her head one more time before heading off to the sales office to finish sorting out some paperwork issue, and I rest against the railing, watching her go. The truth is, I have no idea what I'm doing. I still love Lark, but I haven't figured out how to find an opening in the walls she's built.

If I'm lucky, two weeks of forced proximity will help. If I'm not, haunting is going to be the least of my problems.

As much as I want to wait for Lark to return, it's not in the cards. Javi and his team have the barn set-up well in hand, so I set out to find Bowen. I'm borderline shocked to see him engaging with conversation with a woman, even once I get close enough to see she's handing him a business card.

He breaks away when he sees me coming, and tolerates the bro hug I pull him into. "What was that about?" I ask, grabbing the business card out of his hand. Bowen's been my best friend—mostly against his will—for years now. He *never* talks to people of his own volition. "Realtor? You best not be planning to sell your place."

"The opposite, actually." He runs a hand through his hair, visibly uncomfortable. "Thinking about expanding a little."

"Damn. Didn't know that was even an option." Bowen's moms have a small stretch of land that's just a step above a hobby farm. He's taken on more responsibility lately as his moms have started to travel, and he's done well with keeping it afloat. But there's a world of difference between maintaining and expanding. "I'm impressed, man."

He shrugs. "The last section of the old Wyndham place may be coming up for sale, and I don't want let it go to a developer."

"Can't say I disagree." I do what I can to keep the wariness out of my voice. If he wants to pretend we don't both know why he wants that particular piece of property, I'm not going to be the one to bring it up. But I *can* bring up some other shit. "How'd that date go the other night?"

"It didn't." Bowen doesn't give me a chance to press for details. "How's working in the same barn as the woman who rejected you?"

I grin. "She stomped away the moment she laid eyes on me."

"Smart woman."

"She'll come around." I say it with more confidence than I feel. *Manifestation*, or whatever they call it. Ahead, the restaurant comes into view, and with it the horse trainer I'm about to introduce Bowen to. For Bowen, the family farm is secondary to his growing construction business. Turns out there's plenty of demand for a barn built by someone who actually knows a thing or two about horses. "Now let's get you a new client."

I drag my ass into Racetrack Brews the next morning, not entirely convinced that even the love of my life is worth being in a line this long this early. As the coffee shop closest to the sales grounds, Racetrack Brews is always hopping during the sales—which helps make up for the rest of the year, when it and all the other businesses on this block cling to the cliff's edge by their fingernails. I sneak over here a couple times a week regardless, because there's only so much barn coffee a man can tolerate, but I'm never prepared for this place to be standing room only before the sun has even risen.

As the line inches forward, I scroll on my phone. The group thread I have with Maddie and Bowen is too quiet, so I take a moment to fire off a couple sunrise and good morning gifs. Bowen won't respond—his dislike of conversation extends to texts—but it'll annoy Maddie, which is all I want. I linger over the thread with Lark, which I have yet to unpin despite it going unused since I dropped her off at home that February night, but decide I don't need to torture myself by reading back through the short and impersonal messages she always sent.

It's not like I don't have them memorized already.

The woman ahead of me in line steps up to the register, and my brain finally snaps fully awake when I hear a very familiar coffee order. It takes less than a second for me to confirm what I was too distracted or asleep to notice when I walked in—she's a short Black woman wearing a delightfully familiar shade of blue, with bright pink braids falling down her back.

This is Lark's hired hand. I didn't catch her name yesterday, so I've been calling her Pink Braids because I'm a creative genius.

As the shop's owner tells her the total, I step up next to her. "I got her order, Aiden. Add my usual and a half-dozen drips, large as you can make 'em."

"Wait, what? I don't think—"

Pink Braids's protest is cut off by Aiden telling me the total. I tap my card to the reader before she can interfere, adding a decent tip because there's a non-zero chance I'm about to cause a small scene in his place of business.

Once the transaction goes through, I move out of the way and turn to see Pink Braids scowling at me. "It's too early for whatever this is, so let's say the answer is no and move on with our lives."

I laugh, appreciating that Lark's employee takes as little shit as Lark does. "Just trying to be a good barn neighbor," I say, gesturing between our respective farm polos. "No ulterior motive."

She doesn't look as if she believes me. "Uh-huh."

"Will it hurt my case if I ask for your name?"

"Yup."

"Then it's good I didn't ask." She rolls her eyes, and I make a point of backing up an extra step so she doesn't feel crowded. I had been planning to buy Lark coffee myself, but hadn't figured out how to get it to her in a way that she'd actually accept it. She would never take it from me directly, and she's smart enough that she'd be wary of a coffee left anonymously for her in the barn. There's still a decent chance Pink Braids spills the beans and Lark dumps the coffee out of spite, but this delivery method seems like it has the highest chance of success.

After a few moments of awkward silence, my ability to keep my mouth shut disappears. "If you and Lark need anything this week, just shout. We'd be glad to help."

"You know Lark?" Her suspicion shifts to something closer to curiosity. When I nod—because if I open my mouth, I will say *far* too much—she smirks. "Then you know asking for help isn't a thing she does."

I laugh at that, because she's not wrong. "The offer stands.
"

Aiden slides Pink Braids's order over, and she snags the drinks. She lifts them at me in some combination of acknowledgement and thanks, and I let her leave without pushing the conversation any further. One thing I learned fast about Lark was that she has countless acquaintances but few real friends, which means I doubt Pink Braids knows our history in any real detail.

Hopefully that doesn't come back to bite me in the ass later.

It only takes Aiden another minute to put my order together, and then I'm out the door, too. Despite the way my entire body vibrates with the knowledge that Lark is *right there so close right fucking there*, I keep my eyes on our end of the barn when I arrive. I pass out coffees to the crew, who have all been pulled off of the duties they'd usually have at the farm, and hop in to help make sure all the horses get fed and groomed.

The truth of it is, I'm mostly here as a figurehead—Javi is the one who actually manages the sales crew and the horses, while I'll be pitching in when I can in between networking with prospective buyers and keeping an eye out for any year-lings we might want to bid on ourselves. We don't always have a presence at this sale, which is part of why we were assigned to one of the back barns, but Maddie and my parents have been working through some restructuring, so we're focusing on selling over training this year. I don't know why, exactly, though I'm sure they told me.

I've never been much of a big-picture guy. That's Maddie's thing. I'm just content to show up and do what needs to be done.

Speak of the devil. My phone starts buzzing as I finish picking the hooves of one of our feistier fillies. Once the stall door is safely latched behind me, I pull up the group chat.

> **MADDIE**
>
> Put your stupid gifs away. This morning has been a shitshow.
>
> **BOWEN**
>
> Sucks. Need anything?
>
> **MADDIE**
>
> No, you're good. Nothing you can do about a mare who forgot how fences work.

I wince. It's rare to go more than a few days at a time without a horse finding a new and creative way to risk their life, and I have a feeling I know exactly which one is the culprit this time.

> **ME**
>
> Let me guess. Stars?
>
> **MADDIE**
>
> Yup. I told her I have a glue factory on speed dial, but she just demanded treats.

Which she got, I have no doubt. Stars—short for Stars Immemorial, which is a mouthful no announcer ever had to say, luckily—is one of our best broodmares, despite never running a single race. She is also a being of pure chaos who hears about the glue factory on a near-daily basis.

She loves me and barely tolerates Maddie, which should make the next couple weeks fun.

ME

Tell her I'll visit her tonight if she behaves.

MADDIE

Focus on your own behavior. Leave Lark alone today.

Bowen laughs at the message, and I don't even attempt to not be offended. I've been *so* well-behaved. I even bought her coffee.

Not that they need to know that part.

ME

I haven't even laid eyes on her yet, I'll have you know.

MADDIE

Good. Stay on your side of the barn.

"You."

I whip my head up at the sound of a very familiar, very angry voice. My attempt to find a Scout's honor gif disappears in the face of Lark storming across the barn, a nearly empty iced coffee cup clutched so tightly in her fist the lid is bound to go flying at any second.

She's fury personified, radiant and righteous. I grin, not bothering to hide my admiration.

Turns out, I don't have to leave my side of the barn at all.

My songbird is coming to me.

TWO YEARS AGO

MARK

It was two hours into the Fourth of July barbecue, and I was pleasantly buzzed. This was the only event my family didn't expect me to help run—we each had one—which meant I just got to show up and relax. I intended to take advantage of every second of it.

I grabbed a cider and wove my way between tables covered in food to the retaining wall where my sister and Bowen sat. I hopped up next to them but kept my mouth shut, because Maddie was in the middle of telling a story and if I interrupted, it would probably end with me covered in whatever she was drinking.

She was *so polite* to other people. Just never to me.

"—never guess what she found when she opened the door!" Ah, I knew this story. Bowen did, too, though he at least humored Mads by shaking his head to indicate that he could not, in fact, guess.

"There was a *snake* in her *toilet!*"

I mouthed the words right along with Maddie as she said them, and Bowen had to fight to keep himself from laughing. He was a smart man who had always been a little afraid of my sister. It served him well. "Wow. No way," he said, in a tone that confirmed that he knew this story as well as I did.

Mads scowled. "That was a good story, you know."

"It was a good story about three hundred retellings ago," I countered. I didn't protest when she stole my drink and took a sip, because it wasn't like I couldn't get another one. "You need new material."

"And where am I going to get that? You two are basically my only friends, and you're both boring as hell."

"Damn, that's sad." I laughed when Maddie smacked me in the stomach. "You should probably get out more."

Maddie scowled, ready to snap back, but I got saved by Mom waving her over. "Duty calls," she sighed, handing my cider back to me before hopping down to see what Mom needed. Maddie had the New Year's Eve party off, which meant she was on duty today. The parties were basically Aladyne tradition at this point: four or five times a year, we'd transform some part of the farm into an event-appropriate gathering place. Here in the heat of summer, we were grilling outside the front barn, with misters trying and failing to keep everyone cool. For Halloween, we would be in the back of the farm, where lights were limited and spookiness was exacerbated. New Year's Eve was up at the main house, which transformed into a winter wonderland despite the temperature usually being little more than comfortably cool.

On and on it went, from season to season. The invites were always sent widely, though the Fourth of July party was the one where there were basically no limits. If you showed up, we fed you. No questions asked.

"Dude, who is that?"

Okay, maybe *one* question. But this was an important damn question, because I didn't recognize the smokeshow who just stepped out of a truck. She was with an older couple who I presumed to be her parents, and the pair of them looked more familiar—which meant I probably met them once when I was eleven.

So how had *she* snuck by my notice?

Next to me, Bowen shrugged. "If you don't know, I definitely won't."

Fair. Bowen didn't like—or even talk to—most people. And I doubted he had looked at anyone with more than polite, platonic disinterest in years. That part of him turned off before I even met him.

But today wasn't about my best friend's emotionally stunted self. It was all about the beauty with the sharp, assessing gaze. It was rare for someone truly new to show up, and I was obsessed. Her legs stretched long between her cut-offs and well-worn Ariats, a few inches of her stomach showing beneath her tied-up t-shirt, and my mind had already played out about three hundred different dirty fantasies in which I got to find out what else she might be wearing—or, even better, might *not* be—before she caught me staring.

I tipped my can toward her in a silent, shameless acknowledgement. Her lips pulled into a smirk, her eyes drawing a lazy line down my body in return. Her brazenness made me wonder what, exactly, it would take to make her blush. When she merely shrugged like she had seen better and turned away, I laughed.

Loudly. Appreciatively. "I think I'm in love," I told Bowen. "God help us all."

Determined not to play my hand too early, I stayed next to Bowen, unabashedly watching as she moved around the space. Even though this was my farm, she looked entirely at home. She knew nearly as many people as I did, and I innately recognized the way she braced herself for certain greetings. She didn't just know people—people knew *her*, and she wasn't always thrilled about that.

Maybe it was something we could bond over on our first date.

"What'd I miss?" Maddie reappeared, grabbing my cider again and draining the last of it before shoving the empty can back at me.

"He's in love," Bowen drawled.

"Jesus. I was gone for like half an hour, tops."

I shrugged. "Sometimes that's all it takes."

"Oh god." Maddie groaned. "He's already picturing their babies. This is your fault, you know."

Bowen grunted, and I cut in to redirect her wrath. "I had mostly been focusing on the parts involved in *making* a baby, but now that you mention it, I bet they'd be pretty cute."

"Who is it?"

I nodded in the right direction. "Do you know her?" When my sister remained stubbornly silent, I nearly bounced in place. "You *do* know her!"

"We haven't met," she said. "But I know who she is."

"And that is…"

"Lark Reynolds." *Lark.* Hell, our names rhymed. I could practically hear the wedding bells now. Or at least the overlapping cries when we both came. Potato, tomato. "Her parents took over Landow a while back."

The picture began to fill in. My parents had been good friends with the original owners of Landow Thoroughbreds, so they were the ones I had grown up knowing. But years ago, they ended up selling to a couple that worked for them. The Landows took off for Europe and never looked back. It meant neither Lark nor her parents were new to the scene, but it at least partially explained why I didn't really know them. They were probably swamped with the transfer those first few years.

At least she was here now.

"Any known red flags?"

"Aside from your obvious interest?" Mads shook her head. "Like I said, I don't know her. Though I can make some up if I need to."

"Nah," Bowen said. "Better to let him crash and burn on his own."

"Love the support, guys."

While they continued to give me shit, I caught Lark's eyes skating across our group. She'd been so damn careful not to look back at me—*too* careful, which meant she had to work at it—but moments after a woman joined us, she finally broke?

I had no problem letting her see the smug as fuck grin on my face. Mads and I weren't identical twins—obviously—but we looked plenty alike. She'd figure out she didn't have anything to worry about soon enough, but it was too late for her to recover. She had already tipped her hand.

"I'm off," I declared, once Lark went back to a conversation I now knew she wasn't entirely paying attention to. "Wish me luck."

"No," Bowen and Maddie chimed together. I flipped them off as I pushed to my feet, setting out to loop through the barn before making my approach. A few people were inside, hiding from the sun, and I nodded and patted backs and said hello, but never let myself stop moving entirely.

At least, not until she was back in my sight. I posted up at the end of the barn, crossing my arms and ankles as I leaned against a column to observe her a moment more. Her parents were caught in a conversation a few tables down, and she was busy making up a plate of food. I watched her put her hamburger together, careful fingers darting to most of the available fixings, but instinctively flinching away from the pickles and the cheese.

Noted.

When she was satisfied, she snuck a glance over her

shoulder to where Mads and Bowen were now chatting with some family friends. A nearly imperceptible flicker of *something* flashed across her face when she saw I wasn't there, and I opened my mouth before I could think better of it.

"Looking for someone in particular?"

Her head snapped around like she was a middle schooler caught looking at a dirty picture, her cool mask slow to catch up. "You."

I grinned. "Me."

Heat flared in her eyes as she took me in. I was content to let her stare—turnabout was fair play, after all, and I knew I looked good today. I would have made a real effort today had I known, but my broken-in boots, fitted canvas work pants, and faded Aladyne shirt that fit just a hair too tight in the biceps had yet to let me down.

It wasn't flashy, but it was effective.

When she finally yanked her gaze back up to mine, I inclined my head. "I'm Mark Aladyne."

"Ah." And *there* was the mask. Interesting. I wasn't too proud to admit that my name usually helped my case with those who knew it, but that didn't seem to be the situation here. She just kept making this more fun.

"And you are...?" I prompted, even though I already knew. I was going to get more than one syllable at a time out of this woman if it killed me.

"Lark Reynolds." Her chin raised a couple inches, adding to her armor. "And I'm not interested."

"I haven't even suggested anything yet, Lark." I shifted, standing to my full height and taking a single step closer to her. Not enough to infringe on her personal space, but enough to be noticed. "How do you know you're not interested?"

"Our names rhyme. It's a non-starter."

"I'll pull the name-change paperwork on Monday," I quipped. "What else you got?"

Her lips twitched at my joke, but the amusement faded as she looked me over one more time. "Someone likes you wants a night to brag about or a happy little wife, and I'm not either one."

"Hm. What are you, then?"

"Hungry." She grabbed her plate and practically stomped away, and I let her go with an admiring smile on my face.

Lark Reynolds could walk away all she wanted. We were just getting started.

CHAPTER 3
LARK

I'm going to murder him.

Over *coffee*.

This is not how I planned my morning to go. I told myself today would be better. I didn't spill all over my clothes. My truck started without complaint. Nugent didn't scratch any more of his horses. All squirrels were safe and accounted for on the drive in.

Hell, I didn't even lay eyes on Mark once through the first couple hours of work. Today was as good as it gets.

And then I reminded Alicia to tell me how much I owed her for the coffee she bought me this morning, and she told me she didn't buy it.

That hot white dude who works for Aladyne did, were her exact words, not that I needed her to clarify. And not just because Mark is the only white dude working on this side of the barn.

Suddenly, the coffee that had once tasted like relief and fortitude turned sour in my stomach and I was stomping my way across the barn to find the man responsible for ruining my caffeine boost.

"You," I grit out when I spot him grinning at his phone. The plastic in my hand crinkles, but I tell myself not to break the cup yet. Not until I can dump what's left on the perfect, gorgeous hair on his perfect, gorgeous head.

Because the fact that he's standing there, a little dirty, a little sweaty, but still looking ready to walk onto the set of a photo shoot is what's going to put me over the edge. His crooked smile and that messy hair and those biceps that always look just a bit too big for his sleeves are all lures designed to drag me right back into his orbit, and I can't let that happen.

Not when he wants more than I can give him.

He's a good man. He deserves to have that more, it just won't be from me.

"Morning, Lark." He gives no sign that he's surprised by either my appearance or my anger, which tells me he planned it this way. "What brings you over to our side of the barn?"

"You paid for my coffee." The moment the words leave my lips, I hear how ridiculous it sounds. He did an objectively nice thing, and I'm over here to bitch at him about it.

"I did." His confirmation is accompanied by a warm smile, one that I remember him wearing before his lips would brush against my skin in bed. My body wants to respond in kind, but I send a stern mental warning to my nipples that if they react even the *slightest* bit, I'll never forgive them. "I'm proud of you, Songbird. Consider it a small token of celebration for opening your first sale."

That, right there, is why I can't let myself be around this man. Because while I don't doubt that he knew buying me this drink would get a rise out of me, every word he just said was sincere.

Even after I slammed the door in his face.

Too many responses swirl through my head, at least half

of which involve climbing him like a tree. My anger fades to something softer and far more dangerous, and if I open my mouth, I'll undoubtedly say something I regret.

And my first outing as a professional consigner is not the time to make a scene.

So instead of dumping the coffee on his head, I shove the cup at his chest. His hands come up to grab it, his fingers brushing against mine in the brief moment before I pull myself away. I ignore the fire on my skin in the wake of his touch and hold his stare for a heartbeat too long before I shake myself out of the moment and rush back to the relative safety of my side of the barn.

I only let myself glance back as I turn to duck into our feed stall, expecting to see him on his phone again or throwing the cup away or even just going back to work—anything but what he's actually doing, which is watching me with an intensity that warns me I need to steel my spine.

I'll never regret tonight, Songbird. But one day, you'll wish you had let me in.

His words from that night have never left my mind, existing as a constant whisper threatening to break my resolve. But what's been a whisper for the past six months is inching toward a roar, and I don't know how I'm going to survive the next two weeks with the temptation of him just feet away.

I duck into the most hidden corner of the stall, closing my eyes and taking a couple deep breaths to calm myself. When that doesn't work, I go to step two on my crisis management flowchart, pulling out my phone to call Daphne.

"Uhlo?"

The croak Daphne passes off as a greeting makes me wince; I forgot to account for the time difference before I called. But it's not like I *chose* to be dealing with Mark Aladyne this early in the morning. "He bought my coffee."

There's a long pause before Daphne offers a marginally more coherent, "Who?"

"You know who."

"Babe, it's too early for me to play detective."

If nothing else, my friend's sleepy frustration has cut the sharpest edges off my panic. I decide to back up a few hours. "So you remember when I hung up on you yesterday?"

"It rings a bell." It should. She sent about six texts after asking what happened, all of which I ignored except to say I'd tell her later.

Later just came a little earlier than I expected. "It was because I found out who we're sharing a barn with. You get one guess."

Another beat of silence, and then I can hear her scrambling upright in bed. "No."

"Yes."

"I need you to say it."

Daphne knows all the gory details of what went down with Mark, so I know she's invested now.

"Mark *fucking* Aladyne." His name is practically a growl as it leaves my lips, and I quickly peer out the bars of the stall window to make sure no one heard me.

If I didn't know better, I'd swear Daphne coughs to hide a giggle. "Holy shit. Do you think he planned it?"

I open my mouth to say no, but the word never comes out. I'd like to believe that it's sheer coincidence, but if there's one thing Mark Aladyne has, it's the audacity. "I'll call you right back."

I can hear Daphne shouting for me to just put her on speaker as I end the call and storm back down the barn aisle. In the back of my mind, I have a vague awareness of the looming opening time of the sale, but right now my entire focus is on getting an answer to Daphne's question.

Mark might have expected me the first time, but I don't miss the way his eyebrows fly up in surprise as I reappear. He's hovering in the gap of an open stall door, but his attention is all mine once he lays eyes on me.

It shouldn't feel good to know I can distract him so easily. "Aladyne. A word?"

The smile plastered on my face is supposed to be professional, but I'm sure it lands somewhere closer to unhinged. Regardless, it doesn't seem to faze Mark. "You can have all of my words, Reynolds."

I don't stop to acknowledge his comment because if I do, I'm worried I'll think it's cute. Mark slides the stall door shut and follows me to the end of the barn and around the corner. It's not in any way private, but it's at least out of the direct eye line of any of our employees.

"Miss me already?" When I spin to face him, he's casually sipping the coffee I shoved at him what feels like both seconds and lifetimes ago, his lips wrapped tight around the exact place my lips—

No. No. *Bad Lark. Get your shit together.*

"Did you arrange this?"

"The coffee?" He shrugs. "I'd say I took advantage of the situation more than I arranged it."

"Not the coffee. Forget the coffee." He smirks, because he knows I will not be forgetting the coffee. I barrel forward, gesturing at the barn we share. "*This.* Did you arrange for us to be next to each other?"

"I know I'm not on LinkedIn, but I promise you would've heard if I changed jobs."

Oh my god, I'm going to stab the man. If I thought my parents would actually post bail, it might be worth it. "Did you request that we be in the same barn?" I ask, hoping my language is specific enough that he can't dodge the question.

"Everybody's so suspicious these days." He takes another sip of my coffee, and I'm now regretting that I didn't get to finish it before I found out the truth of its origin. He would look at least twenty-five percent less smug without it. "I can confidently say I made no such request."

I narrow my eyes, deciding if I believe him. I don't, but I can tell that *if* he had a role in setting this disaster up, he won't own it.

Undoubtedly for his own safety.

Maybe Daphne can post bail from Canada?

He raises the straw toward his lips again, and I snap. "That's mine." I snatch it out of his hand and hurry around the corner and back down the barn aisle before he can stop me. He calls an amused, "You're welcome!" at my retreating back, and I ignore Alicia's curious stare as I duck right back into the corner of the stall.

I tap the screen to call Daphne again, and she answers before the first ring. "Bitch, take me with you next time. What did I miss?"

"He did it."

"Whoa. I didn't think he'd actually cop to it."

"Oh, he didn't. But it's too convenient and he was too smug."

I hear Daphne's coffeemaker in the background, which tells me my drama is of sufficient interest that she went ahead and dragged herself out of bed. It's an honor, truly, because Daphne doesn't believe in mornings. "What was the thing about buying coffee?"

"Apparently he ran into Alicia at Brews this morning and insisted on paying for her order."

"Aww, that's sweet."

"No, it's not sweet. It's..." I search for the right word,

finally giving into the temptation to finish the drink I'm holding. The annoying slurping sound quickly tells me there's nothing left, but I'm reluctant to pull away.

Sharing this straw is the closest Mark and I have been since the night I ended things.

"It's what?" Daphne prompts.

"It's presumptuous and overbearing. He's inserting himself into my life."

"Did he ask Alicia to tell you he bought it?"

"No."

"Has he instigated any conversations with you?"

I don't like where this is going. "Not directly."

"Mm-hmm." I brace for the Daphne Truth Bomb that's about to drop. "So if you had just let it go, you would have had a free coffee without interacting with him? Are we sure he's the problem here?"

"What kind of best friend are you?"

"The kind that answers when you call before dawn." She softens her voice. "But all I'm saying is maybe you should think about why you felt the urge to go get in his face about it."

"I don't wanna."

"I know," she says soothingly, like I'm her dog instead of a human being. "Look at it this way: maybe being stuck next to him will be a good thing. Maybe you'll get what you need out of it."

"What could I possibly need from him?"

I don't have to see Daphne's face to know she's holding back. "If nothing else, maybe some closure."

Closure.

I test the shape of the word in my mind, unsure why it doesn't settle quite right. The way Mark and I left things back in February was final, but not complete. Closure should be exactly what I want—what I *need*—from this ridiculous situation.

But the same part of me that stole that damn coffee back just because his mouth had touched it rebels at the finality of it. If we find closure, he has to move on.

I have to move on.

"Yeah. Maybe." A glance out the window tells me my breakdown moment has passed. There's too much work to be done for me to be sitting here, rehashing the end of a relationship that never even existed in the first place. "I've gotta get back to work, Daffy. Thanks for answering."

"Anytime, babe. Keep me updated."

I tuck my phone away, and after a moment's hesitation, I toss the empty cup in our waste bin.

It's just trash.

CHAPTER 4

MARK

"Oh no." Maddie pulls up short when she sees me. "You're too happy. You didn't stay on our side of the barn today, did you?"

Behind her, Bowen grunts. "Doubtful."

They settle onto stools on the other side of the high top, and I scowl as I set their beers in front of them. "Such little faith in me. See if I buy your drinks ever again."

Nestled into the same block as Racetrack Brews is a dive bar called Pretty Penny—at least, that's what the ancient sign out front says. Because everyone in the area has the mind of an immature twelve-year-old, Pretty Penny quickly transformed into PPs and right on into Dicks before I was even born. But it's the closest thing we have out in the sticks to a local watering hole, so Mads, Bowen, and I have made it our usual haunt.

Mads rolls her eyes. "Answer the question, then."

"Turns out I didn't have to. *She* came to *me*." I beam. "Twice."

Honestly, for as minimal as our interactions were today, they gave me hope. Lark wouldn't be pissed I bought her coffee if she were truly indifferent to me, and there was no denying the way she reacted when our hands touched.

She can pretend she doesn't have feelings for me all she wants. I know the truth.

"Jesus. I thought she'd have the good sense to ignore you," Maddie grumbles.

"I'm irresistible and you know it."

Maddie mimes puking as Bowen chuckles. The subject drops—at least out loud, because I personally don't go more than a few seconds without at least thinking of Lark—and the three of us catch up for a while. Our little trio is as good as it gets. My sister is a pain in my ass, but she's the smartest person I know and has saved said ass on more than a few occasions. The years she was off at school were weird as hell for me, because it was the first and only time we'd ever been apart.

But that's when I met Bowen. I was at loose ends without my twin, and he was recovering from whatever went down the summer after high school—which I still don't have the full story on, despite my best efforts. His moms knew something was up and forcibly dragged him to one of my family's parties. It was a classic case of an extrovert adopting an introvert: I sat down next to him, introduced myself, and he's tolerated me ever since.

I should have been worried that the two of them might not get along when they met, but I wasn't. It took them less than ten minutes to gang up on me, and they haven't stopped.

Zero complaints. They can give me shit all they want. They're my people.

"Mom's mad at you, by the way," Mads warns.

"No, she's not," Bowen and I say at the same time. My mother has an exceedingly high tolerance level for me. I don't think I've ever seen her mad at me in my entire life. I'd go so far as to say I'm her favorite, but I don't want to hurt Maddie's feelings.

Even if it's true.

"Fine. She's bordering on annoyed." That sounds much more accurate. "If you don't answer her calls soon, she's going to escalate."

I wince, knowing better than to push my luck. "I'll call her," I promise. "Is something up?"

Even though I still live on the farm, I'm not in the same house as the rest of them. One of the barn apartments opened up while Maddie was at college, and I leapt at the chance to put a little distance between myself and my parents. My sex life certainly thanked me, but it means now I only see my parents a few times a week rather than every day, which puts me out of the loop sometimes, especially during the sale.

"Mom wants to schedule a family meeting to talk about how we plan to rotate the horses to free up your barn. She's hoping you'll be free tomorrow."

As part of our shift toward sales, we realized we'll need more dedicated space just for the horses we're putting into prep each season. The barn I live in has been chosen as the best option, because one half is currently home to our family's personal horses—who are mostly retired racehorses and broodmares who spend 95% of their lives in the fields anyway—and the other half is just storage of junk we no longer need. Getting rid of the junk is easy, but we'd still need to reallocate the adjacent paddocks being used by other barns *and* figure out where our horses will go.

"I'm helping this one"—I nod toward Bowen—"on a job site in the morning and promised Javi I'd handle the afternoon pop-by," I tell her. The sale is closed to prospective buyers on Sundays, but the horses still need to be taken care of, and Javi and the rest of the crew deserve a break. But I'm not entirely sure why this topic merits a full family meeting, anyway. "You mind taking that one for me, Mads? I'm good with whatever you decide."

"It's your barn, Mark."

"It's the barn where I live," I correct. "Not sure that's the same."

"We just want you to be part of the decision making." Maddie exhales and shoves her beer to the center of the table, as she does most nights we come out—she rarely drinks more than a quarter of her beer before tapping out. Bowen shakes his head, so I grab it. One of us usually finishes it off so it doesn't go to waste, and tonight that's on me.

"I am. I'm telling you to make the decision." I give her my best grin. "We both know you have a plan. Just tell them I've already agreed to it."

"Even if it means building a new barn for the retirees?"

I tip my inherited beer bottle at Bowen. "I happen to know a mediocre contractor."

Bowen flips me off as Maddie grumbles about losing the friends and family discount, and I just laugh and enjoy the moment, knowing it can only get better from here.

So long as someday, Lark's at this table, too.

I don't make it to the sales ground on Sunday until almost dusk. Bowen has a handful of guys who work for him full-time, but I pitch in here and there, partially because I know he can always use an extra set of hands and partially because I know it annoys him when I insist on putting pop music on while we work. Today's project ran long—not because of Bowen, contrary to what the homeowner accused—and he bought me dinner after as the only form of payment I was willing to accept.

I'm a growing boy. It's important to keep me fed.

By this time of night, the sales ground is much quieter than it is the rest of the day. A few trucks are in the parking lot, and the occasional security cart drives by in the distance, but otherwise, the only sounds are those of horses settling into their stalls for the night. I make for our barn, keeping my head down as I walk because I don't trust everyone to have dealt with their horse's manure—dog owners have nothing on horse owners for pretending it isn't their giant pile of shit to deal with.

Which is why I turn the corner of the barn and collide directly with Lark. Her forehead slams into my jaw, and we both curse as we process what just happened. "Shit, are you okay?"

"I'm fucking great," she grumbles as she rubs her forehead. "Do you still have all your teeth?"

"Barely."

"Shame."

I laugh, and she gets as far as smirking in return before she fully registers that we're still touching. My arm went around her on instinct, steadying her, and her other hand rests on my chest in a way that's achingly familiar. I remember the first time she touched me like this, in those weighty moments before we kissed like the world would end if we didn't. I can still taste the tang of whiskey on her tongue, feel the curve of her body against mine, remember how she clung to my shirt like she'd disappear without me. This moment echoes that one so sharply that all I want is to lean in—

But she springs back, and I let her, trying to ignore the way my chest caves with the loss of her touch. She's about to bolt, her eyes as wary as any yearling at this sale, but I can't bring myself to let her disappear on me that easily. "Long day?"

Her eyes touch mine before darting away. "They all are when you're basically a one-woman show."

I want to tell her she doesn't have to be, but I know that's the fastest way to make her run. I settle for, "It's good to see you."

"Nope." She turns and strides back down the aisle, her original destination forgotten, and I follow like she's dragging me there herself. When she darts into the stall she's been assigned for storage, I stop in the doorway. Cross my arms. Lean against the doorframe. Flex my biceps for good measure.

The leaning always works on her, even when the biceps don't. I smile when she spins around and sees me, because she can't mask the appreciation in her gaze. "Already desperate to get me alone, are you?"

"We aren't doing this, Mark." Her voice is firm, but I don't miss the way her eyes dart to my mouth, or how her fingers tremble before she curls them into fists. "We're not doing small talk, and we're not going to pretend like everything is normal."

"And here I thought that's all you wanted." I aim for cavalier, attempting to keep the hurt out of my voice, but I have no doubt she can read me like a damn book. And not even a hard one—one of those books meant for kids learning how to read, with lots of pictures. "You wanted to fuck me, not know me."

Her face flashes with emotion—not quite regret, but closer than I expect. It's another brick added to my foolish tower of hope. I step toward her, taking advantage of the cramped space she brought us to. She can back away, but not for long. The stall isn't big enough for her to run. "You wanted me to make you come," I say, with another step. "You wanted my fingers and my tongue and my cock, but you didn't want *me*."

She swallows as she cedes ground, flinching when her back hits the wall. "I never lied to you about what I wanted."

"Maybe not," I allow. "But that doesn't mean you were honest with yourself about what you needed."

She snarls, letting her anger break free. "I don't *need* you, asshole."

"No." I step fully into her space, resting one hand on her ribcage. Her breath blows warm on my skin even as she glares up at me. "You don't need me. You don't need anyone. That's the problem, Lark. You're too scared to need anyone. You're too scared to let yourself love me."

Her heartbeat flutters fast under her skin. "What if I've moved on already? Have you considered that?"

I smirk, pressing my advantage as I slide my hand up her torso to the curve of her breast, my thumb lightly caressing against the edge of her already beaded nipple. She tries to stifle a gasp, and I lower my mouth to her ear when she fails. "No, I can't say that I have."

"Mark." Her voice is faint, her body betraying her, and I press my lips against the thready pulse at her throat. She tries to say something else, but whispers my name again instead.

I might have told my sister I could handle this, I might have even—allegedly—signed my own damn self up for this torture, but the truth is I don't know how to be around Lark without losing myself to her. We've barely had half a conversation tonight and I'm already desperate to be inside her again. There is no *just acquaintances* for us, there is no *friendly colleagues*. For me, with Lark, it's all or nothing.

I'd walk through hell itself for it to be *all*, now and fucking forever. I just have to figure out how to make Lark catch up.

"Two weeks," I say, before I even begin to understand the thought. "Just give me these two weeks."

"You think that's all it will take?" There's a smolder in her voice, the fire heating back up. If I don't get her to agree now, she never will. "Two weeks and I'll magically be in love with you? You could just admit that what you really miss is fucking me and we could get this all over with."

She's right. It's not enough time. Not for everything I want. But the truth is, we've already had months between us. Years, if she really pays attention. I just need her to let her guard down enough to see it. To see me.

To see *us*.

But I know Lark, and I know she won't let herself be vulnerable that easily. I step back, giving us both space to breathe, and present her with the stupidest idea I've ever had. "Let's make it a wager then. If you're so sure sex is all this can ever be, then prove it."

Her tongue darts between her lips and the sight nearly brings me to my knees. Fuck, do I miss being on my knees for her. "How do you propose I do that, exactly?"

"Until the sale ends, you're my girlfriend, in every damn way that matters. It's not fake. You don't fight it and you don't put the damn walls up. For two weeks, you're *mine*."

"That sounds like you get everything you want and I get nothing. Pass."

"I'm not done." I brace my arms on either side of her, staring down with a challenge in my gaze. "You can do your worst, Songbird. Play the damn temptress. Do whatever it takes to break me. If I fuck you before you admit you're in love with me, then I walk the hell away and leave you alone forever."

Her expression darkens as she considers my offer, her eyes darting between mine as she tries to figure out if I'm serious. I hold steady, giving her what she needs, but being this close to her without touching her is torture. I'm on the verge of breaking when she finally offers one single, solitary nod. "Game on, Aladyne."

And then her mouth is on mine. The kiss is all lust and fury, and I make no attempt to control it. Her fingers tangle in my hair, her teeth scrape across my lips. I let her take what she wants, because I've missed her, and because I plan to do the same soon enough.

After all, I've had six months of practice when it comes to not fucking Lark Reynolds.

But I'd bet my damn life that she spent every day of those six months in love with me.

And I have two weeks to prove it.

SEVEN MONTHS AGO

LARK

"I don't understand. *You* want to rent stall space to me?" I tried and failed to keep the skepticism out of my voice. "Why?"

I was having my monthly dinner with my parents, which had grown significantly more stilted in the months since I informed them that I would be leaving Landow to start my own consignment. At first, they assumed I was bluffing, and treated me like a toddler throwing a tantrum. But when I didn't show up to work two weeks ago, they realized I meant business.

And now they were in problem-solving mode.

"Well," my dad huffed, clearly not sure what to do with the fact that I didn't immediately fall down on my knees in gratitude, "it just makes sense to keep it all in-house."

"Exactly," Mom agreed. "That way, when something goes wrong, you can just talk to us. No messy legal drama that way."

"So you're assuming I'm going to fail."

"We didn't say that. But what kind of parents would we be if we didn't protect you from the fallout of your..." Mom trailed off, trying to find something suitably passive aggressive. "Ambitions?"

Dad was pointedly silent.

"It's a kind offer," I said. In their own way, they were trying to protect me. But mostly, they were trying to protect themselves. "But even if I wanted to, I've already signed a contract."

"Contracts can be broken," Dad said with a dismissive wave. "I'm sure our facilities are more suited to your needs."

I didn't have the energy to pursue that particular argument. Landow was a beautiful farm, and I had always been proud of my part in making it that way. But the barns themselves hadn't been updated in decades, while the place where I would be leasing space had been built just over five years ago. Newer wasn't always better, and it was true that it hadn't been designed with Thoroughbreds in mind.

But I had honestly been shocked to discover how reasonable their prices were, for how nice the barn was. It was still expensive as all hell, but it came with enough amenities to be worth it. I had a feeling my parents wouldn't hit the same ratio.

Across the table, Mom realized their initial approach didn't land. She sighed, doing her best to hide a scowl. "We're just trying to be good parents, Lark. I don't know why you can't see that."

"And I'm just trying to run my business, Mom."

"If this is still about Gabriel—"

I cut off my father. "It's about me having already signed a contract."

Mom frowned. "I still don't see why you needed to break up with him. He's such a nice boy."

In this, my mother wasn't wrong. Gabriel *was* a nice boy, and he had been a perfectly lovely boyfriend.

Until he took the promotion that I wanted without

talking to me about it. Maybe it wasn't fair of me, but breaking up with him was better than letting the betrayal fester.

"How about we discuss something else?" I offered. We hadn't even started eating yet.

My parents exchanged a loaded glance, but indulged the request. We talked about the rumors that the old Wyndham place might be broken up into a series of smaller hobby farms instead. It was the sort of topic that could make them grumble for days, so I gladly accepted the new conversational direction.

I made it through the meal with minimal further damage, and reluctantly agreed to stay for dessert. I offered to clear the dinner plates, in an effort to have a minute or two alone, and pulled out my phone the moment I was safely in the kitchen.

ME

Tonight?

I was starting to feel a little itchy after going more rounds with my parents. I needed a reward, and ideally that reward would be a minimum of three orgasms.

MARK

Nine at your place?

The response came within seconds, and I confirmed. Knowing I'd see him soon, I exhaled, my body already starting to relax.

When I returned to the dining room, my father was just putting his own phone down. "Good news," he announced. "Jenny can meet with you tomorrow morning."

It took me a moment to realize he was talking to me. "Sorry?"

"You remember Jenny," Mom informed me. "Our lawyer."

I didn't, but I also didn't know why that was relevant to me. "She's meeting with me because…?"

My parents exchanged a look I saw at least three times a day throughout my childhood. "You said you wanted out of the contract so you can keep your horses here instead. Jenny's going to take a look at it. She's sure breaking it won't be too difficult."

Inhale. Exhale.

Again.

Again.

"That's not what I said."

"Lark, we just want to—"

"It doesn't matter what you want!" I snapped. "I don't want to keep my horses on this farm. I don't want to break the contract. I don't want to meet with your lawyer. Okay? *I* don't want any of that, and that's what matters."

Dad frowned. "You don't have to be rude, Lark."

"Actually, I really think I do." I set the dish full of lemon bars down on the table. "I don't feel like staying for dessert anymore."

I ignored them calling after me as I grabbed my keys off the hook and stomped out into the crisp January air. I yanked my phone out, sending another text.

ME

Plan changed. Get here now.

The drive across the farm back to my cottage took roughly five minutes, and every bounce and dip of the truck along the unpaved paths fueled my frustration. I was used to my parents trying to get their way with everything, though they usually didn't try to overtly gaslight me in the process. But tonight it was like they suddenly decided I had lost all agency in my life. The idea that I didn't know what I was doing when I signed the contract? The idea that it wasn't a *choice* I made?

I knew they'd apologize eventually, and that I'd forgive them because they were my parents. But right now, I was pissed.

I slammed my way around the house once I got home, waiting to hear back from Mark. He was usually annoyingly obnoxious about texting me back—it was part of his whole *this could be a real thing* campaign. So of course, the one time I *wanted* him to text me back immediately, my phone was stubbornly silent. I planned to hold this over his head for the rest of—

Headlights cut across my windows, and I didn't have words for the relief that unfurled in my chest. I threw the front door open, drinking in the sight of his lazy grin as he strolled up the driveway, spinning his keys around his finger. "You summoned me?"

"Fuck off," I said automatically, before admitting, "I wasn't sure you got my message."

He stepped up onto the porch, that grin of his softening as he leaned in to press a kiss to my forehead. "I should have texted back. But in my defense, I was a little busy breaking the speed limit to get here."

"That desperate to fuck me, huh?"

He pressed his fingers under my chin, guiding my eyes up to his. "That desperate to see you, Songbird."

"Don't call me that."

"You like it."

Even if I did, I would never admit it. Not even to myself. "Just get inside already."

"The house? Or you?"

I seriously considered never speaking to him again, but the man had a point. "Both, you asshole."

He chuckled and followed me through the doorway. "As you wish."

Mark's eyebrows raised at the sight of the various cabinets that were still open from my angry, failed search for pretty much any form of chocolate. "You gonna tell me what happened tonight?"

"It's not any of your business."

He stepped in front of me, his face as serious as I'd ever seen it. "That's where you're wrong. I'm not going to touch you until I know everything's okay."

I glared up at him, but he didn't react. His attention was steadying—worse, it was comforting. I didn't want his care, but I knew he wouldn't budge on this. And part of me, a deep, treacherous part of me, wanted to talk to him about it. It seemed possible that Mark, of all people, might actually understand. "It's not what you're thinking."

"It's cute that you think you know what I'm thinking."

"It was just another fight with my parents, okay? Nothing traumatic happened."

"Those two things aren't mutually exclusive, but go on."

I sighed and leaned back against the counter. "I signed a contract to lease some stalls last week."

The joy on his face nearly took my breath away. "That's amazing, Lark. I know you've been working toward that for a long time."

You shouldn't *know that*, I thought, but stopped just short of saying it. The fact that I had told him anything about my plans at all was a slip up on my part. But right now, I was almost glad for it, because his excitement was what I had been missing from my conversation with my parents. His reaction was pure, uncomplicated support.

I needed that more than I was willing to admit.

"Yeah," I said, "it turns out my parents can't wrap their heads around me not keeping my horses here. Dad went so far as to set up a meeting with his lawyer tomorrow so I could break the contract."

"Shit." Mark's lips tugged into an amused smile. "Why did they think you would want that? Have they even met you?"

"Apparently not." It was validating, to have him confirm that what my parents did tonight made no sense. It was also annoying to realize knew me that well. "But that's when I left, and texted you to come over early. Like I said, it's not a big deal."

"We both know that's not true." Mark stepped closer to me, his hands grabbing the counter on either side of me. "But I also know better than to push my luck, so I'm willing to be your distraction tonight, if that's what you're looking for."

I slipped my hands under his shirt, exhaling as I explore the planes of his back. "Please fucking distract me, Mark."

His lips crashed against mine as his hips pinned me to the counter, and the moan that slipped out of me was want and relief, all at once. "You know," he murmured as he kissed his way down my neck. "You should really go on a date with me."

"Answer's still no, Aladyne."

He pulled back to meet my eyes, a wicked grin on his face. "For now. Let's see what I can do about that."

CHAPTER 5

LARK

It's not until I walk into the barn Monday morning and see Mark leaning—that cocky fucker—against Marshmallow's stall with a coffee in each hand that I fully comprehend last night wasn't just some terrible fever dream. "Morning, Songbird."

"Stop leaning on shit," I grumble.

"I will as soon as it stops turning you on." That lazy grin is back on his face, like he's looking at everything he's ever wanted. He holds up one of the coffees, with nary an ice cube in sight. "Figured I'd cut out the middleman this time."

"Should I be concerned about memory loss? It was only two days ago that you bought me an iced coffee."

He shrugs. "It's Monday. You only do iced on the weekends."

How the *fuck* does he know that? I glower at him, confident he's at least gotten the specifics wrong. He's undoubtedly assumed I either drink it black (*like your heart,* I can practically hear him teasing) or that I have some stereotypically basic white girl drink, which, frankly, hasn't always been wrong.

But I take a sip and it's annoyingly perfect. His grin broadens as I glare at him, and he leans forward to press a kiss to my forehead. "You think I don't know my girlfriend's coffee habits? Come on, that's basic stuff."

"I'm not your girlfriend."

"No?" That damn smile of his doesn't break. "Backing down already?"

I take another sip of coffee instead of answering. Last night was...a lot of things. A mistake, mostly. Neither of us should have been there that late, let alone both of us. Colliding with him? A mistake. Letting him follow me to the stall? Another mistake.

Letting him talk to me? Touch me?

Fucking rookie shit. I should have known better.

There was a reason Mark Aladyne was able to talk me into a date in the first place. Last night, he cornered me again. Emotionally and physically.

The worst part is that the whole encounter was frustratingly hot. Emphasis on frustrating, because after the best make out session of my damn life, the asshole just stepped back, said, "I'll see you tomorrow, babe," and walked the hell away like both of our bodies weren't desperate to finish what we started.

And now he's here, with his pretty eyes the same shade as the freaking coffee he brought me, waiting for me to back down. "You only have something to lose if you're wrong," he murmurs. He reaches out with one gentle finger to trace the line of my jaw, and for some unknowable reason, I let him.

"I'm not wrong," I reply, determined to ignore the goosebumps chasing their way down my neck. "And I'm not backing down."

"Then that makes you my girlfriend, doesn't it?" His smug facade softens into genuine relief, and it's a necessary reminder of how desperately he wants this thing between us to be more than it is. I don't actually want to hurt the man—not any more than I already have—but I realized last night that seeing this through might be the only chance I have to set him free.

Give him the two weeks he wants. Prove to him we're no more than chemistry and hot sex. Force him to accept the heartbreak on the other side.

It's not like I *want* to be with him.

"Kind of sad you have to resort to emotional blackmail to get a girlfriend, isn't it?" I quip, pushing past him to grab a grooming kit. Alicia picked up a few mounts today so she isn't coming in for another couple hours, which means I've got to get my ass in gear if I want the horses to be ready by the time the buyers start showing up. The last few days were little more than set up—the real chaos starts now.

Mark doesn't take offense to my comment. "If I had known that's all it would take, I would have done it sooner." He moves with me, opening Marshmallow's stall door before I can ask. He holds out his hand for the filly to smell, laughing when she tries to bite him almost immediately. "Can I help?"

Do I need help? Yes. I'm going to be running myself ragged all week, even with Alicia's support. But do I want help from *Mark*, who's supposed to be running his own damn sale a few doors down?

"No, thanks." I dig the curry comb into Marshmallow's gray fur, smiling as she immediately gives up messing with Mark to focus on the attention I'm giving her. Marshmallow is one I'm going to miss when she sells—she's feisty and smart, but she's a sucker for grooming. Which is for the best, because her silky gray coat is hell to keep clean. "I've got it covered."

"You know where to find me if you change your mind." He lightly tugs me away from the horse to press a chaste kiss against my lips. "Lunch is on me today, so don't go making any plans."

Then he turns his fine, denim-clad ass around and saunters back down to the side of the barn where he belongs, leaving me to swat the filly's roving teeth away as I remind myself of all the reasons I know this is a terrible idea, and all the reasons why I'm going to see it through anyway.

That goodbye kiss ends up on both damn lists.

"I'm sorry about that," I say to Alicia as she returns Windsor to his stall. We just finished showing all three horses to a prospective buyer, but Alicia had to walk Windsor half a dozen times because the dude wouldn't stop staring at her ass long enough to look at the horse. "He was an asshole. I'll send him away if he comes back."

"No, don't cut him off. Interest is interest." She wiggles her hips. "And I mean, who can blame him?"

I laugh, glad it didn't bother her as much as it bothered me. I don't like being in a position where I can't protect my only employee. "I certainly can't. But I mean it. We don't need his money if it makes you uncomfortable."

"It's fine, Lark. We're bound to get some shitheads in the mix."

"Who's the shithead?" Mark picks that moment to stroll up, bags of food in hand.

"No one." I pin a neutral smile to my face as I take him in. He's been in and out of the barn all morning, but his crimson Aladyne Stud polo would still look pristine if it weren't for the small trail of horse snot that runs along the shoulder. His reflective sunglasses frustrate me, both because he wears them well and because it means I can't tell what he's looking at. "You actually brought lunch."

"I said I would." He pauses long enough to set the food on our folding table, then slides his arm around my waist as he turns to Alicia. "Do I get to learn your name this time? I'm Mark Aladyne, Lark's boyfriend."

Alicia's eyebrows skyrocket so fast I worry they might just fly away entirely. "Lark's boyfriend?"

"For the next thirteen days," I clarify, only to realize based on her expression that clarification was not achieved. "It's a whole…situation."

"I'm Alicia," she says, offering Mark a hand. "And I have a million questions."

"Good thing I brought enough food for three, then."

Ohhh, he's good. He knew I'd use Alicia to get out of having lunch with him, so he took that card away from me entirely. I'm going to have to up my game.

Thankfully, the shithead leaving marked the start of the lunch lull. After a brief back and forth during which I refused to sit on Mark's lap—even though that would help *my* cause in our war, I wasn't going to risk clients seeing me that way—he went and stole a chair from the Aladyne side of the barn, which left approximately twenty seconds for Alicia to focus on me.

"You know your names rhyme, right?"

"Trust me, it's impossible to forget."

As Alicia snickers, I take comfort in the fact that she's the one sitting here with me. We're friendly, but she doesn't know the ins and outs of my relationship with Mark, and she's not going to push or ask invasive questions because that's not who we are to each other. Not like Daphne—

Shit. I'm going to have to tell Daphne. She'll never let me live this down.

"Thirteen days seems specific." Okay, maybe Alicia's

going to push a little. Not that I blame her. I would also want to understand the soap opera happening in front of me.

"Think of it as a fling," I suggest.

"My girl doesn't have enough faith in my staying power," Mark declares, catching just the end of our exchange. "I should be offended, because I've demonstrated my stamina to her many times over."

"Gross." I shove my palm into his face, knocking his sunglasses away, and he laughs and grabs my wrist as he sits down with us. "What if we talked about literally anything other than our time bomb of a relationship?"

"She admits it's a relationship. I'll take the win." He presses a sweet kiss to my palm before letting me go. The eye contact as he does makes my insides do a funny hop, and I tell the giddy little bunny in my stomach to go right the hell back to sleep. I'm not *feeling* things about Mark's presence, I'm just not used to it because it's been a while now since my last boyfriend—and even when I was with him, we never really indulged in chaste kisses and casual affection.

This is a new experience. That's all.

"How long have you two been together?" Alicia asks, ignoring my plea for a change of topic. I don't have an employee handbook, but I'll be writing one tonight. It's going to have a long section on loyalty.

Mark makes a show of checking his watch—which is a real watch and not even an ugly-ass smart watch I can mock him for. "About 15 hours and 27 minutes? Give or take?"

Alicia's eyes dart back and forth between us. "I think I'm done asking questions."

"Thank god."

We settle into small talk as we eat, Mark asking thoughtful questions about Alicia's plans when she moves to New York and happily telling her about his family's farm. I cut in with snarky asides now and then, but I spend most of the meal a little stymied from opening my burger and finding it has no cheese or pickles.

Apparently it's not just my coffee order that Mark knows, and that irritates me.

At the end of our meal, we get interrupted by a buyer who wants to see all three horses. Alicia goes to get the first horse ready and I start to follow, but Mark stops me. "I've got it," he says quietly, lightly squeezing my arm. "You stay here."

It's a kindness on his part—with only two of us, it's hard for me to spend much time with the buyers themselves, which leaves me at a disadvantage. Instead of chatting with them and talking up my horses—including the ones that aren't here yet—I'm stuck helping get the horses in and out of the barn.

That doesn't mean I don't hesitate. Mark reads me immediately, dropping his head so his lips brush against my ear. "No walls, Songbird."

I try not to inhale, but the scent of him still finds it way to me. It dredges up dozens of memories of hours spent naked and moaning, and the bunny stirs again. All I can manage is a nod before I step away, accepting that he's probably right.

If he were really my boyfriend, I'd let him help.

"Welcome to Lark Sales," I say, as I join the buyer in the grass in front of the barn. I'd guess she's roughly my age, perhaps a little older, though the full face of makeup and sleek black jumpsuit make it hard to get a real read. Everything about her look is out of place, but there's an intelligence in her gaze that I tell myself not to underestimate. She shakes my hand, introducing herself as Evangeline Rutherford, which is a name I don't recognize. Not an impossible bar to clear, but not common, either. With the pleasantries out of the way, I ask, "What exactly are you looking for this year?"

"Well, my boyfriend came through earlier, and if you ask

him, the answer is everything." I flip through my memory, wondering if her boyfriend might be the shithead. For her sake, I hope not. "We're new to this, and are trying to build out a good portfolio."

I bite my tongue at the description of horses as a *portfolio*, because she already looks so overwhelmed that I can't quite bring myself to hold it against her. "And if I'm asking you?"

"I'm looking for sustainability. Future broodmares, working racehorses. I don't have an illusion of winning the Triple Crown, but I don't want to cheap out, either." As she speaks, her confidence builds. She strikes me as the type of woman who is so used to being hyper-competent that she struggles when faced with something new.

Unfortunately relatable.

"Fair enough. We've got three here now, with six more coming as the sale progresses. Of the ones you'll see today, keep an eye on hips 135 and 152. Their pedigrees aren't the flashiest, but they won't let you down."

For the next few minutes, Evangeline carefully watches as Alicia leads Windsor and Boggy up and down the asphalt pathway between the barns. She asks permission before she films them, which I appreciate, and I offer insight into their bloodlines and family histories.

"*Oh.*" Evangeline's quiet gasp takes my attention toward the barn, where Mark emerges with Marshmallow at hand. For a moment, I think she's fawning over Mark, and the irrational jealousy combined with leftover frustration from the shithead has me opening my mouth to tell her to keep her eye on the horse—only to snap it shut when she gushes, "Look at that coat!"

If I needed proof she's a true amateur horse girl, I just got it. Marshmallow's speckled gray coat has Evangeline sporting heart eyes, and I have a feeling she'll be bidding on the filly in a couple days' time.

Not that I blame the woman. It's a stereotype for a reason.

My own attention stays locked onto Mark, who handles Marshmallow with an ease that does unruly things to my lady parts. I try to tell myself that he shouldn't get points for being good at something he was born into, but when Marshmallow spooks back a few strides and Mark settles her with a gentle pat to the neck and a few quiet words, it's hard to do anything but soften toward him.

I've never actually gotten to see him interact with horses before because I was so careful to keep the lines firm between us. It's probably for the best, or else I would have married him within minutes.

When the pair are at the far end of their walking loop, Evangeline glances at me. "This one is one of yours, right?"

"Correct. Hip 215."

"Perfect. Just wanted to double-check." She nods to where Mark is turning Marshmallow around to walk back in our direction. "The shirt threw me off."

I immediately realize the problem—for all that Mark is helping me out, he's still dressed like he belongs to the farm next door. "Just a little help from a friend," I say, pretending as if I'm not preparing to murder my so-called boyfriend.

Evangeline takes another moment with Marshmallow, then thanks me for my time. "If this is what you have to start, I'll definitely be back to see the rest."

"I'll look forward to it." My sincerity surprises even myself. I don't know this woman at all, but I like her.

She strides off—seemingly bypassing Aladyne Stud entirely, to my surprise—and I turn a scowl on Mark. "Put her up," I order. "Then I want a word."

His mouth tugs into a frown, but he doesn't argue. He returns to the barn, giving the filly a pat on the nose before he shuts the stall door, then follows me as I stalk away from the barn to get out of earshot of anyone who works for either of us.

"Please don't do that again," I whisper-yell once he catches up. His sunglasses now hang between the buttons on his polo, and I almost wish he were still wearing them because looking him in the eye right now is too much.

"You're going to have to be more specific than that, babe."

"I appreciate that you wanted to help. But it's better if you don't do it in the future."

"Why?" His eyes are gentle as he asks the question—it's interest, not accusation.

I take a half-step back anyway, because accusation is safer. "Having you there in Aladyne colors is confusing and makes it look like I can't handle myself."

He pauses in consideration, and I can read the thoughts as they cross his face—counter-arguments and dirty jokes about *handling myself* alike. But I still blink in confusion when all he offers is a soft, "Okay."

"Okay?"

He shifts forward, reclaiming the space I took. "I only want to lighten your burden, Songbird. I never want to add to it."

See, this? This shit right here? This is going to be a problem. My little bunny wants to kick its little feet in response to his gentleness, which means it's time for me to remind him of my part in this game we're playing.

I let him pull me into a hug, sighing despite myself at the way our bodies fit together like lock and key. Then I pull my shit together and lightly nip his clavicle before leaning up to whisper in his ear. "Remember that thing we did at the hotel?"

We've only spent one night in a hotel together, and it wasn't exactly the type of night that would be easy to forget. I smirk when a pained acknowledgement rumbles through his chest, his body going tense and coiled even before I slide a hand between us to tug suggestively at his belt. We're close enough I know the reminder is affecting him, so I go in for the kill. "We can try it again tonight if you want."

I slip out of his arms and walk back to the barn without looking back, leaving him to curse under his breath. The poor boy is going to need a minute before he's presentable again, which is exactly where I want him to be. Two weeks isn't much time, but this is only day one.

He won't give in tonight.

But then, neither will I.

CHAPTER 6

MARK

"What are you doing in my room?" Maddie glares at me from the doorway, her voice the kind of mild that comes right before she snaps and throws something at my head.

"Looking for condoms," I admit.

"Jesus, Mark. It's been like two minutes and you're already hooking up with her again?"

"Not quite." I grin, remembering how pleased Lark was with herself when she left me with a hard dick in the middle of the sales grounds. I have a feeling that's a scenario I'm going to have to prepare myself to revisit with some frequency the next couple weeks. "But I don't want to be caught unprepared if the plan changes."

Her eye roll could be seen from space, but she points to the middle drawer of her dresser. "I hate that I respect that. But why do you need *mine*?"

"Mostly because I assumed your stash might expire before you use them."

"Get out of my room." The order is indeed accompanied by a throw pillow being launched at my head.

I laugh as I retreat to safety. When Maddie came back

from school, she returned to living in her childhood bedroom as she took on more responsibility at the farm. Lucky for her, her room and our parents' room are on different floors. But that condom box looked plenty dusty anyway.

Every bit of knowledge I have about my sister's sex life was learned against my will, but I still worry that she's stagnating here at home. I'd poke at her about it, but I don't exactly have the relationship advice high ground right now.

"I didn't know you were here, Mark!" My mother lights up when I step into the living room, and I lean down to hug her before dropping onto the nearby couch.

"I'm not really here. I have to leave in a couple minutes."

"How was the sale today?"

"Great. Javi and the crew are a well-oiled machine. I think I get in their way more than I help." I ignore the look Maddie gives me as she joins us, having stopped to refill her blunt-force-trauma-sized water bottle on the way. We both know my attention has not been quite as focused as usual this year.

Mom tilts her head. "Then what brings you by? Not that you need a reason, of course."

Mads snorts, and I glare at her. I didn't actually stop just to raid her supplies, although that was a side benefit. "I wanted to tell you I'm bringing a guest to family dinner tomorrow."

"Well, that's a wonderful idea. You know any friend of yours is always welcome here." The inquisitive emphasis on *friend* does not go unnoticed—not that it was supposed to. "You let me know if there are any dietary restrictions I need to know about, okay?"

"Avoid pickles," I say. "Cheese on the side is best. And I'm pretty sure she doesn't like mushrooms. But nothing life-threatening, that I know of."

Mom practically blossoms when I say "she," but tries to

keep it under wraps because she's always been adamant that none of us make assumptions about gender and romantic relationships. *You let people tell you who they are and who they love,* she would tell us when we were kids. *Don't let the cultural hegemony of the world make you lazy or callous.*

I'm still not entirely sure what the cultural hegemony is, but it's reassuring to know even she can quite shake herself out of it. I figure this time, I can let her have her fun. "It's Lark Reynolds, Mom. She and I are together now."

Maddie chokes on her water, and I pat her on the back with a bit too much force as Mom beams. "I'm happy to hear that," is all Mom says, and I revel in the soft sincerity of it.

Carefully ignoring Maddie's face, because I know whatever she's thinking will be less generous, I stand. "Like I said, I gotta go. But you'll see us for dinner tomorrow."

I give Mom a hug, already knowing Mads is going to follow me outside. On the front porch, I sigh and turn to face her. "It's complicated, okay?"

"Then un-complicate it, because last I heard, that woman dropped you with a quickness when you told her how you felt, and you just told our *mother* that you're a couple."

Despite my inner turmoil, I break down and give her the highlight reel of the past few days. For all that I don't welcome Maddie's judgment, she knows me better than anyone. And it's not like I'm good at keeping my mouth shut. "I've got two weeks, Mads," I exhale once I'm done. "It's not much, but it's more than I had before."

To my surprise, it's not judgment on her face when I finish my explanation—it's soft curiosity. "You're really in love with her, aren't you?"

Easiest question of my life. "Yes."

"You're going to get your heart broken. Again."

"Probably." I am all too aware of the risk. "But it can't hurt worse than if I don't try."

I don't give Lark the courtesy of a call or text before pulling into her driveway. Partially because she *technically* invited me earlier, when she taunted me with memories of our night in that hotel room, but mostly because I'm not offering her a chance to talk her way out of seeing me tonight. For all that she agreed to the rules, I know she's going to do her best to break them every chance she gets. And I'm not going to let her.

Even if there is another truck parked in front of her house.

I glare at it as I get out, just on principle, and my glower increases when I spot a man's shirt strewn across the passenger seat. Lark doesn't have siblings, so this had damn well better be a friend. Hopefully one who can take a hint, because I don't want to share her tonight.

When I knock at the door, a dog barks in return, and I hear the low tones of a male voice quieting the dog before the door opens to present a perfectly disheveled Lark: wet hair, a tank top that does nothing to hide her lack of bra, tiny, soft shorts, and bare feet. It's a version of Lark I've never been allowed to see, and I finally understand what people mean when they say they went weak in the knees.

"Mark—"

I step through the doorway and kiss her before she can say anything beyond my name. Her gasp of surprise softens into a quiet moan against my lips as I clutch her face between my hands; her immediate compliance soothes me, because it's something that has never changed.

When it's only up to our bodies, she's always mine.

She parts her lips, begging for more, but I pull back with the restraint of a goddamn superhero. "Hey, Songbird."

Her face shifts through a range of reactions, but I let her go, kneeling down instead to greet the brick house of a pit mix who appears to nudge my knee with his nose. "Hi, buddy. Who are you?"

The moment the dog realizes he has my full attention, his whole body explodes into wriggling joy. I laugh as I try to keep up, only remembering Lark and I aren't alone when an unknown voice answers my question. "That's Angus. He loves everyone, so don't go feeling too special, Aladyne."

The wry namedrop makes me look up to see Gideon Stewart standing in the kitchen doorway with his hands firmly stuffed in his pockets. He is, to my relief, both completely dressed and utterly unbothered by the way I greeted Lark. "Gideon! It's been a minute. How's business?"

Gideon and I are friendlier than strangers, but we've never made it all the way to friends. I've heard he does good work, but about a decade ago, we decided to bring on a full-time farrier to our farm, so we've never had reason to hire him. But you run in the same circles long enough, you end up sharing a beer now and then.

"Sweaty," he answers, because conversations in the summer in Florida always come back to how close we are to the human body's melting point. "But busy. I just came by to drop something off—I'll get out of your hair."

If I were a better man, I'd protest. *Nah, dude. Hang out. Let's catch up.* But instead, I offer him a handshake and a pointed, "It was nice to see you, man."

"Oh my god," Lark mutters. "It's like you've both forgotten I'm even here."

"Trust me." My eyes cut to hers. "I haven't forgotten."

I'm gifted with my favorite sight: Lark's cheeks turning a pretty shade of pink.

"And that's our cue. C'mon, Angus. Whatever is about to happen here is too mature for your innocent eyes." Angus trots happily after Gideon, and the *snick* of the door shutting behind them is the best sound in the entire world.

I take a step toward Lark, whose eyes flare in preemptive defensiveness. She expects some alpha male bullshit about her having Gideon here, but her kiss told me I don't have to worry on that front. No, I have a different concern at the moment.

"Tell me something, babe." Once again, I crowd into her space until her back hits the wall. Two days in a row, I've had her pinned like this. A man could get used to it. I tug her chin up to keep her looking at me. "What, exactly, is sex?"

She blinks, slow to process the question. "What?"

"You heard me. Answer the question."

Her face immediately morphs into her sassiest form. "Has it been so long that you've forgotten? Sex is when you put your penis in my vagina—"

Thank fuck. "You're going to regret that perfect answer."

I take her mouth again before she can respond, and this time I don't stop when she parts her lips for me. My fingers catch one of her wrists, pinning it above our heads; my other hand grabs a bare thigh and hooks her leg around me until our bodies are flush together. She whimpers as her hips roll against me, and I swear the condoms in my pocket are practically screaming at me about how easy it would be to put them to good use.

But we're a long way from her winning this game, and she just gave me permission to have a lot more fun in the meantime. "I didn't expect you to be so traditional," I murmur as I kiss my way down her neck. I slide my hand beneath her shorts, my cock going hard as stone when I feel how drenched she is.

"Mmm?" is all I get in response, and I smile against her skin as I work slow, steady circles on her clit, just the way she likes. I want to slip a finger or two inside her sweet pussy, tease and stretch it so she's ready for me when the time comes, but there'll be time for that later. Her free hand is grasping onto my shirt, her nails digging into my chest, and the noises falling from her lips tell me she's already close to the edge.

I have a feeling my girl has been denying herself pleasure these past few months, and that's a situation I intend to rectify. "Your definition," I continue, my mouth back against hers, my words existing solely in our shared breath. Her hips rock, begging for more, and I increase the pressure from my fingers slightly until I feel her go still right before she explodes.

Fuck, I've missed this. The way she fully inhabits her body in these moments is a thing of beauty—the kind that makes my aching cock meaningless in comparison. Six months without her was six months too long.

I kiss her again, softening my touch as I work her through the final waves of her orgasm. When she bats my hand away, too sensitive for more, I bring the taste of her to my lips, biting back a moan as I do. Before she can fully come back to herself, I release her wrist and brush her pretty blonde hair out of her face. "There are countless ways for both of us to come, Songbird, and you just told me only one of them counts as sex." I would have heeded any line she drew, but I can't say I'm mad about the one she chose. "This is a much better deal for me than I expected."

Her eyes snap open, molten fury in those irises as she shoves me away from her. "You're a fucking asshole."

My laughter only pisses her off more. Maybe I cheated, but I don't care in the slightest. I make a show of adjusting myself, wanting her to see the state I'm in after that encounter. "I only asked a question. You're the one who answered it."

She scowls, returning to the kitchen and the beer she was

having with Gideon when I showed up. She chugs the rest of it in one go, then rinses out the empty bottle and leaves it in her sink. There's something about the tension between angrily finishing the drink and carefully setting it aside to recycle that sums up so much of what I love about her.

But right now probably isn't the moment to bring that word back into our lexicon.

"What is it that you want, Mark? What do you get out of this game?" When she looks up at me again, I see how exhausted she really is, and feel a flash of guilt for pushing her like this when I know she's already pulled in too many directions. If I didn't feel so certain this is my last chance to make this thing between us real, I'd back off.

But it is, so I can't.

"You," I say. "I want you. And we could end the bullshit here and now if you'd just admit we had something real. That we *have* something real."

"I already told you. I don't love you." She doesn't flinch when she says the words, but she doesn't make eye contact, either. She wants to believe what she's saying, but there's a hollowness in her voice that keeps me from believing it myself. "You promised that if I went out with you and it ended badly, you'd leave me alone."

I settle on a barstool next to the island, needing her to know she's not going to run me off. "I promised we'd stop the hookups. Which we did." Did we ever. I don't think my hand and my dick have been this well acquainted since middle school. "But I didn't say a damn thing about giving up on us."

"There is no us!"

"There is until the end of the sale."

"*Just* until the end of the sale."

I nod. "If that's what you want."

She didn't expect me to agree so easily, so she bites her

lip, stymied. Maybe I shouldn't give her such a clear escape route. But the truth is, everything else aside, if she needs to walk away again when this is over, I'll let her.

It'll kill me, but I love her enough to let her go.

"Have you eaten?" she asks after an extended silence, and I stifle an impulse to punch the air.

We're *in this*.

"I could eat."

She mumbles something about that not being the question she asked, but starts pulling food out of the fridge anyway. "Lasagna okay?"

"Sounds fucking perfect."

I offer to help, but she shuts me down—*I pre-made this last week, and I think I'm capable of putting a pan in the damn oven,* are her exact words—so I start to lob questions her way instead. Everything I've learned about this woman over the years has been against her will, gleaned from sifting through tiny scraps she didn't realize she was showing me. I'm desperate to see what I can get when she gives of herself freely.

Still, I start simple, asking about how she came to know Gideon as the oven heats. She tells me that she's known him for years, in the same ambient way that I know him, but they became closer when she hired him as her farrier after she started her own consignment. The fact that she trusts him to take care of her horses while she's at the sale speaks volumes, and I make a mental note to work harder to properly befriend the man.

Once the lasagna is heating up, I succeed in tugging her down onto the stool next to me. Our knees knock together as she restlessly swivels back and forth, and she only stops when I rest my hand on her thigh. When she frowns at me, I grin. "Nervous?"

"Don't flatter yourself."

I don't need to—the way her fingers press flat against the counter as my hand slides a few inches north on her thigh is flattering enough. But I don't push it, mostly because my dick still hasn't entirely given up hope and the last thing I need is to pour more fuel on that particular fire. Once I see her take a deep enough breath that I'm convinced she's settled, I pull my hand away and move onto my next topic of curiosity. "Who was the asshole you and Pink Braids were talking about today?"

I let the topic go when she dodged it at lunch, but I haven't forgotten. Whoever it was cleared out by the time I showed up, and both Lark and Alicia seemed mostly unfazed, but it still bothered me.

"Pink Braids?"

I shrug. "She didn't give me her name at the coffeeshop, so I had to improvise."

"Please call her that to her face."

"I'll consider it if you answer the question."

"I didn't get his name." She frowns. "He claimed to be in a hurry, so I spent half the time in the barn getting the horses ready. And then he spent a solid ten minutes just staring at Alicia's ass instead of the horse."

"Will you point him out to me if you see him again?"

"Why? You want to play hero?"

"I'm smarter than that." When her expression says *doubtful*, I poke her in the side until she smiles. "I know you can handle it. But if that's how he treats people, it makes me worry about how he treats his animals. I don't want to encourage him to buy our horses if I can help it."

There's only so much you can control at an auction, and there's always a risk your horse will go to a shitty owner. But I don't make a habit of glad-handing with assholes, even if they have money. Our horses deserve better.

Lark's eyes study mine for a moment, then soften. "Yeah. If I see him again, I'll let you know."

"Thank you."

I have a million more things I want to ask, but my mind empties the moment she reaches over to run her fingers through my hair. I lean into the gentle scrape of her nails against my scalp, closing my eyes as I do everything I can to memorize the shape of this moment. "I think I'm going to ruin you," she says, her voice regretful.

If being ruined is what it takes for her to touch me like this, then I'll live the rest of my life in pieces.

"I told you, Songbird. Do your worst. Let me worry about the rest."

TWO YEARS AGO

MARK

I didn't see Lark Reynolds again for nearly a month, and it was fine.

It wasn't like I replayed our first conversation in my head on a daily basis or anything. She was hot and funny and stubborn, and was just out there somewhere living her life without me, but not seeing her was fine.

Totally, completely fine.

"God, you're pathetic." Maddie stared at me over the brim of her glass. We were at Dicks, waiting for Bowen to show up. "I genuinely forgot how pathetic you can be."

I glared at her. "Shut up."

Her snort turned into full-fledged laughter. "If that's all you've got, we're really in trouble."

"I just wasn't feeling it, okay?"

A woman had set her eyes on me the moment I stepped into the bar. She was pretty, and her fearless flirting might have paid off in a different situation, but I knew within a few sentences that no part of me was interested. I chatted for a few minutes, let her down gently, and bought her a drink for her inconvenience.

Now I was getting roasted by my sister.

Everything. Was. *Fine.*

"I'm just saying, I haven't seen you like this since high school. And we both remember how well things went with Chloe Cartwright."

"I was fifteen," I countered. "Literally nothing went well when we were fifteen."

"Speak for yourself. I got laid that year."

I choked on my beer, eyes watering. "*What?!*"

She shrugged. "Jason Huang and I hooked up after soccer practice for like two months. I assumed you knew."

"He was a senior!"

Maddie waggled her eyebrows. "I know."

"Great. This is great. I have to belatedly kill a man for hooking up with my sister and then kill myself so I don't have to live with this information in my head anymore."

"I wouldn't recommend it," she said. "Your girl just walked in."

The thing was, odds were high she was fucking with me. I knew that. But that didn't make it physically possible for me to not spin around on my stool to check. Just in case.

And damn if my sister wasn't telling the truth. Lark was hovering inside the doorway, looking like a fucking dream with the way her hair fell around her shoulders. She cast her gaze around the bar as if looking for someone, which meant I got to see the exact moment she did a full-on double take when her eyes skirted by me—then came back, as if to assure herself it was actually me that she saw.

I already had a dopey ass grin on my face, and it only got bigger as she frowned at the sight of me. I raised two fingers in a jaunty wave, taking only minor offense when she rolled her eyes and strode across the room to join a woman I didn't recognize. My jealousy flared, just a bit, but it was soothed by getting to watch her ass sway as she walked by.

"Hey!" Maddie snapped in my face to draw my attention back to her. "You don't get to drool over her yet."

"Right, right," I sighed. Maddie had told me she wanted to talk about some work stuff, and my compromise was suggesting that we do it here at Dicks. If I bailed on her, she'd make my life miserable for the next month. Besides, if I approached Lark now, I already knew she'd shut me down. Restraint would be key tonight. "What's up?"

"Mom and Dad want to restructure now that I've finished my MBA." She paused, waiting to see my reaction, but the truth was I didn't have one. Mostly because I didn't know what the hell that meant. "They want all the financial decisions to flow through me."

I shrugged. "Seems smart." Maddie had always been a numbers person, and now she had the degrees to back it up.

"It'll change the way we do things," she explained. "Ordering, stud fees, sales—all the stuff you run will have a different workflow. Are you okay with that? I'd be the one telling you no sometimes."

"Like that's anything new."

"Mark." Maddie's voice grew sharp, her gaze serious. "This is a big deal."

I rested my arms on the table, spinning my beer in place. I knew she was right. I'd spent the years Maddie had been in school being able to do whatever it was that I wanted, within reason. My decisions weren't always grounded in cost-benefit analyses, but I wasn't frivolous and my parents trusted my instincts. What they were talking about would be a significant change.

But the thing that the three of them never quite understood was that *I didn't care*. I cared about them, and the farm, and the horses, but I didn't need to be in charge. Maddie could make all the decisions. I'd focus on seeing them through.

"I think that sounds great," I said, meeting her eyes with a sincere smile. "We'd be foolish to waste your talent, Mads."

Her smile matched mine—it always did—but faded into something more uncertain. "I just don't want you to resent me."

"Not possible. Not with this."

The words seemed to reassure her enough to crack a joke. "Just with everything else?"

"I've got a running list if you want it. The most recent entry is you telling me about Jason Huang."

"Just wait until I tell you about Cla—"

"Nope." I cut her off. "Absolutely not."

"Sorry I'm late." Bowen finally appeared, settling onto the stool next to me. "What is Maddie not doing?"

"Telling me any more about her teenage sex life."

"Oh, you finally told him about Clara?"

"*Clara?!*" I was basically shouting again, so I forced myself to lower my voice. "Like my ex-girlfriend, Clara?"

"Our," Maddie corrected. "*Our* ex-girlfriend."

"I need another drink," I groaned, not entirely sure if they were fucking with me or not. I left them to their laughter as I made my way to the bar.

While I waited for the bartender, Elsie, to finish the drinks she was working on, I resumed my favorite hobby: shamelessly watching Lark. She and her friend were mid-conversation, their faces alight with amusement. I slowly lost myself in the way Lark twisted her hair up into a bun, thinking about all the things I'd let those graceful fingers of hers do to me.

Which meant I couldn't say how many times Elsie had to clear her throat before she pulled me out of my reverie. "Sorry," I said, with my most charming grin. She was used to my bullshit by now, so she just rolled her eyes and motioned for me to get on with my order. I dropped my card off to open a tab, and ordered another round for the three of us. Then I nodded my head in Lark's direction, and told Elsie, "They're on my tab tonight, too. Anything she drinks goes on my card, even if someone else tries to buy it for her."

Another eye roll. "Whatever you say, Casanova."

I scooped up our drinks, returned to our table, and waited. The gambit took less than an hour to pay off, with a visibly annoyed Lark appearing at our table with her arms crossed. "What do you think you're doing?"

I spun on my stool, framing my legs on either side of her waist even if she wasn't quite close enough to touch, and grinned in genuine delight. "Well, hello again, Lark. Nice to see you, too."

"I left that out for a reason. Why are you buying my drinks?"

"Because I want to." I downed the last of my beer. "It's just a drink."

"That's a load of shit and you know it." She stepped forward, her hip brushing my knee. I had to start thinking some very boring thoughts, and fast. "What did I tell you, Aladyne?"

"Hmm." I pretended to consider. "That you're intimidated by my overwhelming handsomeness and wit?"

Both Lark *and* my traitorous friends laughed at that. Her hand came to rest on my upper thigh, the light caress of her thumb practically a detonation against my skin. She crowded into me further, and at that point there was no controlling my dick's excitement so I indulged in every dirty thought that came my way as she pressed up onto her tiptoes and spoke into my ear. "I'm. Not. Interested."

Before she could back away, I caught her belt loops, keeping her close. I let my eyes drift down to her chest, then over to where her fingers were still gripping my leg nearly hard enough to leave marks. I wanted them to—to have to physical proof of her presence when she walked away. "Your body says otherwise," I murmured, a hair's breadth from her lips.

I could have kissed her. She would have let me—it was in the way her breath caught in her throat, in the way her pupils flared as our eyes met.

"Enjoy your drink, Lark."

I let her go, wanting to give her a moment of being as off-balance as she made me feel. She stumbled back a step, her fire reigniting as her breath restarted. Her lips curved into a sly smile as she walked her way back over to Elsie, and both Maddie and Bowen cursed on my behalf the moment it became clear what she was about to do.

She ordered a bottle of top-shelf whiskey without ever taking her eyes off me, mouthing, *Game on*, in my direction.

I just grinned back, already knowing the night would end with me getting a taste. I'd start with the whiskey, then move onto the woman.

It was only a matter of time.

CHAPTER 7

LARK

"Would you like some more wine, Lark?" From the end of the table, Mark's mother, Diane, holds the bottle, having just refilled her own glass.

The answer that comes out is accidental but honest. "God, yes."

I'd feel worse if it weren't for Maddie and Mark laughing in twin-shaped unison at my response. Mark's arm is casually draped over the back of my chair, fingers periodically teasing my hair, while Maddie sits across from us both, her gaze sharp as she watches our every interaction. Diane and Mark's father, Peter, sit at the respective heads of the table, and Peter is the one who rescues me. "I'd say you've earned it, this being your first solo sale."

"I've survived the first couple days. I'm just hoping I can make it through the rest."

Mark squeezes my shoulder. "Don't downplay it, Songbird. You're working your ass off."

I don't miss the successive moments of meaningful eye contact that pass among the rest of the table at the casual use of my nickname. I'm still not entirely sure how he talked me into coming to a family dinner on the third day of our temporary relationship, but here we are.

Well, that's not true. I remember a little *too* well, if I'm honest. Our empty plates had barely made it to the sink last night before Mark's mouth was back on my skin. I was exhausted and still debating if I had a case for entrapment with how he tricked me earlier, but the moment he slipped a finger inside me I decided I no longer cared.

And when his thumb pressed against my clit to send me into my second orgasm of the day, I would have said yes to just about any question he asked. I was lucky it was a dinner invitation and not a marriage proposal.

Though right now, I'm not longer convinced that just getting married wouldn't be easier than sitting through this dinner. Everyone is so relentlessly *nice*—including Maddie, who Mark warned might try to have fun at his expense—that I'm kind of at a loss. Introducing me to his picture-perfect family is undoubtedly part of his master plan to make me fall in love with him, and the worst part is, I can barely resist the onslaught. Not with his sister laughing at my terrible jokes and his father promising to keep an ear out for potential clients and his mother practically bursting at the seams at the mere fact that I am here with her son.

Dinners with my parents are nothing like this, especially after everything that happened with my ex. They're cold instead of warm, full of critique instead of compliments. I don't remember the last time anyone told a joke, let alone laughed. The Aladynes are a world apart from everything I know.

Which is probably why, when Diane asks for the story of how we got together, I smile sweetly at Mark and ask, "Are we starting with our secret hookups or the fact that this whole relationship is based on a bet, baby?"

Peter coughs into his napkin, Diane's eyes bounce between the two of us like we're a game of ping pong, and Maddie laughs in open delight. But it's Mark who I can't take my eyes off, because he's not rattled in the slightest. He cuts me that crooked grin and replies, "Those hookups were never a secret, baby."

Then, before I can muster a response, he leans closer. His gaze his steady, his words just for me. "There's not a single thing about you I want to hide. Tell them whatever you want, Songbird."

Well. Fuck.

Across the table, Maddie admits, "I already know everything."

Diane shrugs, a smug smirk on her lips that tells me exactly where Mark gets his from. "I have some guesses."

"Well, I don't know a damn thing!" Peter scowls, but his eyes crinkle with laughter. "Somebody catch me up."

"Lark and I met two years ago at the Fourth of July barbecue," Mark begins. His eyes flick to me when I settle my hand on his leg under the table in warning, but he keeps talking. "It was basically love at first sight."

I snort. "Whatever helps you sleep at night."

"Fine, fine, it was more like love at first dismissal. She rolled her eyes and pretended to ignore me—"

"I wasn't pretending."

"—which is how I knew she was the one." I slide my hand up his inner thigh, and he shifts in his seat ever so slightly. "But Lark was intimidated by our connection and wouldn't agree to a date."

"No, I just know a risk when I see one and decided to protect myself." My fingers graze his crotch, and he pretends it's my words he's reacting to when he exhales. "It took him a while to gain access to even the No Strings Attached tier."

"And I said I'd take whatever access to you I could get."

His smile becomes utterly sincere. "That much hasn't changed."

That annoying bunny in my stomach is back, just hopping its way around in glee. The bunny needs to die. I'm gonna murder the bunny.

"The problem is he can't understand basic instructions, so he spent the next year and a half trying to talk me into a date."

"I budgeted five years for that, so I came out way ahead of schedule."

I've stopped paying any attention to his family, entirely wrapped up in the way he keeps flipping our story on its head. He means it all, is the thing that gets me. There's humor and arrogance in the way he talks, but no part of it is a lie. This is just the truth as he sees it.

I wish, for his sake, his truth was compatible with mine.

"He planned a marginally above average date—"

"I fucking nailed it and you know it."

"—but he decided the first date would be the ideal time to tell me he was in love with me."

"Mark!" Diane exclaims as Maddie coughs, "Loser."

"For heaven's sake, son." Peter shakes his head. "I thought I taught you better than that."

I shift in my seat, not quite sure what to do with his family being so firmly on my side, but Mark remains undaunted. "I told Bowen I loved her the first time she looked at me, so I think I showed great restraint in waiting that long, actually."

I told Bowen I loved her the first time she looked at me. I know that doesn't mean anything—he quite literally *hadn't met me yet,* so there was no world in which he *loved* me—but damn if the bunny doesn't roll on its back and kick the air with both back feet anyway.

"I ended things." My voice rasps; I can't bring myself to say more than that. I should—it would probably make his family think less of me, which would make *him* think less of me, which would make this whole situation end more easily. But the bunny doesn't want to put the words I said out for everyone to see. The bunny wants them to like me.

Just the bunny. Not me.

"And we didn't talk again until a couple days ago. She practically ran into my arms."

"He wasn't watching where he was going. I was disappointed he didn't lose a tooth."

"I only ever lose my heart to you, babe."

"Gross," Maddie and I say simultaneously.

"Romantic," he counters, unbothered. "Anyway, I convinced her to give me two weeks to prove this is real. And here we are."

"Malarky!" Maddie's exclamation startles everyone, and she grins. "That's your couple name now. Because I can't go around rhyming all the time."

Mark grins. "I can get on board with that."

Ignoring her children, Diane focuses on me. I expected judgment—this conversation would have been shut down in about two sentences by my parents—but all that shows in her eyes is gentle concern. "Well, I admit my guesses were not quite as accurate as I might have hoped. But I am certainly invested in the outcome. Lark, honey, what is it you get from this whole situation?"

Next to me, Mark scoffs, like the benefits should be obvious, but everyone ignores him in a way that's oddly reassuring. He must be this absurd in all aspects of his life, not just with me.

"He's fed me multiple times so far, so that's nice." I finally move the last inches to place my hand over the bulge in his pants, gratified by the way his knuckles go white around his glass as I squeeze his length. "But don't worry, I have my own rewards."

"Well," Peter says, clearly somewhat baffled after all that information. "We're happy to have you tonight, but I have to confess, I'm rooting for my son. It'd be nice to set an extra place setting indefinitely."

I'm pretty sure the damn bunny just passed out from joy.

"Lark, come with me for a moment," Diane says shortly after, as Maddie starts collecting empty plates to take to the kitchen. "I have something to show you."

I feel bad leaving the cleanup behind, but I'd feel worse not following Mark's mom. I stand, pausing on instinct because Mark rarely misses a chance to be at my side, but he offers me an aggrieved look. "I'll be there soon."

I stifle my laughter as I join Diane. He was the one who agreed to let me sexually torture him, so it's his own fault he's a grown man hiding a boner at his parents' kitchen table.

Diane leads me to a warm and comfortable office, where a black cat twitches its tail on a shelf as it watches us walk in. "That's Pango. He likes his space."

"I know the feeling."

She smiles. "Nothing wrong with knowing what you like."

"I promise I'm not trying to hurt him." I don't know where the words come from, but I don't know how to not say them, either. "I know this two-week thing is weird, but it's not..."

I trail off, not sure how I'd even begin to finish that sentence. Especially when I know this ends with Mark getting hurt, even if I don't want him to.

But Diane just chuffs softly. "Oh, honey, I know my son. There's not a bit of this situation I hold against you. Now come here." She guides me over to the desk, where she opens a thick binder and begins flipping through pages.

It takes me a moment to realize each page is a photo from a winner's circle. The fact that they have a binder full of them —the fact that there's an empty space on the shelf over Diane's shoulder that suggests they have *multiple* binders full of them—makes my chest squeeze. I'm still figuring out what I want my business to be, but it's overwhelming to recognize the difference between my fledgling consignment and the many decades of history here at Aladyne. I might never get into training and racing—I might stay a consigner, or branch out into breeding—but there's a magic to a winner's circle that calls to me anyway.

What might it feel like to have *one* of those pictures as proof of my work, let alone binders full?

"As soon as Mark told me you two were finally together," Diane says as she searches through the binder, "I knew I had to dig this up."

I don't miss the *finally*, and I wonder what it means. If it's that Mark has been as open with his feelings about me to other people as he has been to me, or if it's something simpler—just a mother impatient for her son to settle down. I consider asking, but she lights up as she finds the right picture, and all other thoughts disappear as I take in what she's showing me.

A horse and jockey in silks I don't recognize are in the center of the image, clusters of people on either side. Diane and Peter are there, of course, but they aren't the ones who make my mouth drop open in awe. That honor is reserved for the much younger version of my parents I see standing at their side.

I touch the edges of the picture, tentative despite the protective plastic over top. The date at the bottom marks it as nearly thirty years ago, not long before I was born. The version of my father in the picture is leaner than he is now, his hair shaggier. Mom is leggy and gorgeous, but not her current, immaculate self—her shirt is a bit wrinkled, her hair a halo of frizz around her head that I recognize from seeing my own hair in the mirror each day. Their smiles are broad and beaming, hands gripped tight between them.

They look young. They look happy.

They look like strangers.

Near the date, other text catches my attention. *Trained by Diane Aladyne*, it says. *Owned by Reynolds Racing.*

Reynolds Racing. A name I've never heard before, but one that was good enough to win a race. I stare at the words, unsure what to make of this preserved memory I had no part in.

"Lark, honey?" Diane's voice holds a touch of concern, and I realize I've been staring in stunned silence.

"I didn't know they ever owned a racehorse before they worked at Landow," I admit. "This is…"

For a second time, I trail off, not entirely convinced I ever had a word to finish that sentence. Diane's eyes light with compassion and maybe a hint of regret, but her expression softens before she can say anything. It's the only warning I get before Mark steps up behind me, gently wrapping his arms around my waist. When he laces his fingers with mine, I lean into his form, letting him hold me up.

Right now, I don't mind having him at my back.

"Maybe you should ask them about it sometime," Diane suggests. "I don't know the whole story, just my small part in it."

"What was your part, Mom?" Mark asks, like he knows I can't get the words out.

"I don't know how your parents ended up with the colt in the first place," she says, "but your mother and I ran into each other at the grocery store one day and she said they had a racehorse in need of training. We were doing more freelance training back then, and we had a bit of room in need of filling.

"So we struck a deal, and we trained the colt here for a month or so before he was ready to race. It's been so long I don't really remember the details—I'm not sure how many races they ran him in or what happened to him after. But I knew he won at least once, which meant I'd have a picture of it somewhere."

"Your hoarding is good for something after all," Mark teases. I don't hear the rest of their familial exchange because I'm still lost in the picture in front of me.

Why didn't I know about this? We've had so many conversations—arguments, even—about me starting my own business, and they never bothered to mention they had done it once, too?

But the part that really gets me is that they gave it up. They were building something all their own, together, and the only record of it is this winner's circle picture, tucked away in my temporary boyfriend's parents' house. I never would have known, without Mark's relentless determination.

Mark's arms tighten around me, bringing me back to the moment. His mom is smiling softly at me. "Do you want to keep it?"

"No." As with so much of my conversation tonight, I'm blurting out words before I even have time to think. I try to ease my tone. "Thank you, but I don't want to take the original."

For all I know, my parents have their own copy in their house somewhere.

One of Mark's arms pulls free, leaving something small in me a bit bereft at the loss, but then he's holding his phone, taking a few pictures of the photo for me. I squeeze the hand that's still holding mine, the most thanks I can offer right now, and he squeezes back. "For later," he murmurs in my ear. "If you want it."

To his mother, he says, "Mind if I steal my girlfriend away?"

"Only if you promise to bring her back next week." Diane winks, and this time, my smile is sincere.

"I'll be here."

CHAPTER 8

MARK

"What do you think you're doing?" Lark's face is thunderous, and a smarter man would turn tail and run.

Luckily, I've never been a particularly smart man. "Helping," I say, continuing to pick the stall I'm in, if only to avoid facing her wrath head-on.

"Like hell you are. We talked about this."

I should have known she'd insist on doing this the hard way. I pause, leaning an arm atop the pitchfork. "You said I couldn't help while in Aladyne colors. I'm not in Aladyne colors."

About thirty-three different emotions scatter over her face as she realizes I'm wearing a shirt that is as close a match to her chosen shade of blue as I could get on short notice. I gave serious consideration to raiding her shirt stash to have the real deal, but ultimately decided that was a step too far. She probably only ordered enough for her and Alicia, and odds were low either of their sizes would fit on me. So I settled for a facsimile, for now. "Unlike some of us, you have an entire crew to support, Mark. Go help them."

There's an odd thread in her voice as she chastises me—if

I didn't know better, I'd call it longing. I file it away to mull over later.

"Trust me, they're happy I'm here. I mostly micromanage and get in the way. Besides"—I extend my arm to touch the single row of cinderblock that divides her stalls from ours—"I'm literally this close if they need me."

"I can't afford to pay you—"

"Keep your damn money." That comes out with more force than I intend, but the hint of pink on her cheeks tells me that might be a good thing. "Part of the deal was that we'd be all in, Lark. I can't be here all day, as much as I'd like to be. But as your boyfriend, I want to help when I can. Let me. Please."

When she just glowers at me, I nod over her shoulder. "Coffee's on the table," I inform her, then go back to work.

By the time I finish picking the last stall, Alicia has arrived and Lark is halfway through her coffee as she works on setting everything up for the day. I wait for her to argue with me some more, but she appears to have settled on ignoring me as her current strategy.

I'll take it. If she's ignoring me, she's not actively trying to kick me out.

I still don't push my luck, though. When the buyers start showing up, I make a point of staying in the barn and letting Alicia take the horses out. All three of the horses Lark has here right now will go up for auction in the select sale tomorrow, and by tomorrow night, they'll either be with their new owners or back in her leased stalls, with three new horses taking their place. It's the reason I need to get her used to having me around today—she's going to *need* the extra help tomorrow.

Around mid-morning, I take advantage of a small sliver of peace and slip my arm around her waist, holding her in place so she has to acknowledge me. "My sister wants to bring lunch by today," I tell her. "She'll probably bring Bowen, too. Is that okay?"

It takes her a few seconds before she begrudgingly admits, "That sounds nice."

I smile as I press a kiss to her temple. "Was that painful?"

"Violently."

I'm about to let her go when she leans her head on my shoulder. I freeze, like the slightest shift might send her running for the hills. I'm used to Lark initiating sex, but this kind of affection is an entirely different beast. I refuse to be the one to shatter the moment, because it's the kind I never thought I'd get.

She's watching the Aladyne side of the barn, and I wish I could see her expression. "Mark, I—"

Whatever she's about to say gets cut off by a different voice. "Lark! There you are!"

Lark rockets away from me, her spine going ramrod straight as she spins to face her mother, who is approaching with Lark's father at her side.

"Hi, Mom! Hi, Dad!" Lark's voice is chipper and false, grating on my skin because my girl should never sound like that, let alone with her own parents. I cross my arms and settle against the nearest pillar as I watch her greet them both. If someone had asked me this time yesterday, I would have sworn my plan for dealing with Lark's parents was to push her into introducing me as her boyfriend so that I could show her I fit into her family the way she fits in mine.

But that was before I felt the way Lark stood frozen in my arms as she looked at the picture my mother showed her last night. Lark let more slip about her parents than she realized during the time we were hooking up, but I worry I've underestimated how toxic they are.

So right now, our little game pales in comparison to giving her whatever she needs.

"What are you doing here?" she asks, her hands clasped in front of her. Neither of her parents attempt to hug her, which is unfathomable to me. I'm lucky my mother doesn't get up in the middle of a meal to hug Maddie and me.

"Is that how you greet all your potential buyers?" Lark's mother—Jennifer, if memory serves—raises an eyebrow. I school my face, telling myself she means to be playful and not cruel. "That's not very professional."

"Oh." Lark falters, and my heart squeezes as I watch her expectations recalibrate. "You're here to see the horses?"

"Not all of them, obviously." This is her father, Levi, who doesn't bother to hide the disdain in his voice. "Only the Once and Again filly is worth the time."

I exchange a glance with Alicia, confirming that I'm not alone in my murderous impulses, and she ducks into Marshmallow's stall to dust her off and make sure she hasn't done something foolish like take a nap in her own shit in the time since she's been groomed.

If there's one thing grays love, it's to destroy your hard work as quickly as possible.

"Great! We can definitely do that!" I've never heard Lark's voice reach this particular octave. She glances over her shoulder at me and I nod, letting her know we're on it. The panic in her eyes eases, and she guides her parents out to the walkway.

I meet Alicia in the stall. "I've got her," I say, taking the shank.

She considers me for a moment, then shrugs. "Your funeral."

"It's gonna be someone's," I mutter, leaving her to chuckle behind me as I lead Marshmallow out to where Lark and her parents are waiting.

The situation hasn't gotten any better. "You're lucky we

even found you, tucked so far away like this," Jennifer is saying. "We almost decided it wasn't worth the hike."

Lark laughs weakly, her gaze latching onto me when she realizes I'm the one holding Marshmallow. She scowls, but only after she reveals the depth of her relief.

"Hm." Levi grunts as he studies Marshmallow's conformation. It's the sound of someone with something to say, and I'm hoping for all our sakes he chooses to keep that thought to himself. "Disappointing."

So much for that. I grind my teeth to keep from saying something. This horse is only *disappointing* if you want her to be something she isn't—she's a damn good broodmare candidate, and I guarantee Levi Reynolds knows that.

He just won't admit it in front of his daughter.

"Walk her, please." I didn't know how passive aggressive the word *please* could be until now. But I do as I'm told, guiding Marshmallow into a brisk walk away from Lark and her parents before retracing the path back to where we started. Levi lets out a few more *hms* that make me want to temporarily mute his vocal cords, but at least he avoids other commentary.

"I didn't realize you had more than one employee," Jennifer says. Her tone is impossible for me to read, especially in comparison to her husband's. I don't know if it's curiosity or judgment. "Seems like a lot for your...situation."

Judgment, then.

"Mark's not..." Lark hesitates, looking at me. I offer a subtle nod, hoping she knows I'll back her play, whatever it is. "Mark is actually my boyfriend?"

I don't even take offense at the way she turns the statement into a question. My girl just willingly claimed me, and I plan to ride that high for a damn good while once we get rid of her parents. "I pitch in when I can," I say, putting on as pleasant a voice as I can manage.

Both of her parents seem to move past the fact that she has a boyfriend without even registering the information. "Lark, honey, are you sure it's wise to let an amateur help you like this?" Jennifer asks.

"Mom!" Lark's control is slipping, and I'm rooting for it to slip a little faster. I want the Lark who takes no shit to make an appearance. "Mark's not—"

"Your mother's just trying to offer advice," Levi intones. "It's your first sale, after all, and we don't want you making mistakes."

I've had enough. "I'll make sure to tell my parents you consider us amateurs." Lark's eyes close in exasperation, but her parents both snap to attention at the coolness in my tone. I undercut it by offering them both my fakest, winningest smile.

"Are we supposed to know who you are?" Levi frowns, and I might find it intimidating if it weren't for the fact that it's an expression I've seen thousands of times on his daughter.

"We've met," I confirm. "Mark Aladyne."

Jennifer mouths *Aladyne* as she tries to process what I just said, while Levi rushes to cover their tracks. "Mark! Of course. I can't believe we didn't recognize you, son. It's good to know Lark's chosen wisely for herself—she was so petulant after her last relationship, I assumed she'd rather shoot herself in the foot than accept help from someone who knows what they're doing. No wonder things are running so smoothly over here."

Marshmallow huffs and stomps her feet next to me, picking up on the tension I'm carrying. I press a hand to her neck to calm her, but let my friendly facade fall away as I face Levi down. I don't miss the reference to Lark's previous relationship—which I've been desperate to learn more about for as long as I've known her—but I will not be playing his little game. "I suggest you don't give me credit for your daughter's success ever again."

"Mark." Lark's voice is clear, calling my focus. "Can you take Marshmallow back to the barn?"

I hold her gaze for a moment, trying to read how angry she is—and with whom, because I'm sure I won't be escaping her wrath entirely. But I've already done enough damage, so I gently tug Marshmallow to follow me and return her to the stall. Alicia's eyes are wide as she opens the door. "I couldn't hear all of that but it looked—"

"Worse," I snap. "Whatever you're assuming, it was worse."

Marshmallow tosses her head as I unclip her, and I slip a LifeSaver from my pocket and sneak it to her. She earned it, after being part of that debacle. I give her a few scratches for good measure, then turn to see Alicia holding the stall door closed.

"You good?" she asks, clearly concerned I'm about to go start a fight. She's not wrong to worry.

"I'm good." I'm also all too aware that, for a woman nearly a foot shorter than me, Alicia could give me a run for my money if it came down to a battle of muscles. Exercise riders are no joke. "Please let me out before this horse messes up my hair."

"That would be a national tragedy," she drawls, sliding the door far enough for me to slip out.

"I'm glad we agree."

Lark is still where I left her, now watching her parents walk away. I tell myself to give her space, but my resolve fades when her shoulders slump. I don't bother going as far as the pass-through in the railing—I duck under instead, crossing to where she stands in a few long strides. "You okay, Songbird?"

Her answer comes in the form of a shove to my chest. I

rock back on my heels, then brace for her to try again. She can take out all her frustration on me, if it helps her process what just happened.

But instead of pushing me again, she throws her arms around my neck. I let her sink into me as I circle her waist and pull her close. "I've got you," I murmur.

I get four shaky inhales out of her before she tears herself away without a word, determined to act like nothing happened. She doesn't meet my gaze when she says, "You should probably go do your real job now."

Someday, her dismissals will stop feeling like knives between my ribs. Or maybe that's the entire reason I'm forcing her hand: because I'd take those knives over not ever having her in the first place.

"Okay." I don't argue. After what just happened with her parents, she needs to reclaim her control, and I want her to have the room she needs to do it.

Her grateful smile tells me giving her space is the right choice. And she can have it.

Until lunch.

NINE MONTHS AGO

LARK

"Lark? Are you Lark Reynolds?" The voice that called my name was nasally and uncertain, which didn't bode well. It was a far cry from the deep, confident voice that had been on the dating profile when I swiped right a few nights ago in an attempt to stop myself from texting a certain hot horseman.

And sure enough, when I turned around, the man that greeted me was not the man I expected to see, either. It wasn't a full-on catfish, he hadn't gone that far, but there had clearly been some deeply creative photoshopping along the way. He knew it, too—he held his body like a blow had already hit him as he waited for me to respond.

It wasn't that his actual looks were a problem. Truthfully, that wouldn't make or break a first date for me anyway, and just because he was about four inches shorter than he claimed and lacking a large percentage of the hair he had in his photos didn't mean there wasn't potential there.

Or there would have been, if he hadn't started out by lying. I raised my brow. "Pretty sure you're not the one who should be doubting my identity." I had literally replaced two pictures with updated ones the day we matched. I learned fast that it was easier to provide all of that information accurately and upfront, rather than be the person on the other side of this equation. "I assume your name is actually Rodger?"

He drew himself up a bit, unearned annoyance crossing his face. "Yes, of course it is."

"Great."

When he realized that's all I was going to offer, he motioned to the host stand. "Shall we?"

And now I had a decision to make. The way I saw it, there were three options:

1. Let the subject drop entirely so that we could start from scratch.

2. Go on the date, but make him grovel along the way.

3. Leave now, and spend the night at home with my vibrator.

To be honest, option three was looking pretty damn appealing at the moment, because there wasn't much point in seeing the night through. I wasn't going to date or sleep with someone who tried to trick me into seeing them in the first place, and frankly, the food here wasn't good enough to justify the awkwardness.

I cast my gaze around the restaurant as I considered the best way to say, "Actually, we shan't," when my eyes landed on the last person I wanted to see in this moment: Mark Aladyne.

He was sitting at a table with his parents and his sister, head thrown back in laughter at something Maddie said. He hadn't noticed me yet, and I took a step back, ready to bolt before that could change—but it was as if my movement activated a switch inside him somewhere, because his laughter suddenly cut off as his eyes caught mine.

He tilted his head in inquiry, curiosity of some sort on his face, but I didn't have time to process it before Rodger stepped close to me—too close, nearly making me choke on his overly strong cologne. "Are you ready?" he asked, his hand settling firmly on my upper ass instead of my lower back.

I was about to snap at him and pull away, but I made the mistake of looking back at Mark first. Mark, with his fucking crooked grin, who looked all too amused at the situation I was currently in.

And to whom I now had to prove a point, fallback date with my vibrator be damned. I narrowed my eyes at Mark in warning, before turning my blandest smile on Rodger. "So ready," I lied through my teeth.

I expected him to react with surprise rather than smug satisfaction, so that at least made the fact that I actually had no interest in him much easier to rationalize for myself. He used the act of pulling out my chair as an opportunity to stare down my shirt, and didn't bother to hide his distaste when I ordered a whiskey instead of the cocktail he tried to suggest.

Although I realized as soon as I tasted it that the drink was a tactical error on my part, because it had been a long time since I'd been able to drink whiskey without thinking of Mark. So maybe Rodger had a point on that one.

My chair was, blessedly, pointed away from Mark, so I didn't have to watch him judge my entire date, and he didn't get to see my deeply bored face as I listened to Rodger tell me about his accounting job in excruciating detail. I lowkey lived for spreadsheets, so the fact that my eyes glazed over as soon as he started talking was honestly impressive.

Our waitress proved to be a goddamn angel. She quickly read the terrible first date vibes and made a point of fast tracking our orders, then circled through more than was strictly necessary just to interrupt our lingering awkward silences. I had almost convinced myself I was going to get through the meal mostly unscathed when I saw a familiar smirk over Rodger's shoulder.

Mark's family must have finished their meal, because he was now posted up at the bar, casually sipping a whiskey of his own as he openly watched me. When he saw me looking, he tipped his drink to me in acknowledgement, leaving me to physically restrain myself from flipping him off.

I made it another two minutes under his scrutiny before I interrupted whatever undoubtedly scintillating story Rodger was now telling about the buffet on his most recent work trip—which, I didn't know what kind of work trips accountants had, so I clearly hadn't been paying enough attention—with a terse, "I'll be right back."

My napkin dropped to the floor, but I left it in my wake as I marched over to the bar. Mark's grin only grew wider as I approached, to the point where I was seriously concerned that it might break his damn face. "What are you doing?" I hissed under my breath.

"What does it look like I'm doing?" He asked over the rim of his glass. I watched his throat contract and shift as he swallowed, and had to force my attention away before my eyes continued the journey down to the open buttons on his shirt.

"It looks like you're being a pain in my ass."

"Songbird, if you want a little light spanking, all you ever have to do is ask. You know that."

It was good for both of our sakes that he hadn't set his drink down, because I would have thrown it in his face for that. Not because I was insulted, but because I was pissed at how turned on I was by the lazy promise in his voice.

"I'm having a perfectly nice date"—he snorted at the obvious lie—"and you are intentionally distracting me."

"All I'm doing is sitting at the bar."

"And staring at me."

His eyes swept down my body, hungry as ever, before snapping back up to mine. My freaking knees were probably blushing from the intensity of his perusal. "Someone should be, because you're fucking wasted on that loser."

"Just go home, Mark."

He ignored my order entirely. "You know there's an easy way to solve this problem."

"I'm not going on a date with you."

"Maybe not." He finished his whiskey and motioned to the bartender for two more. "But he's not the one you're going home with tonight."

When the bartender slid them over, he pressed one into my hand. The brush of his fingers against mine made me shiver, and his mouth crooked back into that familiar shape. "Go finish your date, Lark. I'll be here when it's over."

I couldn't tell you what I told Rodger about how I got the drink, and I didn't hear a word of his inane chatter for the rest of the meal. I didn't taste the food I ate, and I damn sure didn't have a good explanation for why my portion of the meal had already been paid for when the time came to ask for the check.

I was too lost in the way Mark's attention drifted over me from moment to moment, in the warmth that flooded my body each time I sipped the whiskey he bought me, in the promise of how this night was already destined to end.

Rodger left, somehow—I wasn't entirely sure I even acknowledged his departure. When the waitress passed by one more time, I asked quietly, "Did he tip you well?"

Her gaze followed mine to where Mark still sat waiting. "He did. And not for nothing, but that one looks like a considerable upgrade."

I drained what little remained in my glass with a sigh. "That is precisely the problem."

And then I gave Mark Aladyne the rest of my night.

CHAPTER 9

LARK

No wonder things are running so smoothly over here.

I suggest you don't give me credit for your daughter's success ever again.

I replay my parents' visit countless times over the next two hours, but those are the sentences I keep coming back to again and again and again. My father, discounting my ability, and Mark reasserting it. The whiplash of being dismissed and supported, by two very different men.

I sent Mark away because he's starting to get under my skin. His annoying face and absurd body and ridiculous clothes. His determination that he won't let a damn thing I do ruffle him. His steady warmth when he touches me. His firm insistence that I get the credit I deserve for my work.

He just keeps *showing up*. It's barely been three days and I'm already starting to get used to having him around.

Getting used to him is dangerous. I got used to having a team once. To being in a partnership at work and at home. When it all fell apart and I realized the costs of that comfort far outweighed the rewards, I threw my walls up fast and high. They've kept me safe ever since, despite Mark's relentless pursuit.

But now I'm supposed to have lunch with his sister and his best friend, and the worst part is that I *want* to. I'm losing our bet and I hate it.

The three of them are easy to spot as they stroll around the corner, an obnoxiously attractive trio laughing and joking with the freedom innate to people who don't mind being seen. *No,* I amend as I watch them approach, *that's just the twins.* Bowen exists quietly in their orbit, their exuberance a cover for his reticence.

"Lunch has arrived," Mark declares. His voice stays light, but his eyes study my face, clearly looking to see if I'm okay. Given that I don't know the answer to that question, I'm dying to know what it is he sees. As it is, he just presses a soft kiss to my lips before gesturing over to his companions. "Alicia, these assholes are my twin sister, Maddie, and my best friend, Bowen."

"You showed up with Mexican food." Alicia shrugs. "You can't be all bad."

She immediately falls into conversation with Maddie, and Bowen sets himself to organizing the food so he doesn't have to talk to anyone, which leaves me and Mark with a moment to ourselves. He settles into the chair next to me, entwining his fingers with mine. "Better?" he asks quietly.

"Getting there."

Another kiss, this time to the back of the hand he's holding. "Good. Come over tonight? I'll make dinner."

"I can't," I say, and the regret in my voice is real in a way I don't appreciate. "Wednesdays are sacred best friend time. I can't bail on Daphne."

Across the table, Bowen's head snaps up. "Daphne? Daphne Wyndham? She's back?"

His intensity is borderline intimidating. "Yes, Daphne Wyndham, but no, she's still in Vancouver." Bowen mouths *Vancouver*, like the word itself is precious. "I didn't realize you know her."

He looks away, suddenly uncomfortable. "I don't. Not anymore."

I open my mouth to ask more questions—this is a *fascinating* development—but Mark squeezes my hand until I glance over at him. A small, sharp shake of his head makes the words fall away. I don't know why he's warning me off, but I do know there is someone else who can answer all my questions.

Daphne will be getting an earful tonight, that's for sure. I pull out my phone and text her.

ME

You have some explaining to do

DAPHNE

???

What did I do?

?????????

LARK??? WHAT DOES THIS MEAN????

ME

Guess you just have to be on time tonight to find out

Leaving her to her panic, I refocus my attention on the people who are currently sitting at the same table with me. Daphne's been gone for the better part of a decade and Gideon works longer hours than I do, so I can't remember the last time I had a full group of people to share a meal with.

The thought tugs my heart a little closer to Mark, fully against my will.

Lunch gets interrupted a couple times by people wanting to see horses, and I practically have to fight Maddie and Bowen to keep them from trying to help, as if it could possibly take five humans to show a single horse—even if that horse is marginally insane, like Boggy. It's big Mark energy from both of them, frankly, which is logical but deeply exasperating. The last thing the world needs is more Mark.

"I still can't believe you told our parents everything last night," Maddie says after the second client leaves. She's leaning back in the camping chair she brought with her, having finished her food well before the rest of us. "I couldn't even bring myself to fuck with Mark after you did that."

"I didn't tell them *everything*," I point out, and both Maddie and Bowen find things to throw at Mark when he winks lasciviously. "But to be fair, I was also trying to fuck with Mark. It just didn't work."

"And you won't fuck Mark until this is all over," he murmurs into my ear.

"Wanna bet?"

He smirks. "Pretty sure we already did."

Maddie pretends to gag. "Oh my god, get a fucking room."

Maybe that's exactly what I need to reset my brain. I turn to Alicia. "If someone shows up before I'm back, put these two to work." Then I stand, walking backward with Mark's hand still trapped in mine. He doesn't protest, happy to let me pull him to his feet.

"Where are we going?" he asks.

I grin. "To get a fucking room."

His smirk deepens. "I can't argue with that."

I lead him halfway down the barn, to the break in the stalls that's lined with three bathrooms on either side. The first one we pass is occupied, so I drag him into the second, not caring if we're seen. Part of me *wants* to be seen right now, so people know Mark Aladyne is slumming it with the likes of me.

God knows that's what my parents think.

He flips the lock behind us as I drop to my knees. "Fuck, babe," he groans when I reach for his belt. He leans back against the door, content just to watch. "I've missed the hell out of seeing you on your knees."

I tug his pants open, feeling him grow harder with every brush of my fingers. He's not the only one who groans when I pull him free, my hand wrapping around his length for the first time in months. At least I don't have to feel guilty about having missed this.

The sex is all that mattered between us.

I stare up at him as I lick my palm as lewdly as possible, taking pleasure in the way he bites his lip to keep quiet. When I begin to stroke him, he curses again. He keeps his hands pressed against the door, holding himself back, but that's not what I want. I grab his wrist and guide it to the back of my head as I wrap my lips around the tip of his cock, exhaling a gratified hum as his fingers grasp the base of my ponytail.

My hand and mouth work in tandem, taking him deeper with each pass, and I keep my eyes on his, wanting to see his desperation for myself. I settle both hands on his hips and encourage him to stop holding back, the sharp tug of hair as his fingers tighten on my head satisfying a need I can't articulate.

"I'm never gonna give up on us, Lark." His voice is rough as he thrusts into my mouth. "Not when every minute with you feels this good."

I tell myself the tears in my eyes are from him hitting the back of my throat, that his confession has no effect on me. Any man would say any damn thing for a blow job this good.

That's all this is.

So when he tells me he's about to come, I give him a few more thrusts before yanking myself back and out of his grip. I overcorrect in the process, falling backwards onto my ass, leaving both of us panting as he stares down at me, hard and aching with the need to finish.

I wipe the saliva off my lip, forcing a wanton smile onto my face despite the emptiness threatening to claw its way through my stomach. I don't know what happened to my exuberant little bunny, but it's nowhere to be found right now as I brace myself to look at the man I just denied an orgasm.

But when I do, there's no frustration or anger. All I see in those brown eyes is wild need cut with an affection so genuine it hurts.

So I try to hurt him back. "You can have the rest when you admit this is all we ever were."

I start to stand, my skin suddenly crawling as I realize just how dusty and dingy this bathroom really is, but Mark's voice cuts through the tension between us, commanding and sure. "Stay."

I freeze, back on my knees. He steps forward, crowding into me. Both his voice and his cock are hard as iron when he orders, "Take off your shirt."

Everything inside me wants to ignore his orders and get away from this situation I created. *Do your worst,* he keeps telling me, and I only fucking win this battle if I stay in control right now. But the voice Mark is using is one I've never heard from him before, and curiosity is overriding my better judgement.

I stare up at him for an interminably long moment, realizing he's not going to move until I do what he says. Realizing, too, that I *want* to do what he says, battle be damned.

Without a word, I pull my shirt over my head.

I'm wearing an old sports bra underneath, nothing like

the fancy lingerie I was wearing on our first—and last—date, but Mark swallows hard anyway. "You're fucking perfect, Lark. And now you're going to watch me come on your body so you know exactly how much I want you."

He fists his cock, and the sight of him finishing what I started is enough to make me squeeze my thighs together. It only takes him a few strokes before he releases across my chest and stomach with a long, low groan. In the aftermath, with the warmth of him still on my skin, he wraps his fist around my ponytail one more time and tilts my gaze up to his.

"That's how much I want your body, Lark. You're wearing the goddamn proof." He lets me go, silently putting himself back together. Once he secures his belt, he grabs a handful of paper towels, dampens them, and carefully wipes me clean. His hands are gentle as he guides me back into my shirt, fixes my hair, and pulls me to my feet. Then he just takes me in, his voice softening when he finally speaks again.

"I want you more than words. More than I've ever wanted anyone. But what you don't seem to understand yet, Songbird, is that I'd never fuck you again for the rest of my life if it meant you'd trust me with your heart."

"I'm so fucked, Daffy. You have no idea."

"Bitch, I love you, and we will get to your problems, but if you don't tell me why you texted me earlier today, I am literally going to explode."

We're fifteen seconds into our FaceTime—Daphne called at precisely seven o'clock on the dot—and already in a stand-off. After a few moments of posturing, Daphne quietly says, "Boom!" When I stare at her, she continues with all the seriousness of a doctor relaying a terminal diagnosis. "That was my spleen exploding. The rest is gonna follow soon, Lark. It's a dire situation over here."

"This was supposed to be *my* two weeks," I grumble. "But fine. You want to tell me why Bowen Campbell basically passed out when I mentioned your name today?"

Her eyes turn into little moons, they go so wide. "You know Bowen?"

"He's Mark's best friend," I explain. "He came to lunch today."

"Oh. Wow." She nods. A lot. Like she's a bobblehead running on a battery pack. "Wow. How is he?"

"Quiet. Hot. Very interested in whether you were back."

"Wha—what did you tell him?"

"The truth? That you still live in Vancouver?"

"Right. Right. Of course. Good. That's good."

"Hey, Daffy?"

"Yeah?"

"You good?"

She exhales, laughing shakily, and answers sounding more like herself. "Yeah. I'm good. Sorry, it's just been a while since I've thought about Bowen."

That is a nice little lie she's telling both of us. But I know Daphne well enough to know self-delusion is her second-favorite coping mechanism, so I'll let her live in it a while longer. "How do you know him?" I ask instead.

"I don't anymore." I decide not to mention how perfectly that echoes what Bowen said earlier today. "He went to high school with my brother."

"That was a lot of panic for a friend of your brother's," I point out. Daphne and her brother, Leon, went to different high schools, so I have a feeling I'm missing a few puzzle pieces here.

"I wasn't panicking," she lies. "I was *processing*."

"My mistake."

Daphne throws back what looks like an entire glass of wine in one go, then points at me. "Your turn now. Something tells me I've missed a lot of developments in your game of relationship chicken."

I snort at the description of what we're doing as *relationship chicken*, mostly because it's pretty damn accurate. I broke down and told her about the deal Mark and I struck on my way home from the barn on Monday. She laughed so hard I hung up on her, and this is our first time getting to really talk since. "Fuck, I don't even know where to start."

"Mmm, always start with the juicy stuff."

Well, in that case. I recap the encounter Mark and I had in the bathroom at lunch today, and by the time I'm done, Daphne is staring at me, mouth agape, with those moon eyes all over again.

"Holy fucking shit, Lark. You need to marry this man *immediately*."

I glare at her, wishing she weren't thousands of miles away so it would be more effective. "You keep choosing the wrong side."

"No, this is me being as Team Lark as it gets. It's in your best interest to let that man claim you."

"That's not the point and you know it."

She rolls her eyes and turns her camera so I can see her dog, Millicent von Muesselburg. Millicent is a brown and white mutt who in no way lives up to the stature of her name except for her ability to give intense side-eye, which she is currently doing. "See? Millicent agrees with me."

Daphne also insists that Millicent always be called Millicent. No nicknames are allowed. *A dog deserves dignity*, she told me once, as we literally watched Millicent get so confused by having successfully caught her own tail that she just fell over. It's the only dignity the dog has, so maybe Daphne has a point.

Before I can delve into what it is, exactly, that Millicent thinks, Daphne relents and asks to hear all the less juicy stuff, too. So I tell her about dinner with Mark's family and the winner's circle photo his mom showed me, and how much it proved I don't know about my own parents. Then I tell her about Mark's insistence on helping at the sale, and the way my parents behaved, and how Mark defended me. I even tell her a bit more about lunch with Maddie and Bowen, though I mostly leave Bowen out of it because I don't want her fainting dead away while she's living in another country.

When I've finally told her everything, she sighs. "You're gonna be pissed, but I stand by my advice."

"Daphne, come on. Be serious."

"I am." There's the smallest bite in her tone that tells me I'm about to shut up and listen. "Put all the games aside for a minute. Why are you so against being in a relationship with him, Lark?"

"You know why," I say. I stand up, tablet in hand, to take her with me as I pace. This conversation cannot be had while sitting. "After everything that happened with Gabriel,"—god, it's been a long time since I've let myself say that name out loud—"I can't give Mark what he wants."

"And what's that?"

"He wants a relationship." And that's the last thing I have time for right now, even if I wanted to be with him.

Which I definitely don't.

"What do you want?"

"I don't want people thinking my business is a success because of who I'm sleeping with." My parents *already* think that. Again. "I don't want to spend all my time checking in with someone and planning around them only to disappoint them when I'm not perfect. I don't want anything to distract me from getting my business off the ground."

"Lark, honey?" Daphne's voice is sugar sweet.

This is a trap. "Yeah?"

"That wasn't the question I fucking asked."

"…What?"

"I didn't ask what you don't want. I asked what you *do* want."

It takes her putting it that simply for me to even realize there's a difference at all. That cuts me off at the damn knees, and I drop to sit cross-legged right where I am in the middle of the hallway. "Oh."

"Exactly. So what is it that you want?"

"I want…" I spin the words around in my head. Until this very moment, I didn't realize just how contrary I've let myself become. When was the last time I focused on my desires instead of my frustrations? "I want to show everyone I can make this work. I want to prove to my parents that I was worth trusting."

"Still focusing on other people, but that's a start. What else?"

"You're supposed to be a photographer, not a therapist."

"What. Else."

"I want to be in control of my own choices." I think about that winner's circle photo. "I want to have a place to belong in the industry."

"You will," Daphne says with the irrationally supportive confidence of a best friend. Then, with the brazenly *annoying* confidence of a best friend, she imitates my voice. "*I also want to get railed by the hot guy who's in love with me.*"

"That's not what I sound like," I protest. "And even if it is, I've been saying that the whole time. The sex isn't the problem."

My skin warms just thinking about the way he stared me

down in that bathroom, his mark on my chest. No, the sex has definitely never been the problem.

"Uh huh. Come back down to earth, lusty eyes." Daphne's amusement fades, her face shifting back into *shut up and listen* mode. "I guess what I'm asking, Lark, is if you're judging Mark based on Mark, or if you're judging Mark based on Gabriel. Did you even bother telling him any of this before deciding a relationship just isn't possible? How do you know it won't work, if you don't even try?"

"We are trying," I grumble. "For two weeks."

"And has he stopped you from making your own choices so far? What did he say when you told him about tonight?"

I break eye contact. "He was happy that we make each other a priority." *Preserving that time with your friend is smart as hell*, were his exact words when he asked me more about it over lunch. *Maybe Bowen and I will copy you.*

She kindly skips the told-you-so as she pushes forward. "And has he kept you from doing your work? Or has he helped make your job easier?"

I pick at the rug beneath me. "No comment."

"Has he taken credit for your successes?"

Fucking low blow. "I get it, okay? I get it."

Daphne snorts. "Sure you do, babe. Listen, I'm not saying you should marry the man—"

"That's exactly what you said."

"Hyperbole, bitch. I'm not saying you should marry him tomorrow. What happened with Gabriel sucked ass. I won't deny that. I just don't want you to deny yourself something good out of sheer stubbornness. Have a real conversation with the man. See what happens."

Forcing my eyes back to the screen, I offer a tiny shrug. "I'll think about it."

"Good. Because you can pretend you don't care about him all you want, but you're literally sitting in your hallway right now. That's some *I'm secretly in love with him* shit if I've ever seen it, babe."

"I'm hanging up on you now."

She cackles. "No, you're not."

No, I'm not. But I get up and leave the hallway anyway, because Daphne's wrong. I'm not secretly in love with Mark Aladyne.

I refuse to even consider it.

CHAPTER 10

MARK

ME

> Can I take you out tomorrow night?

I stare at the text for a solid five minutes before I send it. It started as something more like, *Can I take you out to celebrate tomorrow night? Or commiserate, but I'm pretty sure it'll be a celebration of how much ass you're kicking. And only after your work is done, obviously, and I'll get you home in time to sleep, I promise,* but I edited out all the unnecessary word vomit in an attempt to not make her panic any more than she already will at the prospect of another official date.

Of course, once I send it, I stare at it for another ten minutes before reminding myself she's busy with her friend tonight. So I do exactly what I told her I would, and text Bowen.

ME

> Dicks tonight?

Getting Bowen out of the house after dark is always a crapshoot, but odds go up if we hit up Dicks, despite the awkward texts it requires. It'll be busier than usual tonight, but even at its busiest, Bowen won't have to worry about interacting with strangers.

BOWEN

Pass. I've already dealt with your lovesick
ass once today.

I send a few middle-finger emojis in return, and when he doesn't rise to the bait, I push harder.

ME

Please? If you don't, I might get bored
enough to start asking questions about You-
Know-Who.

BOWEN

I don't know what you're talking about.

ME

And you never will, so long as you meet me
at Dicks in an hour.

BOWEN

Fuck off

You're buying

Huh. I don't actually have it in me to bother him about Daphne—the microscopic bits of info I've collected across the years have been enough to tell me whatever happened between them is too big to make light of. But I'm starting to wonder if that's the wrong play. Maybe he needs a push.

I set that aside to consider later, pulling up my sister's contact. When she answers, I get straight to the point. "Drinks at Dicks tonight. I'll pick you up in thirty."

"I *just* changed into PJs, you asshole."

"Love you, too! See you soon!"

By the time we get to the bar, I still haven't heard from

Lark, but I've only checked about three dozen times, so I'm being totally chill and normal. Bowen is already inside, which is a surprise, but it makes more sense when we spot him sitting with Gideon.

I brighten, delighted by this turn of events, even as Maddie mutters, "Oh good, more testosterone."

"Gideon, my man. Twice in one week! That's a new record."

"Aladyne." He nods at me, then spots my sister. "Second Aladyne."

"I'm older," she declares. "I'm not second anything."

Gideon raises his hands in apology, and I clap them each on a shoulder before my sister can scare the man off. "First round's on me. What're you drinking?"

A few minutes later, the four of us have claimed a table, I've procured beers all around, and I'm trying to subtly interrogate Lark's friend. "On a scale of one to ten, how close would you say you and Lark are?"

In my defense, subtlety isn't my strong suit.

"Close enough to know she'll have my ass for speaking out of turn."

"What would you have to speak out of turn about?" I hope my smile lands on pointedly friendly rather than utterly deranged, but the look Bowen and Maddie exchange doesn't bode well for me. "If you're just friends?"

"Oh my god." Maddie sends a pleading look Gideon's way. "Put the man out of his misery or else it'll be our collective misery for the rest of the night."

I nod. "What she said."

Gideon laughs. "You're just so easy to torment, dude. Nothing has ever happened between us."

It shouldn't matter, but the relief I feel at knowing that is not insignificant. Lark and I both have histories, and I have no interest in being that dude. But her friendship with

Gideon is new in the time we've been apart, so I appreciate the hell out of having that context.

"I've been turning her horses out at night this week to help her out a bit," he continues. "She's got a lot on her plate."

"She does." I tamp down on the part of me that wants to be jealous that she lets him help her so easily. "I'm glad you've got her back."

"What's y'all's deal, anyway?" he asks. "Just fuckin', or what?"

Maddie groans. Bowen shakes his head. I grin. "How much time do you have, my friend?"

For the next couple hours, we sit around and shoot the shit. I give Gideon the Cliff's Notes version of the situation with Lark, at which point he shakes his head and declares he won't be drinking for the rest of the night to make sure at least one person at the table can make good decisions. Maddie plies him for gossip from the various farms he works at, Bowen nodding along and even tossing in a punchline now and then, and it starts to feel like he might have a place with us. We've been a trio for so long, it's hard to make room for other people.

But I'm making room for Lark, so we may as well bring Gideon along for the ride, too.

"So you're effectively freelance," Maddie observes, after he tells us about a day where he had to do six emergency stops at five different farms. I might not know the man well, but it's obvious he has a hard time saying no when people need his help. "Is your model sustainable long-term?"

I slap a hand over my sister's mouth. "She's a math nerd." She tries to bite my fingers, so I yank my hand away. "You can ignore her nosy-ass question."

Gideon chuckles. "It's fine. I've got no secrets. It's a tough balance to strike, if I'm honest. I had a major client get out of the business last month, and I'm still trying to figure out how to replace them."

"Pick up one big client or a lot of smaller ones?" Maddie muses. I can see her finance brain whirring away.

He nods. "Pros and cons. There's stability in the larger outfits, but I like knowing the people and horses I work with, which is easier small scale."

"Well, you do good work, man. Lark's crew looks great."

Gideon tilts his bottle at me in acknowledgement, and the three of them spin off into a new conversation. But I don't bother paying a lick of attention, because I've finally—*finally*—gotten a text back from Lark.

SONGBIRD

It's a date

Tomorrow night, I get to take my girlfriend on a second date. Things are looking up.

"Breathe, Songbird." Lark is next to me, teeth worrying her lower lip as she watches Marshmallow enter the auction ring. "You've got this."

When she doesn't give any sign that she's heard me, I reach over and un-claw her hand from around the armrest of her chair and grasp it in my own. She spares me only the smallest glance, but she doesn't pull away, either.

For now, that's a win. It's been a morning for my girl. Windsor didn't meet the reserve his owners set—despite Lark encouraging them to drop the reserve one step, which would have been just enough to get him sold. It wasn't the most encouraging start, even though it wasn't her fault.

Then Boggy decided to be a handler's worst nightmare in

the outer rings, constantly rearing and shying. Lark kept him well in hand, and she was never in any real danger of losing hold of him, but her arms were shaking by the time she handed him off. When he sold for five thousand over reserve, it helped make up for some of his drama—and it turned out his new owners hadn't even seen him until he started causing a ruckus outside—but it still set her on edge going into her final horse of the day.

Especially because all of us have developed a soft spot for the gray filly.

My own day has been equally hectic, as I raced between helping Lark as much as I could and doing my actual job. While I preferred being in the barn with the crew, most of my energy went to being a face person whenever our horses get called up to the ring. Friendly smiles, handshakes, subtle nudges to people looking for what our horses could provide…it was usually something I enjoyed, but it didn't feel the same this time.

Not when I could be at Lark's side instead.

Which is why I'm sitting next to her now as the bidding starts, even though my phone is buzzing in my pocket and one of our own horses is only a few hips behind.

Marshmallow was perfect on the way inside: alert and spirited, without any of the chaos of her barn mate. Her gray coat was spotless and shining, which meant she had plenty of last-minute interest, which in turn made the existing eyes on her more focused. But none of that will matter if the bids aren't there.

As the auctioneer finishes his introduction, Lark squeezes my hand even tighter. The delay before the bids start is always fraught, even if it only lasts a couple seconds. But then the first bid rolls in, and then the second and third. I can see all the bidders in the room, which means they're real and not the reserve.

Then the reserve—one Marshmallow's owner intentionally kept low—is in the rearview, the bids keep coming, and Lark's death grip starts to relax.

For approximately ten more seconds, until the first bidder drops out and I lose feeling in my hand again. "Hang in there," I murmur.

"Shut up. I'm panicking."

I chuckle softly, content to stop watching the board and just watch her face instead as the bids finally stall. The number isn't massive, and she may well do better before the sale ends, but for today?

She's filled with fucking wonder as she stares at the total, and that's the only thing that matters as the gavel falls.

But there's no time to revel in the moment—she's on her feet within seconds, rushing to retrieve her filly as she exits the ring. I trail behind, giving her the chance to murmur quiet affirmations to the horse who just helped make Lark's dreams a little more possible.

"Aladyne!"

I stiffen at the sound of my name from across the ring, debating whether I can ignore it or not. But then I hear my mother's voice join in. "Mark!"

"Duty calls," I sigh, offering Marshmallow a congratulatory pat. "See you for our date tonight?"

She beams at me. "I won't even be drowning my sorrows."

My chest squeezes as I press a kiss to her temple before reluctantly letting her lead Marshmallow back to the barn without me. I allow myself a few seconds to stare longingly after them before I stride off to find my mother.

Turns out both of my parents *and* Maddie are here, unbeknownst to me. Next to them is a man I haven't seen since the two-year old sale earlier in the year. "Domingo. Good to see you."

"I was just asking your parents where you were hiding,"

Domingo says, offering his hand. He's a few years older than me, and his jockey career was cut short when his leg got stepped on by a horse after a fall mid-race. His mobility aids vary each time I see him, but today he's sporting a dapper cane with a vicious-looking horse carved into the handle. "Been a minute, man."

"That it has. What brings you to the sale? Looking for anything in particular?"

He grins. "Don't worry, the Apple Butter colt is on my list."

Sometimes there's just no professional way to say a horse's name, and it's even worse when the horse in question is one of the best studs our farm has ever produced. I tell everyone Maddie named him, but the truth is, it was my fault. I just *really* liked apple butter at the time.

I was also eight. I refuse to apologize for it, even if I will shift the blame to my sister any chance I get.

"Glad to hear it."

We shoot the breeze for a few minutes, my parents and sister flitting around the immediate area as our next horse moves up in the ring. Despite how much I usually enjoy Domingo's company—the man's a shit-stirrer, but he's a hell of a horseman—I'm only half paying attention, the other half of me already anticipating getting Lark alone tonight. So it takes me a moment to clock when he turns the conversation. "You got any inside details on this job your parents were hinting about?"

"Hmm?" I'm lost in an inner debate over how far to push our date tonight, but my spine straightens when I belatedly process his question. I cut a wary gaze his way. "Say again?"

He frowns. "Maybe I read it wrong. It just felt like your parents were feeling me out for a potential job."

"You probably got it right," I allow. "But I've got nothing

for you. I'm pretty far down the decision-making tree these days."

"Fair enough." Domingo shrugs off my lack of knowledge, his gaze shrewdly assessing the Apple Butter colt in question, who was now being guided through some final laps before going into the sales ring. "Not sure I'm in the market for that big a change, but I'd hear you guys out."

"I don't know what their plans are, but we'd be lucky to have you. You ever decide you *want* that change, let me know."

He dabs me up before ducking inside along with my parents as our colt gets called to the ring. We have another horse due up in just a few minutes, so Mads and I stay outside, and I snag her between conversations. "What job were Mom and Dad trying to poach Domingo for?"

Because if there's one thing I know, it's that our parents aren't the most subtle people. If Domingo thought they were feeling him out, they definitely were.

Maddie scrunches her forehead. "Did he not tell you?"

"Did who not tell me what?"

"Javi is planning to retire next year."

"No shit."

"We've got some time, but if we keep pushing the sales, we're going to need to replace him."

Losing Javier will be a blow to Aladyne—he's worked at the farm for decades, and he knows more about our horses than anyone. "We'll probably need to hire about five people to make up for his absence."

Maddie grunts in agreement before lowering her voice. "We're also retiring Apple Butter after this coming season."

"Jesus." I try to process that, realizing I've clearly missed some conversations while chasing Lark around this week. "Can we even survive without the income from his super sperm?"

She smacks my bicep. "Do you really have so little faith in me?"

As the closest thing we have to a CFO, Maddie has been tracking every damn cent in and out of the farm the last few years. I could ask her how much any random item in one of our barns costs, and she can rattle off the answer, plus or minus a dollar or two.

Which I ask her to do, a lot, because it annoys her so much.

"I trust you more than anyone." It's the honest truth. She might spend half her life rolling her eyes at me, but she's always had my back. "Just seems like a lot of big changes at once."

"Honestly, I think there's more—"

Whatever Maddie was going to say gets cut off when one of our old trainers walks up. For the next few hours, we network our asses off, sometimes with our parents in tow, sometimes on our own. I itch to get back to Lark, but the one time I make it to the barn, she's nowhere in sight and I don't have a chance to look for her, because I have to help get a filly ready to head up to the ring after one of our crew took an ill-timed kick to the thigh and got sent home to rest and ice it up.

The moment I'm no longer required, I hurry back to my place for a desperately needed shower. I'm not sure the human body is supposed to be capable of producing as much sweat during any given day as we do during these August sales. But at least half of my day was spent figuring out what to wear tonight, so getting dressed doesn't take long at all. So much of my life is spent in work clothes that I enjoy being thoughtful about the rest of my wardrobe—the fact that a good outfit always puts Lark a little on the defensive is just a bonus.

I fight the urge to break the land-speed record on the

drive to her house, and take a steadying breath before I knock on the door of her little cottage. Her smile when she answers is so unguarded I feel it in my soul. "Sorry, I just got home," she says, her eyes tracing the line of my button-down sleeves, rolled up to the elbow partly because I want to avoid heatstroke and partly because I live for the way her pupils flare when she studies my forearms. "I still have to get ready."

"Take your damn time, babe." I kiss her—no tongue, if only for my own strained threads of control—and she laughingly shoves me away.

She's in a good mood. What a fucking gift.

"So who bought Marshmallow?" I ask as she moves through her living room, which is chaotic and lived-in and comfortable. For a moment, I let myself imagine what it might look like with my shit intermingled with hers. My boots resting next to hers, the quilt my grandmother made for me draped across the back of her couch. It's a good image.

"Remember the woman looking to build her *portfolio*?" Lark still can't hide her disdain for the term, but the rest of her looks excited. "Evangeline Rutherford. I still can't figure out if she's a pinhooker or if she'll have Marshie for the long haul, but we exchanged numbers. She promised to keep me updated, and I told her to let me know if she needs anything."

"I'm happy to hear that, baby." Lark isn't as worried about her other horses, but she's got a soft spot for the gray filly, so I'm glad her new owner is open to future communication. It's all a crapshoot, especially given that Lark has no ownership stake in any of the horses she's working with. I worry, sometimes, that she might be too soft-hearted to do consignment forever, but there's time for her to figure that out.

For *us* to figure that out.

I follow her through the small space to post up in the doorframe of her bedroom. She's clearly fresh from the shower, in an outfit not dissimilar to the last time I was here—sinfully short cotton shorts, a tank top damp from her hair, and little else. She crosses her arms over her chest, hiding those peekaboo nipples I can't wait to play with later. "I take it I don't get any privacy?"

I grin. "Don't get shy now, Songbird. I've seen it all before."

She scowls, but there's no heat behind it. "Do I get any clues about this date?" she asks. "I'd like to dress appropriately."

Before I can answer, her phone starts to buzz where she left it on the coffee table. I snag it for her, catching Gideon's name on the screen before I toss it her way. "Hey, Gideon," she says as soon as she answers, her brow furrowing. "What's up?"

It's no more than a few seconds before she freezes in place. "Are you okay?" The worry in her voice has me shifting closer, even though I can't hear the other side of the conversation. "No, go home. I'll turn out tonight." After a short beat, she repeats herself more firmly. "Gideon! Go. Home." Whatever he says satisfies her, because she softens. "Call if you need anything, okay?"

Her apology is on her face before she even pulls the phone from her ear. "About our date..."

I wave that away. "What happened? Is Gideon hurt?"

"Apparently he got pinned today. All he'd cop to is some bruising, but the fact that he even told me means he's probably broken something. Stubborn man." She rests a hand on the flat of my stomach, her eyes genuinely regretful in a way that fills me with hope. "But it means I have to go back to the barn tonight. I'm sorry."

"Don't be." Her visible relief is a sensation I want to chase forever, so I add, "I'll drive."

It's not the second date I had planned, but it'll do.

ONE YEAR AGO

MARK

"I thought you said she wasn't going to be here."

Maddie's words activated my Lark Reynolds radar, and I lost my damn breath when I saw her entering the room. She trailed behind her parents, wearing a floor-length sapphire dress with a slit practically up to her hip, and I immediately had about forty-seven different ideas for what to do with that long, tempting slope of her thigh. There was a hint of metallic sheen in the fabric, which meant she quite literally glimmered with every step she took.

I loved that dress nearly as much as I wanted to take it off her.

"I didn't think she was." I shifted in my boring charcoal tux, suddenly wishing I had dropped the money on the designer one I had been eyeing when I picked this one up earlier today. It wasn't that I thought Lark cared about clothing labels, but I had a feeling me showing up in a hunter green suit would have made her have a low-level coronary, and that would have been fun to watch. "But I've never been happier to be wrong."

Maddie sighed. "Well, that sucks."

"Since when do you not like Lark?" That reaction was new, and would be a problem if it continued. It had been just over a year since the first time I met Lark, and I was still fighting to get her to actually date me. But once I won that fight—and I *would* win that fight—I didn't want to have to choose between my sister and my girlfriend. I wasn't sure of anything other than I would be the loser in that scenario.

"It's not Lark I don't like. It's you pining after Lark and leaving me alone all night that I don't like."

"I don't *pine*." With immense effort, I forced my eyes off of Lark and brought my attention back to my sister. She had eschewed a dress in favor of a sleek black jumpsuit, and I knew she was nervous about the choice because she had actually asked if she looked okay before we left tonight. Maddie didn't *do* insecurities, not like that, and I had initially written it off as her being out of practice with dressing up— like most of the people here, frankly.

But now, as I took in her clenched jaw and defensive glare at the rest of the room, I realized that wasn't the issue. She could have shown up naked or in her most comfortable jeans and she'd be feeling the same way about being in this space. "And I won't leave you alone."

She huffed, clearly not believing me, and I resolved to keep my Lark obsession in check for the night. Sibling loyalty mattered. "Is there a particular person who has you ready to explode? If tonight ends with me throwing a punch at someone, I'd rather know in advance."

Maddie's disdain was practically a physical thing as it landed on me. "Please. We both know which of us has the better right hook."

That was, unfortunately, true. It took until college for Mads to become the bookish type. She got into multiple brawls on the soccer field in high school—and at least one fight off it, which we somehow managed to keep from our parents. Given that Maddie had a black eye and bloodied knuckles, that was quite a feat.

"Ignoring the question, I see." A waiter came around with a tray full of champagne flutes, and Maddie and I both snagged one. She drained hers and replaced it with another before the waiter had gotten five feet away.

"I just hate this shit," she said. "It's a *fundraiser*. Why can't we just cut a check?"

I shrugged. "Rich people love a gala."

Maddie was right that the whole thing was a bit absurd. One of the newer players in our local scene, a New England transplant who inherited his family business after some sort of tragedy, was making a big deal about wanting to *give back to the community*. Which was a mission I could get behind, even if he chose the most pretentious and bland way possible to go about it.

Invitations arrived for the *charitable event of the season* a couple months ago, and here we all were: absurdly priced tickets purchased, formal wear on, pretending like any part of this was a normal Saturday night. We were in the only place in the area with a formal ballroom, which was the hotel in the equestrian complex that typically catered to the high-end hunter/jumpers, with its gaudy chandeliers and ornate windows. Each farm had even been comped a room at the hotel for the night—no doubt to encourage us to drink enough to loosen our control over our wallets.

Our parents were supposed to be the chosen sacrifices to attend, but Mom very conveniently came down sick and Dad insisted he needed to stay home to take care of her. "Aladyne Stud *has* to be there," Mom declared between coughs when she called me last night, and I had an abiding suspicion that she was making her voice weaker on purpose. "You and Maddie should go have fun."

And now here we were, Maddie clearly prepared to hit

someone at the slightest provocation, and me desperately trying not to notice every shimmering movement Lark made across the room. Good times.

Maddie's mood perked up when the appetizers started circulating in earnest, and she even willingly participated in a few brief conversations as various acquaintances greeted us. If anything, she was the more effusive of the two of us once the champagne began to lift her spirits. I developed a peculiar itch anytime my eyes grazed past Lark and found her engaged in conversation with, well, anyone. I wasn't discriminatory in my envy—I wanted to take the place of literally every single person who felt the wash of her attention fall on them tonight.

It left me a bit disgruntled, frankly, and I knew Maddie didn't miss my mood even if I upheld my promise to stay by her side.

"Oh, thank god," Maddie muttered when the staff began to politely shepherd us all toward the secondary ballroom where dinner and what I assumed would be a range of self-serving speeches would be held. "I think the waiters were under orders not to walk by me with any more of those mini-quiches."

"With good reason." I was pretty sure she had eaten about ten of them before the poor staff even realized what had happened. "The whole tray wasn't meant just for you."

The flow of bodies stalled as people paused to read the seating chart on their way in; luckily for me, a former jockey stood in front of me, giving me a clear view of the sign. I grinned over at Maddie. "I've got good news."

"She's at our table, isn't she?"

"That wasn't what I was going to lead with, but yes. More importantly, we're the table furthest away from the stage."

Maddie's desire to be close to the food meant that we were among the first to be guided into the dining room, and

I walked with purpose toward our table as soon as I saw that not just tables were assigned, but seats were, too. I circled the table twice, once so I could palm Lark's place card, and again so I could swap it with the one on my other side. Only then did I sit, not concerned in the slightest about any chaos that might come from switching things up. The tables were big, with entirely unnecessary centerpieces in the middle, and I wasn't going to be at the same table as Lark and not be able to see her, or hear her, or touch her.

A man could only take so much.

Now that we were settled at a table with the promise of real food on the horizon, Maddie dropped more of her distaste for the situation. She started happily talking with the people sitting on her other side—old family friends, who were always pleasant enough to be around. Unfortunately for them, I only had eyes for the slow sway of Lark's hips as she approached the table.

Her eyes danced around the table, searching for her name. The slight wrinkle of confusion between her eyes when she realized she wasn't next to her parents made me grin, just in time for her to look up and see me. Her eyes held mine as she stepped around the table, fingers light against my palms as she let me guide her into her chair. The neckline of her dress gave me a fucking tempting view of the perfect curve of her breasts, and I had to steady myself as I returned to my own seat when the memory of having them in my mouth just a few days ago threatened to knock me on my ass.

"Something tells me this isn't my intended seat," she murmured, her body leaning toward mine of its own accord. Lark wasn't the type to admit her desire for me this fast, not when she was aware of it. "Maybe I should tell them there's been a mistake."

"The only fucking mistake would be this night ending without me stripping that dress off your body," I said the words as casually as I would ask about the weather, enjoying the way her tongue darted across her lips as she pretended to be unbothered.

"In your dreams, Aladyne."

"Every damn night, Reynolds."

There. A slight pink flush spreading across her face. I counted every moment I got to touch her as a win, but I only considered the blushes as victories. They were a rare gift, and it made me want to trace the path of them across her skin with my tongue. This time, when I leaned in and whispered as much in her ear, the blush only deepened.

I was starting to understand the appeal of a gala.

For nearly two hours, I slowly tortured Lark while delighting in my own stupid luck. I wasn't foolish enough to mistake this for a date—when I took this woman on a date, I certainly wouldn't be sharing her with strangers, like the ones on her other side who kept trying to draw her into small talk. But she couldn't politely ignore their questions, nor could she cut me out of the conversation entirely, which meant I got to ask questions of my own. I knew at least half of her answers were lies, but some of them weren't. And that was enough for me to start with.

Especially when my hand teased the bare skin of her thigh through that damn slit of her dress any time I thought she was telling the truth. If the honest answers got more frequent as the meal went on, I only had Pavlov to thank.

When the wait staff came to clear away the dishes after the main course, Maddie snapped to get my attention, a necessary reminder that I had, in fact, entirely ignored my sister during dinner. "Yes?"

"Give me your keys," she said.

"Why?" I asked as I dropped them in her hand. She replaced them with the keycard for the hotel room we had been given—neither of us had planned on using it, so she had just stashed it in her purse when we came in.

"Because we both know you're not going home tonight."

I could have argued, but there was no point. "Will you be good to drive?"

She nodded toward the water that had just been refilled. "I'll be here a while longer and this is all I'm drinking the rest of the night."

"If you're not—"

"Mark. I'll be fine." When I hesitated a moment longer, she patted my arm. "You get credit for holding out until I had food in front of me. I solemnly swear I won't give you shit for abandoning me."

"Thanks, Mads." I tuck the keycard into my wallet.

"You're welcome. I never want to hear a single detail."

Dinner did indeed end with a few speeches, but I found myself respecting Mr. Gala Thrower a bit more when he revealed that one of the charities our donations would serve was designed to provide legal aid for undocumented farm hands. Had he announced that in advance, plenty of assholes would have dropped out of attendance, but he was clever enough to wait until tickets were purchased and silent auction bids had closed.

He might not be as boring as I thought.

After dessert, I caught Lark's hand before she could run away from the table entirely. Her fingers flexed around mine —another impulse, if the way she flinched was any indication —and I brought them to my lips for a long, heated moment.

In the ballroom, a string quartet began to play the moment my lips touched her skin, and I took that as a sign from the universe for the both of us.

"Dance with me, Lark."

CHAPTER 11

LARK

I should have sent him home. But before I had even fully processed his offer to drive, he was tossing jeans at me and buckling me into the passenger seat of his truck.

And now it's too late, and he's going to see the other side of my tiny, fledgling business. The one that's barely a drop in the ocean compared to his.

The one that started to feel worryingly possible today when the gavel fell.

As if he can hear my thoughts, Mark glances over at me. "I fucked up earlier," he says, "because I didn't tell you how proud of you I am before I got pulled away."

I duck my head, hoping my still-damp hair hides the blush threatening to take over my cheeks. My treacherous nervous system and its desire to roll around in the idea that *anyone* is proud of me needs to be reined the hell in.

All I've heard from my parents is a single text from my mother that said, *At least you're not taking them all home,* making it clear that one horse not meeting its reserve—which I've been reminding myself all damn day is *very common*—matters more than the two who sold.

But now I have Mark next to me, celebrating my success, and I'm stuck on my conversation with Daphne. *Have a real conversation with the man. See what happens.*

It's tempting. The pull of these kinds of moments between us is real. Squeezing his hand to death as I watched the number climb when Marshmallow was in the ring today helped calm me in a way I'm not brave enough to articulate.

But I already know the outcome Mark wants. He's been telling me in a thousand different ways since we met. He wants it to end with *us*.

At which point I don't know what happens to *me*.

Past experience suggests it doesn't go well.

It would all be so much easier if I didn't like the stupid tiny birds embroidered on his button-up so much. He's got the sleeves rolled up to his elbows, like an absolute fucking menace to society, and I'm never going to forgive him for any of it.

I don't realize how long I've been staring at him until his lips crook up. "Take your time with the view, babe."

"Fuck off." I swallow my own smile as I tear my eyes away to look out the windshield instead. In yet another example of the man knowing too much, he didn't have to ask for directions or an address—he drove straight to where we needed to go.

I'd call him a stalker but it would only boost his ego.

The truck bounces as he pulls onto the gravel driveway, and I point him toward the third barn. We're late enough that the farm is mostly quiet—there's a bit of movement in the front barn, but otherwise, we're the only ones around. I was just here this morning, well before dawn, but I suddenly realize how much I miss my evening routine, too.

It's not dark yet, but the crickets are already singing as we enter the barn. "Hey, everyone," I call, flipping the lights on. A series of nickers go up from inside, only some of them from horses in my care. I have about half of the stalls in this barn to use, and a few of the other horses are indoors full-time rehabbing right now.

Having Mark with me makes light work of the evening feed—by the time I finish filling a bucket, he's delivered the previous one and is back for the next. The comfortable rhythm of teamwork makes me realize how isolated I've become in the time since I left my job at Landow.

The thing they don't tell you about making it on your own is just how lonely it is.

I would normally start picking stalls while the horses eat, simply to move things along, but Mark tugs me back into his chest and I just…stay there. "You run a tight ship, Reynolds," he says. "You're killing it."

"I'm glad someone thinks so."

His exhale doesn't quite become a chuckle. "Permission to speak freely?"

I snort. "Sure thing, Cadet Aladyne."

He turns me in his arms until he can see my face. "I don't like how your parents speak to you. I know you love them, but you don't deserve to be dismissed."

"I'm used to it by now." I trace one of the birds on his shirt, the shape of the small wings pressing into my finger.

"Are you?"

My eyes snap up, my defensiveness easing when I see that it's genuinely a question—he's not asking if I just lied to him, so much as he's asking if I just lied to myself. "No," I admit. "I should be, but I don't think I am."

His expression darkens, but his voice is careful. "I don't think *should* is the right word, Songbird. Not for something like this."

I step away, and he lets me go. If I immediately regret leaving the safety of his arms, that's not something I'll admit to either of us right now. "They don't mean to be cruel." It's a line I've told myself a thousand times since they chose Gabriel over me. "This is just how they worry."

"Mm." Mark doesn't push, for which I'm grateful. I still have the memory of his family dinner in my head, the way they were all so *kind* to one another. How odd it felt. "Have you asked them about the picture?"

"Not yet. I'm supposed to have dinner with them this weekend. I might bring it up then."

Mark's face grows expectant, almost eager. When I stare back, stoic, he smirks. "Lark. Come on."

"What?" I know very well what.

"You know very well what."

Fucking mind reader. "You could just ask."

"That wouldn't be the same and you know it." He traces his fingers down the length of my arm, shoulder to wrist, teasing and light. "I'm your boyfriend, remember?"

"For nine more days."

"Those nine days include this weekend."

"Fine." I huff. "Do you want to come to my parents' house for dinner with me?"

He shrugs. "I'll have to check my schedule."

"I'm never touching you again," I warn, but his laughter is already softening my annoyance.

As does the way he catches my fingers and presses a kiss to my knuckles. "I would love to go with you."

It takes me a few moments to fully collect myself and avoid swooning, at which point I realize the horses are mostly done eating. I reluctantly tug my hand free, returning my attention to the reason we're here.

"We've got eight to turn out," I inform Mark. Five of them are due for the sale; the other three will be going up in February. Sales prep for them will ramp up in a month or so, but keeping them inside during the worst of the heat seems like the least I can do. I hold a lead rope out to Mark, then pause. "Are you sure you want to risk getting your douchey date clothes dirty?"

He laughs, the insult sliding off him like he's made of teflon. "I knew you liked this outfit." He grabs the rope. "And we both know a little dirt will only make me harder to resist."

I don't dignify that with a response, because he's right. He had a streak of dirt on his forehead for a while this morning and it was all I could do not to lick it off.

I have use of two fields, neither of which are immediately next to the barn, so it takes a few minutes to turn out each pair. We're quiet for this part, the setting sun casting a glow of pink and orange over our skin as we walk. The horses are eager for their freedom, necks stretched and steps brisk.

Everything is fine, until it's not.

On our third trip, we start on the colts—I have Minnow, a rangy chestnut with the scraggliest forelock, and Mark has Grasshopper, a pure bay who's heading to the sale tomorrow. We're approaching the gate to the second field when one of the barn cats comes screeching through the grass, darting between Grasshopper's legs. Minnow startles, flying back a few steps, but it's Grasshopper who lives up to his barn name. He fully panics, rearing up briefly as Mark fights to give him his head without letting him go, before throwing himself into a sideways buck. Mark doesn't have time to get out of the way, falling into the fence right before Grasshopper crashes into him. The colt finally comes to a snorting, tense stop as one of the fence boards cracks and gives way.

"Fuck!" Mark's voice is pained, and it sends my heart lurching into my throat.

"Are you okay?" I'm trying to keep Minnow at a safe enough distance to avoid riling Grasshopper up again, but it's making it hard to see Mark because there's an entire horse between us. "Mark, are you okay?"

"I'm fine. But his leg is trapped between boards, and I doubt he's gonna hold still for much longer."

"Shit." I can't do much with Minnow in hand, and I can't let Minnow loose in the field without risk of him setting Grasshopper off, to say nothing of the newly broken fence. "Can you buy me enough time to get to the barn and back?"

"I'll try," he says. "But I'd suggest you hurry."

I'm moving before he even answers. I give them a wide berth, and once we're a safe distance away, I tug Minnow into a trot. I'm hoping the novelty of the new pace will distract him from the fact that we're going back to the barn when he was so close to romping around for the night. It works reasonably well—I only lose a few seconds bickering with him about going back in his stall—and then I duck into the feed room in a desperate search for something that will help with the fence.

It feels like an eternity before I locate a small, handheld crowbar and go flying back down to where I left them. The colt still stands frozen, blessedly aware of how precarious his position is, and I can finally lay eyes on Mark, who is squeezed between the fence and the trapped horse. His eyes light up when he sees the crowbar. "My brilliant woman. We're gonna need that."

"Are you okay?" I ask again as I slip through the gate to enter the field.

"I'm fine," he says through gritted teeth as Grasshopper shifts impatiently. "But I should warn you, you're going to see blood." When I curse, he tosses a hopeful look over his shoulder. "If it helps, I'm pretty sure it's all mine."

"Why would that *fucking help*, Mark?" I struggle to keep my volume level as I kneel by the nearest fence post. It becomes very clear that this situation could have been avoided entirely if someone knew how to build a goddamn fence in the first place—whoever replaced one of the boards when it last broke nailed it back in on the wrong side of the fence posts, leaving a perfectly sized gap for a young, panicked horse to fall into.

"I just assumed you'd be more worried about the horse than me."

"I'm not a goddamn sociopath," I retort.

His grin is so pleased, I'm ready to accuse him of planning this entire fiasco. "So you're saying you like me more than your horses?"

"It's still murder even if he deserves it," I sing sotto-voice instead of answering, because right now I need the damn reminder. I'm careful as I work the crowbar against the fence post—the last thing we want is *more* sudden movement right now, so I alternate between sides, loosening the board as much as I can without pulling it free entirely.

Mark lets me work in peace, but I hear him murmuring quietly to Grasshopper, telling him to be calm and quiet. "I'm going to pull the board away now," I warn. "He's gonna want to move, so be ready."

"On three," Mark says, and we count together. From there, it's all over in a few seconds. I pull the board away, Mark follows Grasshopper's instant retreat, and the colt paces for a moment before letting out a deep sigh of relief.

I hurry around to take him from Mark, my eyes searching them both for injuries. "I'm fine," Mark promises again when I can't hide my reaction to the dark red stains on his shirt. "Let's get him inside and we can figure everything out, okay?"

Mark refuses to let me look at his injury until everything else is handled. "It's just a scratch," he promises a half-dozen times. I don't fully believe him, but I obsessively watch the blood stains on his shirt and they don't seem to be getting any bigger.

A thorough check of Grasshopper proves he's not hurt, which is a fucking miracle—explaining to his owner that he got injured literally hours before shipping to the sales grounds would be a nightmare. He is, however, royally pissed to be back in the barn, which means there's still a chance he ends up hurting himself just for the hell of it.

I call Maria, the barn manager, to fill her in; she offers to send someone over to fix the fence—which is down to only a couple functioning boards—but I am eager for the excuse to hit things with a hammer, so I drive to the back of the farm where the extra supplies are kept instead and do it myself. Mark uses his phone as a flashlight for me in the increasing dark and laughs freely every time I hit the board instead of the nail, but he doesn't try to take over.

At least I put all the boards on the same damn side, unlike whoever did it last time.

It's fully dark by the time it's safe to turn the colts out again. Mark tries to grab a lead rope to help, but I stare at him with violence in my eyes until he sheepishly puts the rope back on the hook. Grasshopper is a handful on the way out, and he shies a bit around the section of fence that tried to kill him a few minutes ago, but he bucks happily across the field when I let him go. The remaining colts follow suit, and my section of the barn is finally empty—

Except for Mark, who started picking stalls while I was turning out. "The shit can wait, Mark. Get out here."

He dutifully follows me into the feed room and over to the sink, where I dig out the first aid kit and start dampening some paper towels. "Shirt off," I order.

"If you want to have your way with me, you're going to be disappointed." He winks, then unbuttons his shirt with an efficiency that shouldn't turn me on. There's something mesmerizing about the quick, controlled movements of his fingers and the ever-increasing amount of his chest that's revealed with each button.

But when he winces as he tries to slide it over his shoulders, I'm reminded that he got hurt helping *me*. "Hold still," I grumble, guiding the shirt down his right arm so I can focus on the injured side. The fabric sticks against his skin, so I take a moment to soak it with the wet paper towels to loosen everything up. "If I find out this requires stitches and you've been sitting here refusing to let me look at it for the past hour, I'm never going to speak to you again."

"Then I really hope it doesn't need stitches."

I look away from the sincerity in his expression as he says that, and begin to carefully pull his shirt free from his bloodied arm. He doesn't make a noise, but I can feel how tense he is as I work one particularly stubborn part free. We both relax once I get it off, and I take a moment to process the wound across his upper arm.

Lucky for him, stitches appear unnecessary. But the broken board did a number on him when he got shoved into it, leaving a series of angry scrapes that have started bleeding again after pulling the fabric away. There's also a handful of not-insignificant splinters tucked into his skin.

"How's it look, doc? Am I gonna live?"

"Unfortunately for everyone, the answer is yes." I dab at some of the unbroken skin, clearing away dried blood. "This might take a minute, though, so you'd better get comfortable."

His free hand comes up to brush against my hair. "Trust me, I'm plenty comfortable with you this close."

"Is that so? Here I thought I had a different effect entirely."

His breath catches when I clean one of the cuts, but his

eyes stay alight with mischief. "Something tells me you're going to enjoy this a little too much."

I laugh, flirtatious and casual, to hide the fact that I'm actually spiraling inside as I slowly dab at his skin. Horses are unpredictable, and shit like this happens. It's not that it's a major injury—he'll be mildly annoyed for a few days, and then it'll be like it never happened. But every part of me is screaming that I could have prevented him from getting hurt if he hadn't been here in the first place.

"Hey." Mark waits for me to look up at him. "I really am okay. You know that, right?"

At some point along the way, I'm going to have to accept that Mark sees every emotion I try to hide. "Yeah." Suddenly, the one syllable is all I can manage.

Because the other part of it, the part that lurks underneath every *almost* moment around horses, is the *it could have been worse*. Grasshopper is okay. Mark is okay.

But what if he wasn't?

What the fuck would I do with myself if Mark Aladyne was ever not okay?

"Lark, baby. Are *you* okay?"

"Mm-hmm."

"The deal was no walls, Songbird. Two weeks where I get all of you." His hand curves around my face, not letting me look away. "That includes whatever is going on in here right now." He taps a finger against my temple, and I break.

"I'm freaking out that you got hurt and it's my fault, okay?" The words have teeth, because I hate saying them aloud in the first place. "If you hadn't come with me, none of this would have happened to you, and it's pissing me off."

"Okay."

"That's it?" He keeps doing that. Just accepting what I say. I hate it. "*Okay?*"

He gives me a sideways smile. "You're allowed to freak

out. Frankly, I've been losing my shit knowing it's usually you or Gideon out here doing this all alone. If there hadn't been two of us here, it would have been a lot worse."

I push his hand away, returning my attention to his arm because I refuse to acknowledge that he has a point. Doing this job alone isn't just lonely—it's risky. I finish cleaning off the blood, then dig around for tweezers before I deal with the splinters. Once I pull the biggest one free, I hold it up to him. "Your trophy."

"I'll keep it with all the other trinkets in my Lark Reynolds box," he says, tucking the small sliver of wood into his pocket.

"Please tell me that box isn't real."

His face tinges ever-so-slightly pink, which tells me enough. This time, I *do* relish his hiss of pain when I wipe the scrapes down with disinfectant. I cover them with gauze and vet wrap, just to make myself feel better even though it's overkill, then take a step back. "There," I say, "you're all finished."

But I immediately regret the distance, because I'm suddenly able to see the whole damn Aladyne portrait. He's got his hip cocked against the counter, his hurt arm braced next to it while his other hand is tucked casually into his pocket. His hair is disheveled—this time properly so, rather than the pretend kind he's so good at—and his ruined shirt with those damn little birds lies rumpled on the ground next to him. His fitted dress pants sit low on his waist, leaving his torso entirely on display for me to ogle.

And ogle I do. I haven't seen him properly shirtless in months, and you'd think it was a rainstorm in a desert with the way my body reacts to the sight. *Some* part of this whole landscape is getting wet, that's for sure.

Mark's not a gym rat; he's not built out of bulging muscles and an eight-pack you can bounce coins off. He's made of lean, functional muscle instead, the strength he has from his work living more subtly under his skin—he's never had much need to prove it's there, and I've always been mildly obsessed with that display of confidence.

I don't know when I make the decision to close the gap between us again. I don't know when I decide to touch him, to press my lips to his throat, to lick the sweat salt from his skin. All I know is that the urge to claim his body again, to mark it with the proof of my passion rather than injury, is nearly setting me on fire.

If this relentless, unrestrained *need* for him were love, I'd never be able to walk away.

When he tugs my mouth to his, pouring his own desire into me, I push away the relief that he's safe, and the tears that threaten at his nearness, and the comfort that comes from his reciprocal touch. I focus on the wetness between my legs, and the hard length of him against my hip, and the way his body becomes the literal air I breathe.

It's just lust, I tell myself again and again and again. *It's just lust.*

Love can't possibly feel like this.

CHAPTER 12

MARK

"You ready to head to the barn?" I flip my keys in my hand as I stroll toward Lark, who's doing a last top-off of water for her three new arrivals. We both stayed busy with our respective jobs today, much to my annoyance, but I saw enough to know Lark had a steady stream of interested parties today. "We should probably ride together. Better for the environment and all that."

"No need," Lark says, pulling the hose back through the stall window. She wraps it back around the holder, huffing a small laugh when I step up behind her and wrap my arms around her waist. She can deny the way she melts back into my body all she wants—it's as instinctual to her as breathing at this point, and we both know it. She's still a little damp from getting caught in the thunderstorm earlier, but I have no complaints. Her fingers come up to lightly scratch my jaw, and it's all I can do not to nuzzle into her like a cat. "Gideon's pulling that stoic manly crap and insisting he's fine, and Maria feels guilty enough about last night that she's promised to be there to supervise."

"How does Gideon feel about having a babysitter?"

"I'll let you know when he finds out. Dealing with him is part of Maria's penance."

"So that means I can take you to dinner before drinks tonight?"

She turns in my arms, and I steal a kiss that has me longing to be anywhere other than in public right now. She's a little starry eyed when we finally pull apart. "I do owe you a date."

"Oh, is that what this is?" I slowly walk her back toward her extra stall. "Just a little quid pro quo among friends?" I use my heel to nudge the door shut behind us, moving us back to the same corner where we struck our deal in the first place. Hard to believe we're closing in on the halfway mark. "Because if that's the case..."

I kiss her again, and her mouth opens to me without hesitation. Claiming her is the most natural thing in the world, and I'm soon kissing my way down her neck to the hollow at the bottom of her throat, loving the steady vibration of the quiet whimpers she makes with each swipe of my tongue. She murmurs my name as I unbutton her jeans, and I nip lightly at her skin in return.

"Do I have to work for it tonight, sweetheart? Or are you wet for me already?" Her breathing goes unsteady as she rocks her hips toward me for a touch that hasn't even started yet. I slip my fingers beneath her underwear, but keep them far from where she wants me. "Answer the question, Songbird."

Her eyes flare with defiance that turns to amusement. "Scared your kiss left me cold, Aladyne?"

"No." I slide my fingers lower, growing smug when her hands tighten on my hips. I capture her mouth again, deep and intentional, rolling her lower lip between my teeth as I pull away. "But you're going to need to admit you want me before I touch you."

"I always want you, Mark."

It's only as I hear them that I realize those words aren't the ones I want to hear. She can want me and hide her heart from me all at the same time. But that doesn't change the way hearing that confession makes me feral.

My hand finally reaches its destination, and her cry as I slide my middle finger through the wetness at her core makes my dick leak. I tease her for long moments, offering only fleeting, light caresses. I wait until her hips don't stop moving, until her hands claw into my shirt, until her head tosses back as a plea for *more* drops from her lips.

Then, and only then, do I push a finger inside and begin giving her exactly what she needs. Her gasp sharpens into a moan, and I kiss her to keep her quiet—but as she rides my fingers, I'm desperate to look at her, so I replace my mouth with my free hand, muffling her cries.

Every version of Lark that I've been blessed to fuck has been perfect in its own way. Quick and eager, pressing her up against a door we barely got closed. Hard and intense, bending her over whatever horizontal surface we could find. Slow and unhurried, loving on every inch of her the night she broke things off.

Whatever you call what we did in that damn bathroom a couple days ago.

But there's something about this, here: both of us fully clothed, barely hidden from prying eyes, my fingers alone enough to make her desperate with need. Maybe it's as simple as the fact that it feels more illicit, more salacious— my hand covering her mouth, keeping her quiet, keeping the extent of her pleasure hidden from the world.

When I press another finger into her, the base of my palm rubbing against her clit as she writhes, I try to memorize everything about this moment. The build up, the anticipation —it's all going to be worth it in the end. For both of us.

It has to be.

Because the moment she's ready to come apart, I pull my hands free and step away. Her eyes darken immediately as she takes deep, gasping breaths. *"Fuck."*

"You think you're the only one who can play dirty?"

I half-expect her to finish herself off—a show I will gladly be in the audience for—but she considers me with heavy eyes as she buttons her pants back up instead. "Is it weird that this makes me respect you a little more?"

My laughter echoes in the barn even after we leave.

"So if—in theory—a person had entirely hypothetical questions about...relationship...things...would that be a conversation someone else might potentially be open to discussing in the right possible context?"

Lark and I are sitting on her porch steps, the thick weight of the night air less oppressive than in the daytime but still heavy against our skin. The scent of citronella burns on the breeze, a fair sacrifice to keep the mosquitos at bay. Her head rests on my shoulder; my arm is settled around her hip. The silences between us have been contented and easy, neither of us in any particular hurry to draw the night to a close.

We had a quiet dinner in town, both of us exhausted after the events of the week, and then spent the better part of two hours at Dicks with Maddie, Bowen, and Gideon. Gideon looked like shit but refused to acknowledge it, and spent a solid ten minutes bitching about the fact that Maria hadn't left him alone even once. Bowen tried not to flinch any time Lark dropped Daphne's name in conversation, which I think she did on more than one occasion specifically *to* make him flinch. Maddie seemed only half-present, distracted and drinking even less of her beer than usual, but I knew better than to press her on it in public.

And in between everything else, Lark kept giving me looks that ranged from contemplative to indignant, even when I hadn't done or said anything. She clearly also had something going on in her head, but I wasn't able to figure out what it was—I assumed it was going to be some new form of torture.

Instead, I got an algebraic word problem.

"Could you try that again with more specific nouns?" I teased, despite the raging inferno of hope exploding in my chest.

Her scowl is audible. "You know what I mean."

"I like to think I do," I admit. "But—hypothetically—I would want that conversation to not happen in code."

"But code is so much *safer*," she whines. I laugh, but otherwise give her the time to find what she wants to say. In this, I refuse to pry. She has to come to me. Her voice is a near-whisper when she finally continues. "Daphne gave me annoyingly good advice on Wednesday, and I can't get it out of my head."

"What was the advice?"

Her words have the air of a quote she's memorized a thousand times over. "*Have a real conversation with the man. See what happens.*"

I make a mental note to send Daphne a fucking phenomenal present. "I think I like your best friend."

"I think your best friend likes my best friend, too."

"Nice try," I say. "I'm not that easily distracted."

"Damn."

"So this real conversation. Can I assume it's about what happens if we take the expiration date off of our little game?"

"You know what they say about assumpt—"

"Lark."

She sighs in annoyance. "Hypothetically. Yes."

It physically pains me, but I pull myself away from her and turn so I can actually see her face. Neither of us drank much tonight—me because I was driving, her because the last thing she needs is a hangover right now—but it's still reassuring to see the clear-eyed focus when she looks back at me. I won't have this conversation with a version of Lark that doesn't feel in control of herself.

She'd never forgive me for it, and I wouldn't blame her.

"I'll talk to you about anything, Songbird. But I don't want to hide behind hypotheticals. A conversation isn't a promise. You're still entirely in control of the outcome. But if we're going to talk about the future, we're going to talk about it like it's a real thing. Because the only future I want with you is one I can genuinely have."

I wait, wary, for her to retreat. But something in what I said keeps her from slamming the door. "It's really not, Mark. It's not a promise, okay? I don't want you getting your hopes up because I ask a few questions."

"I hear you," I say. "My hopes are my problem, anyway."

Her eyes narrow, clearly unsure about my answer, but it's the best I can do without lying. There's nothing either of us can do about my irrational daydreams. "Promise?"

"Promise."

She chews on her lip, and I settle against the porch railing, content to wait. I won't get many chances like this, and I'm going to do my damnedest not to fuck this one up. "What do you want our relationship to look like?" she asks eventually, hesitance in every word.

I tuck away the burst of pride at the fact that she is making herself have this conversation, because I know she'd take it as condescending rather than sincere right now. "I don't think that's a question I get to answer alone."

Lark rolls her eyes. "If you're going to dodge the literal first question, there's no point in even doing this at all."

"I'm not dodging. That just feels like the kind of thing we decide together, you know? A relationship should work for both of us, and me rattling off a list of things I want without any consideration for what *you* want isn't going to make that happen."

"But there has to be something that's important to you!"

"Yeah." I stare at her, making sure she's with me as I answer. "*You.*"

She's not sure what to do with that, and I know she's about at her limit with this particular approach, so I change tactics. "You're coming at this the wrong way, Lark. Put your fears on the table. Ask me what you really want to know. Throw it all at me. I can take it."

That settles her a bit, because she thrives under a challenge. I try not to smile as she slings her first question at me like a dart. "What happens if I don't text you back right away one day? Or if you try to call and I don't answer?"

"That depends."

"For fuck's sake. Depends on what?"

"Whether it's because you're busy or because you're ignoring me. I don't need to be coddled, but I'd like to hope that if we're together, you'll actually want to talk to me."

"And if it *is* because I'm busy? I work a lot, Mark. We won't always be in the same barn day in and day out."

If only. What a dream that would be. "I'm not going to get mad at your for doing your job. I've been watching you work your ass off for two years, baby. I'm not going to get in the way of it now."

"You would be the first." Her words are mumbled low enough I can barely hear them, and I want to chase that thread so badly—to know exactly what kind of past fuckery I have to make up for. But I let her think I don't hear her, because right now, I want this to be about us.

We can deal with her ghosts later.

"I don't want—" She cuts herself off, shakes her head, then sighs deeply. "Fucking Daphne."

Amused, I ask, "What'd she do this time?"

"I was telling her all the things I don't want from a relationship, and she asked me what I *do* want instead, and now I can't stop thinking about the difference."

"Far be it from me to challenge Daphne's wisdom, because I'm a huge fan, but I happen to want to know the answers to both of those questions."

Her eyes drift down to my arm, and the scratches hidden under my sleeve. The only time they've hurt today is when Domingo slapped my arm as we greeted each other in passing, but I can still see the guilt she's nursing over the whole incident. "I don't like relying on people," she says. "I don't want to report my whereabouts or ask permission to do the things I want to do. And I'm scared I'll disappoint you by not being that person for you."

I sit with that for a moment, knowing I can't rush this answer. "I'm asking to be your partner, not your jailer. Will I want as much time with you as I can get? Yes. Of course. I'm a needy fucker and I've been obsessed with you since we met, if you haven't noticed." I'm hoping for a smile, but I only get the merest twitch of her lips. "But you don't ever need to ask for my approval to live the life you want. I don't want to own you. All I want is the chance to live my life next to yours."

"That's easy to say." She meets my gaze with a challenge. "It's harder to do."

"You think I don't fucking know that?" I snap, but wince the moment the words leave my mouth. "Sorry, I—"

"No." Her voice is firm. "Say it. Finish that thought."

"I spent a year and a half at your beck and call, Lark, and

then six months not seeing you at all. Showing up when you wanted me, leaving you alone when you didn't. Grabbing desperately for any crumb of yourself that you would let fall. I damn well know it won't always be easy to give you your space, because it hasn't been easy for the past two years."

She parts her lips, whether from surprise or a need to respond, I don't know. I don't find out, either, because I push forward, determined for her to hear this now.

"I about lost my damn mind, Lark. Ask my sister, ask Bowen—I spent half my life checking my phone in the desperate hope you'd ask for me. You know how many times you responded when I reached out first? Zero. It was always on your terms. Every time. And I *still* fell fucking head over heels in love with you.

"So you want to know what my deal breaker is? What I want from a relationship with you? I want you to want me back. That's it, baby. End of list. Every other damn detail is negotiable, if you let yourself care about me."

Her mouth ticks down into a frown; she doesn't retreat, but my words landed a blow. Part of me wishes I had softened it, but my gut tells me she needed to hear it. When she finally speaks, her words are soft, contemplative in a way that tells me she's genuinely worried about my answer. "What if I can't meet you on your timeline, Mark? What if two weeks isn't enough?"

"Then *ask*. Ask for more time, baby," I plea. "You can have it."

"You say that, but what if it's six months from now and I still haven't said it back? A year? What then?"

"The night we…" I search for the right word. You can't break up with someone you never really dated, even if that's what it felt like for me. "The night we stopped, you told me you *can't* love me. Was that true? Because we need to have a very different conversation if you don't do romantic love at all."

I had done a fair amount of emotional, panicked research in the months we spent apart. Other than that one word that one time, Lark's never given me reason to think she's aromantic. But something tells me my mom's warning about the cultural hegemony applies here, too, so I want to leave space for Lark to articulate what she meant.

"It's not that. If I were to fall in love with someone—" She hangs her head, exhaling, and I know the unspoken end of that sentence will keep me up tonight. "I don't want to give you false hope," she whispers, worry in her eyes as she forces herself to meet my gaze again. "That's all."

"I'll give you a lifetime if you need it, baby." My voice is raspy, but I don't attempt to clear it away. "I want your love honestly, or not at all. I'll wait as long as it takes for you to feel what I feel."

"Hypothetically," she jokes, clearly desperate to slip out from under the weight of the last few minutes.

I hold her eyes, determined to keep her here with me a moment more. "No, Songbird. You aren't a hypothetical to me. Not now, not ever."

Our chests rise and fall in sync with one another, two long cycles. She bites her lip as she finally looks away. "I think I need to go to bed."

This time, I let her escape. She needs time to process everything I just told her.

Truth be told, so do I.

ONE YEAR AGO

LARK

"Just follow my lead."

The fact that Mark Aladyne could not only say that but *mean* it made me want to quit life altogether. He swept me into his orbit the moment we reached the dance floor, his arm sliding tight around my waist.

And then he started fucking *waltzing*. I stumbled over my feet for the first few bars of the song, despite the deftness of his guidance. But with his hand at my hip and his voice in my ear, it didn't take long for me to settle into the rhythm he created. This was not what I expected when he asked me to dance, and the softness of it all threatened to wash me out to sea entirely.

His eyes were steady on mine as we spun around the room, and I had to fight not to give into their pull entirely. It was already looking to be a losing battle, but I refused to give up the fight so early. "Were you a cotillion kid, Aladyne? Is that what this is?"

"Why? Are you trying to get to know me, Reynolds?" I frowned, annoyed by my slip. His grin grew into a delighted beam, then he leaned in, his lips brushing against the shell of my ear. "Don't worry. If you ask nice enough, I'll tell you anything you want."

The shiver down my spine was nothing but an ill-timed coincidence, and I planned to go to my grave saying as much. But coincidence aside, the atmosphere of this moment was deeply, wildly romantic. We were both dressed to the nines—the way his tux sat across his shoulders could make a freaking nun weep—and surrounded by luxury, drowning in champagne. His left hand held my right with the surety of a man who knew what he wanted; his right, against my lower back, weighed heavy with the promise of unspoken potential. We danced with such purpose it was easy to believe the music played only for the two of us.

I wasn't entirely sure it didn't.

When he leaned down and pressed his lips to mine, I didn't stop him. A room full of people I knew—a room with my *parents* in it—and all that mattered was the man who was so damned determined to catch me. It was a fleeting kiss, a brush of lips, a whispered promise.

It was more than I wanted, and nowhere near enough.

The song came to a close, and our waltz with it, but Mark didn't let me go. "No running away tonight," he murmured. "There are a few people I want you to meet."

I pulled away—or, at least, I tried. But it ended up feeling a bit more like being caught by him, when his arm at my back didn't budge. A hint of fondness edged into his expression. "Not like that," he chuckled. "I just know some people who are considering working with consignments in the future. Thought you might be on the lookout for some potential business."

I bit my lip, unsure how to proceed. It would be stupid to turn down the chance to talk to people who could hire me someday. But I didn't want to have my fate attached to Mark Aladyne any more than I wanted it to be attached to Landow. There was networking, and then there were favors, and this had the potential to end up in the muddy, brackish waters in between, if not on the wrong side entirely.

"A middle ground, then," Mark said, once it became clear to both of us that I was frozen in place as the gears in my head overheated as they spun. "I get another dance, and you stay in my room tonight. In return, I discreetly point out the people I have in mind and you approach them on your own."

"While you brazenly ogle me from across the room?"

"My sister called it pining. I prefer admiring."

I snorted, then shook my head in reluctant, annoyed acceptance. The truth was, we both knew I'd end up in his room tonight, so all I was giving up was a second dance. And right now, that didn't seem so bad.

"Another dance," I agreed. "And I'll *go* to your room tonight."

His hand brought mine up, pressing my fingers against his neck before letting go. Then he used both arms to pull me flush against his body, my breasts molding against his chest, his length already hardening against my abdomen. When we began to move, it was only so we could dance in slow, intimate circles. It wasn't a waltz this time. It was fucking foreplay.

Mark's breath was hot against my skin as he spoke, too soft for anyone around to hear, but with a stern rumble that made me hear his words down to my bones. "You'll *stay*, Lark. It's a hotel room, not a wedding vow. The whole point is that it doesn't last."

"Fine." I exhaled, my sigh shaky despite how frustratingly steady I felt in his arms. "I'll stay."

His lips pressed against my hair, and he somehow pulled me closer, one hand still teasing the boundaries of impropriety as it lingered at the curve of my ass, the other pressing warmth into the sliver of bare skin between my shoulder blades. My hands began clasped behind Mark's neck, but soon I needed to explore, too. I slid my left hand up, twisting the soft edges of his hair, and my right hand down, teasing the skin beneath his collar. Feather-light, just on the wrong side of chaste. Just enough to make his body shudder.

"You keep touching me like that, and we're not even going to make it to the room before I'm inside you," he murmured against my skin.

I tugged at his hair, just lightly enough to claim his attention. "You promise?"

His eyes bored into mine. "You've been taunting me with that slit in your dress all fucking night. It's not a promise, Lark. It's a goddamn threat."

For someone who seemed so determined to get more out of me, he was *very* good at the one thing I actually wanted from him. My pussy practically whimpered, but my voice, at least, held steady. "Then you better get moving on your end of the deal."

He did. For the rest of our dance, in between filthy narrations of what he wanted to do to me, he pointed out the people he thought I should meet. Then, when the song ended, he stepped away and left me without a backward glance to go rejoin his sister, who seemed to be in the middle of a tense conversation with Wesley James, the host of this entire event.

Him walking away like that might have been the hottest thing he had ever done. I fully had to take a moment to gather myself before I could rejoin the general populace.

I found my parents talking with some old family friends in the corner; my father exclaimed, "There you are!" with such surprise that I realized he had no idea I had even been on the dance floor, let alone that I had been on the dance floor with Mark Aladyne. I had no need to correct that over-sight, so I settled for making small talk until I had a moment to assure my parents I wouldn't be needing a ride home. If they wondered why, it didn't show.

The next couple hours were lost to a series of bland, mostly unproductive conversations. I greeted some of my own contacts; I didn't try to talk shop, I just wanted to be fresh in their memories for any decisions they would make in the next few weeks. In between, I made forays at intro-ducing myself to the people Mark identified for me. One of them, a middle-aged man in an ill-fitting suit who carried himself with an air of unearned arrogance, brushed me off immediately. He would have talked to me, had Mark been at my side, but I preferred this version. At least I knew where I stood from the start, rather than finding out after a contract had been signed.

The second person I approached was friendlier—about the same age as the first man, and a similar level of outclassed by the formality of the event, but without the chip on his shoulder. We made pleasant small talk, and he was intrigued when he heard I would be starting my own consignment. I left him with one of the handful of business cards I had tucked into my clutch, just in case.

The last of Mark's trio, Eileen, was the most enthusiastic. She was older than me by a few years, probably in her early thirties, and nailed her soft butch aesthetic even in formal wear. She recognized my name—she knew of my parents and Landow, she admitted, but mostly it was Mark that had told her about me.

When I asked what he said, she just smiled enigmatically and said something about "only good things." But then her smile became a knowing smirk, and she added, "He doesn't have to say much when he looks at you like that."

I tried *so* hard not to snap my head around to look at him.

I really did. But it was instinct, pure and simple, and my throat went dry at the pure *desire* on his face. All the other usual suspects were there, too, bolstering its intensity—heat and lust, amusement, curiosity—but the longing of it was what got me.

He didn't just want my body. I'd known that for a while now, and I mostly tried to ignore it. But Eileen was right: the expression on his face right now spoke for itself. He wanted more than I would ever be able to give him. I knew then I should break it off. I promised myself that I would—that I would try to date again, make sure that I had a real reason to end things for good.

But, I reasoned with myself, I had already promised him tonight. It would have been deeply unfair to back out now.

So I found him a few minutes later, and let him pull me away from the music and the fancy clothes. I let him yank my thong down my legs and tuck it in his pocket the moment we were in the elevator, his fingers wringing an orgasm out of me that I had to silence with a palm over my mouth. I let him pin me to the wall outside the hotel room, him fumbling to get the key in the door, me fumbling to roll a condom onto his cock. I let him see to the fulfillment of the threat he made on the dance floor, sinking all the way into me with a guttural groan before he finally got the keycard to work and we stumbled inside the needlessly luxurious room.

I let him fuck me on every surface in the room, both in and out of my dress. I let him murmur in my ear about how wet I was, how tight I clenched around him, how good it felt to be inside me. I let him tell me to scream for him, to cry his fucking name when I came apart.

And, in the early morning hours, I even let him tuck my body close against his as he drifted toward sleep, his voice a hazy chorus in my ear. "You always sing so pretty for me when you come, Lark. My songbird."

I let him hold me, his body wrapped around mine like a blanket, or a cocoon, or...a cage.

I snuck out once he fell asleep, wondering the entire ride home whether a songbird could ever grow to like its captivity, or if being held could never be anything other than a beautifully gilded cage.

CHAPTER 13

LARK

I try to cancel, but no one will let me.

I started with my parents, casually dropping a few hacking coughs into my call to my mother to "confirm" the details for the dinner she demanded last week. It took about five of them for me to realize she wasn't going to ask if I was sick, so I broached the subject myself. "I'm not sure where this cough came from," I lied, "but maybe I shouldn't come over. I wouldn't want to get you sick."

"You won't."

That was it. The entirety of her response was a delusional level of confidence in her immune system. I tried again before hanging up, going for a different approach. "I know you're super busy right now. I don't want to put you out, if you'd rather wait until the sale is over."

My mother wasn't having it. "Honestly, Lark. Are you trying to get out of dinner with your family?"

"Of course not."

I've never told a more obvious lie in my life, but my mother is oblivious. "Then stop projecting your own inability to manage your workload onto us. We'll see you at six."

With that insult ringing in my ears, I turned my attention to Mark. I knew that would be a losing battle before I started, and he answered the phone with laughter in his voice. "You're not uninviting me to dinner, Lark."

My angry silence suffused the line as I contemplated approximately twelve different places I could bury his body. "I wasn't going to cancel," I lied again.

He snorted. "Like hell you weren't. I've been waiting for this call all morning. But while I've got you, what kind of wine do your parents like?"

"The kind made from grapes. Why?"

"If I show up to their door empty-handed, my mother will be disappointed in me for the rest of this life and all of the next."

What I knew of Diane suggested that was true. "If you want them to like you, ditch the wine in favor of port."

"Mmm." The noise in the background told me he was looking over options as we talked—the soft clink of bottles as he picked them up and set them down almost made me wish I was there to have this conversation in person, to see what label just made him grunt in disapproval. "And if I want *you* to like me?"

"The most obnoxious rosé you can find. They have this personal vendetta against rosés for not picking a side."

He chuckled. "Sold."

Somehow that call ended with me glad I hadn't been able to talk him out of it. But now he's minutes away from picking me up, and all I can think about is that conversation on my porch last night. Honestly, I haven't stopped thinking about it yet.

It's Daphne's fucking fault. I wouldn't have said anything if she hadn't put the idea in my head, and now I have to live with the ramifications of opening that door. Because the truth is, it's not his answers to my questions that I can't get out of my mind—it's the unvarnished hurt in his voice when he called me out for never once being there when he asked for me.

I told myself I was setting boundaries. Protecting my peace. If he wanted me, he could have me on my terms and my terms only. But I never considered what it must have felt like to him, to know that I would never give him the same courtesy. I used him for sex; the rest of him, I ignored. The man wants me to love him, is convinced I already do, but the very thought of it claws at something vital inside me.

What is my love even worth, if that's how it manifests?

It's better this way. I just have to hold out a little while longer, and then he'll be free.

He deserves more than me.

I remind myself of that again and again as I watch his truck pull up my driveway, as he steps out and leans against the hood, as he hungrily peruses my body while he waits for me to approach. His fitted black jeans have a small rip across one thigh that nearly makes me swallow my own tongue, and he's paired it with a houndstooth polo that I know—from the time months ago that I touched it just long enough to yank it off his body—is absurdly soft. It's a combination that neatly straddles "appropriate for a dinner with my parents" and "destined to drive me insane," and the worst part is that I know it's going to work.

That damn sliver of thigh is going to wreck my entire shit tonight.

"Eyes up here, Songbird." His crooked grin is waiting for me when I snap out of my thigh-induced reverie, but in a rare bit of grace, he doesn't belabor the moment. "Are we walking or driving?"

In theory, it's a fair question. My parents' house sits just under a mile away from mine, and it's entirely walkable, setting aside the swampy air. But as soon as he asks it, I realize I haven't walked to my parents' house since the moment I moved into my cottage, and for good reason. "Driving makes for a faster get away," I declare.

"No arguments here." He walks around to the passenger door of his truck, motioning for me to climb in.

He takes his time as he follows my directions down various pathways between fields, and I find myself watching him as he takes in the farm that's been my home for as long as I can remember. The one I no longer have anything to do with—but still, for some reason, want him to appreciate. "It's no Aladyne Stud," I say eventually, but he must hear something in my voice because his smile is gentle as he looks over at me.

"This is the place that made you," he says. "There is no comparison."

The place that made me. The words resonate in my chest, because they fit. I've lived somewhere on this farm for nearly my entire life—first in the farm manager's house, then in the main house when my parents purchased the farm outright, and now in the little cottage on the edge of the property. This place is in my bones, in the DNA of who I've become as a person.

And yet, as far as my parents are concerned, I'm not good enough to manage even a small piece of the farm myself, let alone own it.

It's a unique kind of heartbreak.

"Do you feel that way about Aladyne?" I ask, needing to escape my own loss.

Mark's gaze flies to mine, his surprise that I'm asking a real question of my own accord evident on his face, a reminder of just how carefully I've kept him at arm's length. Still, he doesn't rush to answer. For a man so quick to join me in battle, he takes his time when the stakes are real.

"Yes and no," he says. My parents' house is in front of us now, and he drives slower, as if he can extend this moment that's ending before it had a chance to begin. "It's always been there, and so have I. It's why I admire what you're doing with your business so much, Lark. I've never been that ambitious about anything. I've never needed to be."

For some reason, that answer rings hollow. Maybe it's that after two years of Mark fighting so hard for us, it's odd to realize he doesn't feel the need to fight in all the other aspects of his life. Or maybe it's because he admires a part of me I wish I never existed in the first place.

How do you explain that the thing you're pouring your soul into was never your dream?

But I don't have time to pursue that thought, because just as Mark opens the truck door for me, an all-too-familiar figure steps out onto my parents' porch. It's been a while—around when I quit my Landow job, I'd guess—since I've laid eyes on my ex, let alone been close enough that interaction is inevitable. He jogs lightly down the porch steps, with the casualness of a man whose done it hundreds of times before, only looking up when he hears the thud that accompanies Mark closing the truck door.

"Of fucking course," I mutter when, instead of veering off toward the nearest barn, he breaks in our direction.

"Friend of yours?" Mark's lips brush against my ear, the soft contact almost enough to distract me from the incoming disaster.

"Not anymore."

"Understood."

"Lark!" Gabriel offers a wave and a smile as the gap between us vanishes. He looks the same as he did when we first met, back when I still thought there was a chance for us to have a future. Open expression, sun-darkened brown skin, wavy hair kept just a little too long. Hell, he's even wearing the Mexican National Team shirt I bought him our first—and only—Christmas together. "What a pleasant surprise."

"Not sure I've ever been called pleasant, but okay." Next to me, Mark huffs a laugh. I should probably take his agreement personally.

Gabriel wisely lets that one go by, his gaze landing on Mark. "I don't think we've met," Gabriel says, hand extended. "Gabriel Rojas. I'm the operations manager here at Landow."

Mark shakes his hand as I absorb the weight of that title. Gabriel has been promoted, it seems. Again. "Mark. The boyfriend."

God, it's petty to be so turned on by the fact that he chose to associate himself with *me*, rather than his farm. It's enough to keep me from elbowing him in the stomach when he wraps an arm firmly around my waist and pulls me tight against him.

Just this once, I don't mind being claimed.

Gabriel doesn't seem surprised or put out—not that I would expect him to be, given how long it's been since we broke up. Instead, he just continues to smile. "It's great to meet you, man." His attention lands back on me. "I hear you've got your business up and running. That's awesome."

How much easier this would be if Gabriel was ever an intentional asshole, instead of just an accidental one. "Sounds like I'm not the only one who's had some career changes."

He has the good grace to wince slightly. "Yeah. It's new." To his credit, Gabriel quickly realizes that if he's waiting for a congratulations, he'll be waiting at least until his bones turn to dust, if not until the heat death of the universe. "I'll let you two get inside. It was good to see you, Lark."

I can't quite bring myself to say it back, so I settle for a nod and a quiet, "Have a good night."

He strides off, and I let Mark bundle me in his arms for a hug. Burying my head in his chest is as good a way as any to process that interaction—a deep inhale of laundry detergent and cologne and *Mark* helps settle my soul. "He seems nice."

I sigh. "Unfortunately, he is."

"Want me to punch him anyway?" I nod without lifting my head. "Consider it done. Next time I see him, it's on sight."

We both know he won't do it, but the promise makes me feel better anyway. So does the fact that he's not pushing for answers yet, even though I know better than to think he won't ask eventually. "We should go inside," I say, with no conviction in my voice. "My parents will be mad if we're late."

"Pretty sure they live their lives mad, babe." His arms tighten around me. "We'll go inside when you're ready, and not before."

I'm glad he can't see the smile that sneaks across my face. "We might be here a while, then."

"Fine by me, Songbird. Fine by me."

The atmosphere around the dining room table is ripe with discomfort. Everything is staged beautifully—the meal my parents ordered from a chef they share with a few other families has been carefully contrived to look homemade, fresh-cut flowers adorn the centerpiece, and we're eating from the dish ware my mother considers *formally casual*. It's all an attempt to make everything appear welcoming and charming, like my parents and I are a big, happy family who eat meals together all the time.

But having finally seen what that *really* looks like, over at the Aladynes', I can see through the rotted facade to what it really is: two people desperate for the kind of position and power they thought they'd never have.

Mark sees it, too.

He plays his role perfectly. He's charmingly deprecating as he presents the bottle of rosé, which he wrapped in an obnoxious ribbon just to make me laugh. He offers genuine compliments about the decor and asks thoughtful questions about the farm's operations. He keeps the mood light, never lets the conversation grow stagnant.

But he also watches me with a ferocity that borders on relentless. Every small dig from my mother, every passive aggressive comment from my father—he notes them all, checking in to make sure I haven't reached my limit. Unbeknownst to him, I have developed quite a tolerance over the years.

It's a fact that seems to displease him, if the increasingly false curve of his lips is anything to go by.

"Oh, Lark darling, we wanted to talk to you about something." My mother announces this the moment we finish our entrees, with all the subtlety of the Kool-Aid Man blasting through a wall. "Perhaps we can borrow you for a few minutes before you leave."

Translation: *we don't want to have this conversation in front of Mark Aladyne.*

"Why not talk about it now?" I ask, playacting ignorance.

"Some things are better discussed among family, Lark." My father injects a plausibly deniable amount of disdain into his words—he wants me to hear it, but not my boyfriend. The tick of Mark's jaw tells me he missed the mark by a mile.

"Mark's my boyfriend." I swear the gleeful little bunny in my stomach got a high when Mark held me outside, because I come far too close to calling him family. "I'll just tell him what you say when we leave, regardless."

A curious look flashes across Mark's face, like he can't decide if I'm telling the truth or not. I can't entirely blame him, based on our relationship thus far, but despite knowing how this all has to end, my walls are falling fast.

"Well, there's no sense in going on about it," my mother tuts. "We just want to know when you'll be out of the cottage."

"When I'll what?"

Dad sighs, like this conversation is already tedious. "We recently promoted Gabriel."

"So he said." I bite the words out, not liking where this is going.

"I hope you congratulated him," Mom says. "He's worked hard for the position."

"What does this have to do with my cottage?" I try to keep the conversation on track, because a conversation about what Gabriel *earned* is not going to end well for anyone. Across the table, Mark's expression is growing increasingly stony, his usual grin nowhere to be found.

"Part of the compensation package is on-site housing."

I'm going to crack a tooth—or ten—if I'm not careful. "Doesn't he already live above the foaling barn?"

My father waves a hand. "That was fine when he was barn manager. He deserves something nicer now."

"So you're going to kick me out of my house."

"*Our* house, Lark. You don't own it. We do."

Mark's knuckles are white, his eyes furious. It's for the best I didn't tell him the full story before we came inside. If I had, he wouldn't have even this much control left.

The last time they promoted Gabriel, I effectively lost my job.

This time, I'm losing my home.

"So you're evicting me," I repeat. I need them to say it—to *own* it.

"It's not as crass as all that," Mom says, her eyes darting to Mark. "But you made your decision when you quit your job here. You have your little business now. The cottage was never supposed to be yours forever."

No, it wasn't. When I first moved in there, it was with the hope that someday—years from now—my parents would leave me the farm, and this house would become mine.

That's what makes me ask a question I wasn't sure I'd ever be brave enough to ask. "What happened to Reynolds Racing?"

Across the table, in the midst of the shocked silence I've sent my parents into, Mark's anger softens. He gives me a single nod, a gentle reminder that, for once, I'm not alone here.

"How did you hear about that?" Mom demands.

"You *shouldn't* know about that," my father adds, making it clear this was no small oversight, but a deliberate secret.

In an attempt to keep Diane out of the conversation, I settle for a simplified version of the explanation. "I saw a winner's circle photo recently. I didn't know you ever had your own business."

"And what do you call this?" Dad gestures in the air, his motions clearly encompassing not just the house but the lands around it, too.

"You know what I mean."

"No, I don't think I do." Mom's voice has gone cold, the polite sheen it usually carries nowhere to be found. "How is this farm we've poured our whole lives into not *our own business?*"

"I didn't—" I pause, already exhausted. Leave it to my parents to evict me and then make me out to be the villain in the same conversation. "All I meant was I didn't know you had something under your own name before you came here. It took me by surprise that you never talked about it."

"Yet another conversation that would be better among family," Mom mutters. The smile she pastes on to give Mark is so brittle it's already shattering. "I apologize for my daughter's indiscretion."

Mark's eyes don't leave my face. "There's never a need to apologize to me on your daughter's behalf."

There's a beat of harsh silence, only broken by my father's annoyance. "Fine. If you must know, we attempted to set out on our own. We were young, inexperienced, and ambitious—always a dangerous combination, as you well know."

I don't miss the implication in his words or the weight of his gaze—nor does Mark. But I push to keep my parents talking. "What happened?"

"We took the little bit of money we had and bought a couple racehorses. We practically had to beg, borrow, and steal to get them trained—that's how I first got to know your mother." My mom's smile to Mark looks more genuine this time, but the firm press of her palm on the table as she steadies herself belies her discomfort. "We had a little luck with one, but the money disappeared fast."

"It didn't take long to learn that all anyone cares about in this business is the name on the silks." Dad picks the story back up, making no attempt to hide his bitterness. "There was no point in doing it on our own. We sold the horses, took the money we had left, and worked ourselves to the bone to be able to make this place ours when the Landows were ready to sell. Landow Thoroughbreds is a name people know and trust. The name Reynolds meant shit-all then, and it means even less now."

That punches all the air out of me, and he's not even done.

"That's why we told you starting your own business is a fool's errand, Lark. You could have had a place here, but you threw a temper tantrum when we promoted Gabriel and you left. You're naive enough to want to do it all on your own, but when it comes crashing down, you'll wish you had a place to fall."

"Are you fucking serious right now?" Mark's voice is hard, and there's an undercurrent of anger in it I've never heard before. It seems we found the limit of his patience. "You can say that with a straight face after you just *evicted* your daughter?"

"Now, son, I know you care about her," Dad starts in, ignoring the obvious flinch on Mark's face at being called *son* in this moment. "So you surely understand."

"Understand what, precisely?"

"It's…sweet that Lark wants to branch out on her own. But if she matured a little, she'd know there's no reason to bother. You can't tell me it's not easier for you to work on your family's farm than to try to create your own from nothing."

Mom adds, "We just want to save her from herself."

"I don't need *saving*," I snarl, at the same moment Mark snaps, "She doesn't need to be *saved*."

Our eyes meet, the slightest hint of warmth peeking out from behind his fury, and I realize with sudden, horrifying clarity that I am, in fact, not quite as not in love with him as I want to be.

"Don't be dramatic," Mom sighs. "Obviously it would be lovely if you succeed."

"You just don't think I will."

"We know how hard it is from experience. How long do you honestly think you can make this one-woman show last?"

"Do you want to take this, Songbird, or can I?" Mark's anger has yet to abate—if anything, it seems to be coiling into something more intense. But he still looks to me first, giving me a choice, and something about that self-control hits a new series of dominoes in my heart. I might not need saving from myself, but a small, fragile part of me wants to be saved from *this*.

"It's all yours, babe."

The endearment makes another flash of pleasure appear under his rage before he starts talking. His voice is steady and controlled, ringing with the surety of a true believer. "I would advise both of you not to confuse your past failures with your daughter's potential. Because I have spent the past week watching her work her fucking ass off, and what you don't seem to realize is that it's not for some ambiguous future—she's already made her success happen. She's *living* it. It doesn't matter if her business lasts another week or the rest of her life. She'll never be a failure. So maybe you should stop anticipating ways it could fall apart and start thinking about how you can show the fuck up for her in the meantime." He pauses. "Pardon my language."

All three of us stare at Mark, although I'm pretty sure I'm the only one who's currently imagining all the very dirty things I want to do to thank him later. I didn't realize how *vital* it would feel to have someone speak up for me until this perfect, awful moment.

It's my father who finally speaks. "Those were pretty words, son, but I think you'll find we know our daughter's potential—or lack thereof—better than you."

The silence, and my heart: in that moment, my father breaks them both.

CHAPTER 14

MARK

"I think you underestimated your getaway speed," I say when I catch up to Lark. She bolted, her father's dig about her potential the final straw on an already broken back, and I stayed back just long enough to inform them that the next communication they have with her should be in the form of an apology and snag what remained of the bottle of wine I had brought before taking off after her. But that was enough of a head start for her to be what feels like a quarter mile away, because she's powered by the dual engines of spite and hurt. "Fuck the truck."

She pulls up short. "Shit. Your truck."

I wave that away. "Like I said. Fuck the truck. I'll get it tomorrow." I hold out the mostly full bottle of wine. "Can't drink and drive, but we can drink and walk."

"Valid point." She grabs the bottle and takes a hefty swig before clutching it to her chest and resuming her angry march. I fall into stride next to her, glad for a reason to walk off the worst of my own fury over that encounter. The fact that *that* is what Lark's been dealing with this whole time has me longing to punch something. "So that's what my family dinners are like."

"Can't say I'm a fan."

She snorts. "You wouldn't be, Aladyne."

"Lark—"

"They picked him over me." She cuts me off. Her speed finally lessens, but she's clinging to the wine bottle, wrapped around it in a way that tells me it's the only thing tethering her right now. "I used to spend summers working in Kentucky. My parents' idea. They wanted me to get experience outside of Landow. You won't believe me, but I loved it. Loved working with everyone, loved learning from people who forgot more about horses every day than I could ever hope to know. God, just watching your crew makes my chest ache with how much I miss it sometimes.

"But right before I was supposed to go one year, I find out they had hired this new guy. They asked me to stick around, show him the ropes. A few weeks in, he asks me out. I'm reluctant, not sure I want to cross those streams, but he's sweet and charming and my parents like him. Eventually I say yes. One date turns into another, and then those dates turn into a serious relationship."

I don't like where this is going, and not just because I know at least part of how it ends. She's disconnected, empty in a way I've never seen her, and it takes everything in me not to tell her to stop. But she needs to purge this from her system, and all I can do is listen.

"We were talking about living together. He even mentioned his grandmother's ring once." I tamp down on the flare of jealousy that brings. "Then one of the barn managers took another job. We had just lost one of our best broodmares to colic. My parents blamed me. I was the one who turned her out that morning, so we didn't notice until it was too late."

"Jesus, Lark." Colic is a bitch of a thing in horses. You can do everything right and still lose them. "It wasn't your fault."

"Oh, I know." Her laugh is bitter. "It took me a while to see it, but it was a convenient excuse. If it hadn't been that, it would have been something else. They constantly talked about how much I needed to prove myself, how much I had to learn. How they couldn't just *give* me anything. Anyway, they promoted Gabriel to the barn manager position instead of me."

"But you grew up here. You *trained* him."

"Yup."

"Fucking hell. And he just accepted it?"

"Of course he did. Better pay, better hours, small but free barn apartment. He was pumped."

I was mostly kidding before, because I'm a far better lover than fighter, but I might really punch the man next time I see him.

"Anyway," she continues, "I broke up with him, like the nepo baby having a temper tantrum I was, and started making plans to launch my consignment. Convinced myself it was all for the best. That I actually *wanted* to do it all on my own. Moved on. Gave up the camaraderie of a crew in return for complete control.

"But now I have to move out of my house because taking my home from me once just wasn't enough for my parents."

Her voice cracks at the end of that sentence, pain manifesting in one haggard exhale. I want to ask questions, to comfort her, to soften the sting of the hits she took tonight, but her anger isn't done with her yet, so I settle for keeping pace at her side as she walks. The silence between us is loud and ominous, but I let it breathe.

If I push too hard, she might push back. Push me away. And what I want more than anything is to still be at her side when that ticking time bomb in her chest finally hits zero.

The explosion starts the moment her cottage comes into view. She freezes in place, leaving me to stumble to a stop next to her. She's staring at her house, a stricken expression on her face, but it only lasts a few seconds before she rears back and fucking *yeets* the wine bottle toward her cottage. We're nowhere near close enough for her to actually hit it—the bottle glances off a nearby fence post instead before it thuds to the ground, rolling slowly in a half-moon arc.

The action seems to finally shake her out of the stasis she's been in since she stopped talking. Her eyes land on me, distant haze replaced by pained clarity. "That whole thing was bad, right?" There's a thread of broken laughter to the words. "I'm pretty sure it was bad."

"Yeah, honey. It was bad."

"Yeah." She starts to nod, then just keeps nodding. "Yeah. I thought so. Yeah."

I can't stand not touching her anymore, not when she's spiraling. I catch her nodding head with my palms, holding her face in my hands. When she stills, then exhales, I'm not surprised by the tears that line her lashes. I am surprised they took this long to appear.

"What do you need, Songbird?" My voice is rough as I pose the question, because I already know I'll give her anything she asks for right now. Hell, not just right now.

Always.

Everything about her softens as I brush my thumbs across her cheekbones, catching tears as they fall. Some of the pain she's holding dissipates in this moment that hovers between us. "You," she whispers. "I just need you."

"You've got me." In every fucking way possible, whether she knows it or not, she's got me. "I'm not going anywhere."

"Take me to bed, Mark," she pleads, and I catch her mouth with mine for a soft kiss that she sighs into with such relief that I almost cry, too. Then I settle her hand back into mine and we finish the walk to her cottage. I open the front door, guiding her inside. "Go get in bed, baby," I murmur. I linger for a moment as she scurries down the hall; I pull the door shut behind us. Lock it for good measure.

What she's asking for is the end of this stupid game we've been playing. If I walk down that hall after her, I'm giving up the last days I have to prove my point about how good we can be together, giving up the chance to make her say the words I need to hear.

But no part of me hesitates.

The Lark who needs me right now is more real than the one I've been trying to create, and I love this Lark too much to walk away.

All I can hope is that what I've already given her will be enough to make her stay.

Any effort I put into readying myself as I followed her down the hall is shattered when I step through her bedroom door to find her perched on her bed, naked. "Fucking hell, Lark." I fully stop in my tracks, drinking in the sight in front of me. She's leaning back on her wrists, breasts on full display, with her legs spread just wide enough for me to see just a hint of what awaits. "Do you have any idea how perfect you are?"

I nearly lose my mind at the pink that warms her chest as she listens to my words. I spend half my time trying to make her blush with jokes and innuendo, and apparently all it takes is me saying a few true words.

The pleasure she takes at the compliment undercuts the eye roll she gives me. "Are you just going to stand there and stare all night?"

"I fucking might," I admit. "It's a hell of a view."

This has always been one of the drawbacks of the walls Lark threw up between what we could and couldn't be: so little time to *linger*. She never wanted to talk, never wanted to breathe, never wanted to rest. Not with me, anyway. So a moment like this? Where I can just stop and look at her?

I'm in no hurry to bring it to an end.

But damn if there isn't something to the needy way she groans my name when she can't stand the silence any longer, too. I smirk at her impatience and cross to stand between her thighs, batting away her hand when she reaches for my shirt. "Later, baby." I lean forward until her back falls to the bed. "I'll give you everything you want tonight, but I'm not going to rush a single moment."

Not if it's the last time you let me have you. I keep that thought to myself as I kiss her, slow and unhurried. She melts back against her unmade bed—I don't think I've ever seen it otherwise—and parts her lips for me, her tongue meeting mine in a teasing little game. My hands trace ever-so-light trails up and down her side, leaving goosebumps in their wake as her skin comes to life under my touch.

My dick is already threatening to resign in protest at being told to wait, but there's too much pleasure to be had in kissing my way down her throat, tasting the perfect curves and planes of her body. I've never been a man particularly dedicated to academic studies, but I could spend years memorizing the minute difference in her gasps and never grow bored of it. I'd get a fucking PhD in Lark Reynolds, just for the way she cries my name when my tongue finds her nipple—and then I'd do it all again for the way she bites her lip when I draw my thumb across her hip bone.

I take a slow, meandering path down her body, and for the first time, she lets me. She doesn't push to pick up the pace, to move things along. She just relaxes into my exploration, her fingers content to tangle in my hair and dance across my scalp in a sensual massage as I worship her stomach.

When I'm finally kneeling in front of her spread legs, I've

already lost all sense of time and place. The world in its entirety consists of me, Lark, and this eternal present we're in together. I kiss each of her inner thighs, determined not to take this for granted. "It's been so long since I've gotten to taste you properly." I breathe the words against her skin, tortured by the sight of how wet she already is, how eagerly her hips rock in anticipation of my touch.

"Then you'd better make up for lost time," she says, and underneath her usual sass, there's just a hint of something different. A sincerity, I realize—or, if I'm lucky, an admission. An acknowledgment that the time we spent apart could have been better spent together.

Or maybe that's my own desperate hope for a miracle. "Tell me what you want," I demand, my voice rough. "Tell me how you want to come."

"Start by putting that mouth of yours to work, and we'll go from there."

The time for leisurely exploration has passed. I drag my tongue up her folds, flicking lightly against her clit, and the soft tang of her in my mouth makes me groan. "Fuck, Lark. You better hang on tight."

And then I lose myself in her, determined to make her as eager for my mouth as my mouth is eager for her pussy. Her hands come back to my hair, but this time her fingernails bite my skin as she grasps on for dear life. I press a finger inside her, fucking obsessed with the way her walls cling to me, and tease and curl until I find the spot that sends her flying.

It's never subtle when that happens, and this time is no exception. Her back arches with pleasure, a string of filthy expletives leaving her lips before she begins to beg. "Please don't fucking stop, Mark. Please don't stop."

I don't stop, but I do add a second finger. My cock aches to be inside her—hell, for any relief at all—but I tell myself it's worth the wait. Lark's hips begin to rock and grind against my face as her orgasm builds, and I throw myself into giving her exactly what she needs. If this is all she wants of me, then I'm going to make damn sure no one else can give her more or better than I can.

"Yes," she whimpers. "Just like that, Mar—" She chokes on my name as her release tears through her, her pussy clenching around my fingers in long, shuddering waves. I urge her through it, my fingers and tongue relentless until she's fully spent, but even then, I don't stop. I shift the pressure, my attention back to slow and teasing around her freshly sensitive nerves, but I've missed having my head between her legs too much to stop at just one.

"Fuck, I can't, Mark." She's practically boneless from pleasure, and her words take on a charming, exhausted slur. "I can't."

"The fuck you can't," I snap, lightly biting her upper thigh to make her gasp again. "I told you we're not rushing this. If I want to get you off a dozen times before I put my cock in you, then that's what we're doing."

"I don't think that's—"

I bite her other thigh, this time slightly harder. "No more thinking," I say, and go back to work. It takes time, a slow and steady build, but this time when she explodes, her thighs clench tight around my head and I nearly fucking come myself.

Going for a third is tempting, if only to prove I can, but when she tugs at my hair with a barely audible, "I want to kiss you," I instantly give in.

She exhales happily as my body settles over hers, and I let her lead the next few minutes. Lark's never kissed me gently before, but this time she does, and I tuck the memory of it away for all the rest of my days, for any dark moment when I need to be reminded of when I had this one, precious thing.

Her hands roam around my body, and this time I don't stop her when she peels my shirt over my head. When her hands reach for my waistband, I roll to my back, letting her strip me until the only thing between us is the air.

I hiss in tortured relief when she finally wraps her fingers around my cock, her hand steady and sure as she strokes me, as unhurried with me as I was with her. A sting sharpens in my chest, worried that this is her way of saying goodbye, but I'm helpless to stop it. I couldn't have stopped myself from telling her I loved her six months ago, and I can't stop myself from letting her take what she needs from me right now.

A lifetime of heartbreak for me in exchange for a night of distraction for her is a deal I'll take every time, no matter how unbalanced it might be.

God knows I'm getting more than my share of pleasure tonight. She works me with her hands and mouth until I'm one feather-light touch away from coming all over her, but this time when she stops, it's because I beg her to. "I wanna come inside you, baby. You have to stop."

"So picky," she teases, but she gives me the reprieve I need. At least until she shifts, straddling me with a smirk, and begins to grind her hips against me.

"*Fuck*, Songbird." My cock was already slick from being in her mouth; it takes seconds for it to be drenched in the moisture between her legs, too. "You're killing me here."

Her grin sharpens, a hint of our usual combativeness finally returning to her face. "Then it's working."

I flip her onto her back again, reveling in her carefree giggle as I dig through the pockets of my discarded jeans for the condoms I've been carrying everywhere the last few days. I toss them on the bed, then return my attention to my girl, who sobers as she watches me. "You okay?" I ask.

"I will be," she says, brazening her way through like she always does. I study her for a moment, trying to read how true that statement is, but she uses my hesitance as an excuse to start touching herself, and the sight of her fingers slipping inside her wet pussy is too much for me to resist.

I kneel in front of her again, pulling her hand away and replacing it with my own. She parts my lips with her slick fingers, and I suck her clean before sliding back up her body, my fingers taking the chance to stretch and tease her one more time before I claim her with my cock. I press my forehead to hers, knowing it's a gamble but unable to prevent the quiet, "I love you," from leaving my lips. But I kiss her before she can panic, matching the rhythm of my tongue to the thrust of my fingers as I kiss her, groaning from my very soul when I finally pull away long enough to reach for a condom.

But the moment my fingers brush the foil packet, I hear Lark's voice. "No."

I look at her in surprise. Condoms have always been a non-negotiable for both of us—I'm stupid in love with her, but I'm not stupid about sex. As tempting as the idea of being inside her with no barriers between us is—and *fuck*, is it tempting—I frown. "Not sure that's a rule we should change in the heat of the moment, baby."

There's an odd look on her face. Regret, maybe, with a little fear thrown in for good measure. But she just shakes her head, her voice hoarse. "Don't fuck me tonight, Mark."

The sting of fear in my chest becomes a stab of incoherent hope. "I thought that's what you wanted."

"It is. God, it's the only thing I want right now."

"Then you win, Lark. It's a stupid fucking game in the first place."

"*No.*" The force of her objection catches even her off guard. "I mean, yes, this bet is ridiculous. I just…"

She trails off, looking away until I reach out and draw her chin back in my direction. "Finish the thought. Please."

"I just don't want you to lose yet."

Keeping the dopey-ass smile that's threatening to take over off my face is an act of pure valor. "Does that mean you want me to win?"

"No." This time it's a scoff. But the derision is half-hearted, at best, and underneath it lies a layer of pure vulnerability. "It means I want you to keep playing. That's all."

I don't know if she's going to regret this later. I don't know if *I'm* going to regret this later. But right now, the promise of maybe is a hell of a drug.

"Then let's fucking play, Songbird."

EIGHT MONTHS AGO

MARK

"Dude."

The single word was all Bowen said, but I heard every-thing it implied. Judgment. Exasperation. Sympathy.

Mostly judgment, though.

"I know, I know." I swiped a hand through my hair. "But it's been a month, and I'm dying here."

Bowen raised his eyebrows at me, the "dude" silent this time but just as expressive. We were sitting on the tailgate of his truck, having just finished installing a pair of new water troughs at his place. If we were at Aladyne, I'd have just hired his crew outright, but because it's for his family, I got dragged into helping him. It's the friend tax, but I don't mind paying it.

"You didn't see the guy she was on a date with, Bowen. He looked like he lost his hair trying to climb into his own pocket protector." Was that maybe the shittiest thing I'd ever said about another person? Yes. But it was far kinder than how I really wanted to describe him, after seeing the way he leered at and lectured her in equal measure.

Bowen grunted. "But he was the one on the date with her, not you."

I think I preferred the *dude* from before. It felt less like a knife to the back. "Jesus Christ, man."

He shrugged, clearly unconcerned with the betrayal he just inflicted. "It's true."

"But she *left* with me," I pointed out. "That's what matters."

At least, that was what I had been telling myself every day of the past month of radio silence from Lark. We'd had a damn good night that night—my truck was still recovering from the various ways we defiled it until I was sober enough to drive her home—and I had assumed it would be enough to make her text me again soon. God knew I was desperate for another round or ten the moment she kicked me out at three in the morning.

But instead: nothing.

This was nearly the longest I had gone without seeing her since we met, and I was growing restless. And on me, restless became impulsive. Which was why I had added Lark and her parents to the list of invitees for the New Year's party without telling the rest of my family. Because the party was held in the main house, we typically made a point of running any new names on the guest list by everyone in the family, just to avoid any unexpected surprises.

Bowen clearly didn't understand, but he would. Eventually.

Because I wasn't about to give my family a chance to say no before I gave Lark a chance to say yes.

"Just you wait," I said, with far more confidence than I felt. "She'll be there."

"She's not here." I was tucked into the corner of the living room, which served as both a convenient hiding spot for antisocial Bowen and a direct line of sight on the front door for me. "Why the fuck isn't she here?"

"She's probably out with her boyfriend."

I glared at Bowen, trying to determine if he was fucking with me or actually had inside information. I relaxed—*slightly*—when I decided it was the former. "You don't know she has a boyfriend."

"You don't know she doesn't," he countered.

"Just for that, you have to stay until midnight."

He ignored my threat, his eyes flicking over to a woman who lingered on the threshold between rooms. "Maybe you should move on."

I pretended to scan the room, taking in the woman who was openly watching me along the way. She was hot, and she was certainly interested. Add in the magic of a New Year's kiss, and it probably wouldn't be hard to seal the deal.

But the truth was, I had already tried. A *lot*. I had flirted, stolen kisses, gone on dates. I spent the better part of the first few months after we met trying to get my mind off Lark. I knew how shitty it was of me to refuse to take her at her word when she said she didn't want to date me.

The problem was that nothing I tried worked. The dates were tedious and boring, the kisses staid and passionless, the flirting rote and exhausting. It was like my body and brain had decided that as long as Lark Reynolds existed in the world, nothing else mattered.

And so it didn't really matter if the woman across the room was a ten or even if she was my fucking soulmate. I was doomed to live in my longing, and there was no point in dragging anyone else down with me.

Other than my best friend, anyway. "Moving on's not in

the cards for me. Do you want me to wingman you? One of us should get laid tonight."

He shook his head. "Nah, I'm good."

I bit my tongue, determined not to say something stupid. Even offering that much had bordered on pushing more than I liked to do with him. Bowen deserved better than the isolation that he liked to live in, but he heard enough about it from his moms. He didn't need me adding to the pile.

"Well, damn," Bowen sighed. I looked at him, curious at the change in tone, but I was already processing what I was seeing out of the side of my eye. "So much for peace in the new year."

Just inside the front door, Lark was handing her coat off to a man I didn't recognize but had already decided wasn't good enough for her based on the entire everything about him.

He was just so…not me.

"Don't worry," I assured Bowen. "I'll behave."

"No." His voice was shorter than usual. Which was saying something. "Ruin his night."

I was already planning on it, no matter what I said, but I now had the endorsement of my recalcitrant best friend. "Do I want to know why?"

He swallowed, his eyes unfocused for a split second before he shook himself free of his thoughts. "No."

It was *her* again, then. Daphne. Someday I'd get him to tell me what happened, but in the meantime, I was all too happy to give him the outcome he wanted.

As Lark took in the space, I ducked out of sight. I had to wait for her to show up, so now it was her turn to wait.

Fortunately for her, my patience was limited. It took about half an hour for the loser on her arm to step away—and that was long enough.

"I wasn't aware you had been given a plus one," I

murmured as I stepped up next to her. "I should probably kick him out."

She didn't startle—instead she instinctively pressed into my palm hovering at her back, like she knew it would be there. "It's not very hospitable of you to expect me to spend my evening alone."

"Oh, Songbird." The nickname hit her in a satisfying way—she tensed, but didn't pull free from my touch. "I was never going to let that happen. Now come with me."

She turned, but I didn't let go, letting my arm loop around her waist instead. Her hip pressed into mine as she leaned back to look up at me. "I'm here with a date, remember?"

"Believe me," I said, my voice rough. "I remember."

Her eyes flared with heat, but her expression stayed fixed into place. "You don't get to interject yourself into all my dates, Aladyne."

I shook my head and tightened my arm just enough to make her breath stutter. "*You* don't get to bring another man to my party and expect me to be a gentleman about it."

"Oh?" She blinked up at me, those long lashes so fucking pretty. "What can I expect, then?"

This woman was a fucking hazard to my health. But she'd tipped her hand too fast—now I knew she was intentionally provoking me, which meant this just got way more fun. I pulled my arm away and stepped back, just as her sorry-ass date started making his way back across the room. "That's not the question, Lark."

"It's not?" She tried to sound disinterested, but she failed.

"No. The question is what are *you* going to do about it?" Then I turned to her date and held out my hand with a beaming smile. "Mark Aladyne. Pleasure to meet you."

If he was at all concerned about what I was doing with Lark while he was gone, it didn't show in his face. He took my hand and met me with a smile of his own. "Leon. Thanks for having us."

"Leon is my best friend's brother," Lark explained. When I quirked my lips at her, amused by her sudden need to clarify, she looked away.

Not a threat, then. Not to me.

I made small talk with the man for a few minutes, determined to drive Lark a little batty in the process, before finally stepping back. "Enjoy your night, Leon." Then, as I passed by Lark, I added in a voice low enough for only her to hear, "See you at midnight, Songbird."

Later, when everyone started the countdown, Lark Reynolds crossed the room to meet me. I didn't wait for midnight to kiss her, because I wanted to end this year *and* start the next with her lips against mine. Hell, I wanted to do that every year for the rest of my damn life.

As far as I was concerned, we were inevitable.

And it was high time I made her see that, too.

CHAPTER 15

LARK

I wake up in Mark's arms. It's still dark outside, the sun not quite ready to rise, but I've been getting up by 4 a.m. for the past week, so there's no chance of me sleeping until daylight. For a moment, though, I wish I could. A few more hours tucked against Mark's warm body doesn't seem like too much to ask.

Except for the fact that asking would reveal how badly I want it, and I'm not sure I'm ready for that yet—even if I am closer to ready than I've ever been.

Mark grumbles softly when I try to slip away from him. "Not yet." His arms tighten around me, his lips press against my hair, his words thick with sleep. "We'll get up soon. But not yet."

Turns out, when Mark's morning voice makes the plea, giving in becomes easy. "Five more minutes," I murmur back, my eyes already closing.

His lips curve into a smile against my skin. "Five more minutes."

Soft tendrils of pre-dawn light are sneaking in through the window the next time I open my eyes, the space beside me empty, and I sit up in a panic. I tell myself my worry is because I never oversleep, that I have work to do—but when footsteps approach from beyond my bedroom door, my relief is so profound that I have to accept the truth.

I didn't want Mark to be gone.

I'm so fucking fucked.

"Morning, Songbird." Mark takes a sip from his coffee, and something about the sight of him drinking from a joke mug Daphne got me years ago—one that says *buck you*, with a terribly drawn horse flipping off the viewer—knocks me off my axis, if I was even on it in the first place.

When he offers me my coffee in my favorite mug, with a reassurance about getting me an iced coffee while we're out, I suddenly start to wonder if this is what I've been denying myself: being seen so clearly that he reaches for the right mug without having to ask. I've spent two years scared to let Mark in, but he's here now, and I don't hate it.

There's something to be said for not having to make your own coffee on a Sunday morning.

He leans against the doorframe, his unbuttoned jeans hanging low on his hips in some false attempt at modesty. I take another sip of coffee to remedy the dry mouth I develop just from staring at his bare torso, but his smirk tells me he isn't fooled in the slightest. He motions for his shirt, which is on the floor next to me, and I toss it to him.

"Wake yourself up and get ready," he says. "I'll go get my truck, and then we have horses to feed."

"Breakfast after?"

The expression that crosses his face is so achingly happy it makes my chest hurt. "Yeah, baby," he says. "Breakfast after."

We feed out at the farm, taking a little extra time with the horses who are due to be shipped to the sale later this week, and then drive across to the sale and feed both sides of the barn, since he gives his crew Sunday off. The work goes faster with Mark at my side—or it would, if he stopped trying to corner me into kissing him every few minutes.

The fact that it works every time is beside the point.

We eventually find our way to a diner down the road. A couple blocks away from both Dicks and Brews, it's the literal definition of a hole in the wall, attached to an ancient gas station. Longer than it is wide, the diner holds about six tables normally but can cram in up to nine during the sales. The place is hopping this morning, filled with familiar faces who had a similar plan—take care of work early, then celebrate with food. A harried waitress waves us through to the one open table, and I glare at Mark. "If you try to sit on the same side as me, I will castrate you with a butter knife."

"Seems needlessly messy, but point taken."

I finally order my iced coffee, we both ask for way too much food, and I try to relax into the moment as we eat together. He doesn't push us to talk about last night, for which I'm grateful. I'm not even sure where we would begin: do we start with me seeing my ex and all the history I dumped on Mark as a result? With my parents' insults and insistence that my business is doomed to fail? With the fact that I apparently need to find a new place to live?

With the reality that I could have ended this entire farce of a relationship *and* gotten railed, and chose—practically begged—not to do either?

No, it's far better if we ignore it all. Right now, we have bacon and eggs and pancakes galore, and that's enough.

Halfway through the meal, my phone buzzes with an incoming call. I flip it over, unsure if I'm hoping or dreading to see one of my parents on the caller ID, but it's Daphne's face that grins up at me instead. It's not unusual for her to call me in the morning—she knows I'm far more likely to answer now than I am late at night—but it's still super early in Vancouver and she didn't text in advance at all, which is worrisome. "It's Daphne," I tell Mark. "Do you mind?"

"I'd mind more if you didn't."

That eases a knot in my stomach I didn't even know was there as I asked the question. I slide my thumb across the phone screen before the call can drop. "Hey, Daffy," I say, right as all the noise in the restaurant explodes at once. Someone drops a plate at one table, a group of people burst into laughter at another table, and a chime signals new arrivals as the door opens.

Daphne pauses at the cacophony. "Where the hell are you?"

"I'm at breakfast."

"...Alone?"

I close my eyes and brace, knowing I have to bite the damn bullet. "No. Not alone."

"Are you with *Mark*?!" she exclaims, the diner now so suspiciously quiet that Mark can hear her clear across the table.

He grins and leans forward. "Hi, Daphne."

I scowl at him while Daphne gasps in my ear. "Does this mean you *spent the night* with him? Lark? Does it? Answer me!"

With a heavy sigh, I say, "Yes."

"Holy shit. Holy shit. You spent the night with him and are eating breakfast with him the next morning. Holy shit."

"Damn, it's like she's in my head," Mark quips, casually taking a sip of his coffee.

"Is there a point to this?" I ask the woman who is no longer my best friend.

"There was, but it's changed. I want to talk to him."

"Absolutely not."

Mark had stopped listening, but my adamant refusal has his head popping up fast. I try to turn the volume down, but

I'm not fast enough to keep him from hearing her demand once again that I put him on the phone. His hand reaches out to snag it from me before I can stop him, and he sits back with a smug grin as he says, "It's a pleasure to finally get to talk to you, Daphne. I get the impression I have you to credit with some of our recent progress."

I throw a piece of potato at his face when I realize *he* has successfully turned the volume low enough I can only hear his side of the conversation. The fact that he manages to catch the projectile in his mouth and wink at me in the process only pisses me off further.

If this is how the two of them together are going to be, I'd better call the whole thing off now.

"She hasn't admitted anything yet," Mark is saying, "but we've got an entire week left. I'm not worried."

I kick him under the table, and he laughs. The fact that I can't tell if he's laughing at me or my best friend is *deeply* frustrating. "Our girl is growing violent," he observes. "So I better give you back. But hold on one second." I watch him swipe into my phone, typing in my password with ease before his fingers move across the screen swiftly enough that I've barely attempted two swipes to reclaim my phone before he returns to the call. "I just texted you my contact info. Apparently I'm in her phone as Mark Fucking Aladyne, which is more complimentary than I expected."

He wasn't supposed to *know* that.

When he hands my phone back to me, I say to both him and Daphne, "I'm never talking to you again."

"Oh, calm your tits." Daphne isn't the slightest bit worried about my threat, which is, unfortunately, entirely reasonable of her. She knows too much about me to ever be kicked out of my life. "I just wanted to introduce myself."

"We both know you had chaos on the brain, so how about

you stop pretending otherwise and tell me why you called in the first place?"

"You're no fun. I thought you'd be more fun now that you're getting laid again."

There's no way to correct the nuances of her assumption without Mark overhearing, so I decide to let that go for now. "Tell me or let me eat biscuits in peace."

"Fine." She sighs, her voice becoming a softer, more vulnerable presence. "I was going to tell you about my date last night."

"You went on a date?" My surprise catches Mark's interest, curiosity mingling with something else on his face. "Like, a real date?"

Last time we talked, Daphne had still been in the midst of her spiral about whether she should say yes to a date with the hot, not-quite-unethically rich guy. It's a dance we've danced before. Most of the time, that spiral ends with her running far and fast from the date in question. I've known her for half my life, and she still hasn't let me in on what makes her so gun-shy about dating, even though if anyone would understand, it would be me. I just know it happened the summer after we graduated high school, right before she began her vagabond journey around North America.

If my math is right, it was also right around when she knew Bowen. It makes me wonder if his sudden appearance in my life is why she said yes to the date this time.

But that's a conversation better left for our Wednesday friend date.

"Okay, drop the judgment, she-who-lives-in-denial." I scowl, but have to let that one go, too. "Yes, a real date."

"How was it?"

"Weird," she says. The word sounds wistful, and I wish I could see her face now, because I know she'll have processed it enough by Wednesday that I won't get the real emotion out of her. "But okay, I think?"

"I'm proud of you. I know you hate when I say that—"

"I hate when you say that."

"—but it's true."

"Thanks, Lark. I'll tell you everything on Wednesday, okay? Enjoy your breakfast and don't do anything stupid in the meantime."

Before I can protest the insult, she hangs up. "I apologize for whatever she said to you." I immediately go on the offensive as I set the phone down. "Daphne doesn't always remember to use her filter."

"I like her." Mark grins. "We're gonna be friends."

"Great," I drawl. "Sounds perfect."

"Just..." He trails off, and that look I couldn't read from when I mentioned Daphne's date is back on his face. "Be careful mentioning her around Bowen, okay? I don't know what she's told you—"

"Basically nothing. It's very annoying."

"Sounds like as much as I know." He shakes his head. "But whatever happened between them, it left its scars. I'm excited to get to know her, but I don't want to make things harder by throwing her in his face."

His plea is clarifying. On its surface, this is what I've been afraid of: him asking me to make myself, my *life*, smaller to fit into his. A week ago, I would have become instantly indignant at the idea that I should have to avoid talking about *my* best friend to make *his* best friend happy.

But now that we're in this moment, I realize it's more complicated than my fears want it to be. He's not holding a grudge against Daphne or trying to shut her out—he just gave her his fucking number so that they can continue to torment me without my phone as the middleman. And he's not telling me to pretend she doesn't exist, or to cut her out of my life.

He's just asking me to take care with his friend's heart.

After the time I've spent with Bowen this week, it's a request I'd be inclined to grant anyway, for his sake alone. I like the quiet man, and the last thing I want is to hurt him.

But what scares me is that I don't want to do it for Bowen. I want to do it for Mark. I want to give him this thing he asked for, because I can, and because I care about him.

Maybe, a small voice suggests deep in my head, *that's how a relationship is supposed to feel.*

Maybe he won't ask for more than you want to give.

Maybe, just maybe, this is what love can be.

CHAPTER 16

MARK

Lark lets me stay with her Sunday night, too.

We eat and we fool around and we talk. We feed our horses and we watch TV and we never go more than a few seconds without touching, not if we can help it. It's the most I've ever had of her, the most open and relaxed she's ever been around me, and it makes me happier than I've ever been.

It's also never been more obvious that she's still hiding from me.

I'm not even sure she knows she's doing it. All of it is small stuff, easily deniable. Insignificant enough that I'd call myself paranoid if I didn't know her so well despite herself.

When we swing by Aladyne to let me pick up a proper change of clothes, she sends me upstairs to my apartment alone. She wants to play with the horses, she says, but something tells me she also doesn't want to see where I live. She doesn't want to envision herself there, to risk imagining a future she's trying so hard not to want.

When I ask if she has plans for expanding her business, she murmurs a few sentences about it being a long-term work in progress and changes the subject. I try not to obsess over the hints she's let slip that she's not actually happy running her own consignment, but anytime I even brush up against the topic, she darts away.

When she asks what Aladyne is planning to do now that we're retiring Apple Butter, and I admit I haven't been at those meetings and haven't thought to ask, she keeps her expression bland and unchanging, even though I *know* that answer pisses her off.

So yeah. She's hiding. And Monday arrives before I can figure out how to make her stop.

The morning passes in a blur of work. Javi knows I basically defect for the first few hours of each day now—longer, even, if I can manage it—and Lark has mostly given up arguing with me about whether I'm allowed to help so long as I wear the right colors, which means I'm still on her side of the barn when my sister rolls in around nine.

Maddie casts an appraising eye at my shirt, as if she hasn't seen it before, and Lark catches the expression from where she's filling water buckets. "This is all him," she clarifies. "I never asked for his help."

"You *should* ask for his help," Maddie snarks. "We clearly don't give him enough to do. Are you coming to family dinner tomorrow?"

Lark's usual confidence softens at the question. "I was planning on it?"

"Good. We'll need the backup." Without explaining what that means, Maddie turns back to me. "I need to talk to you."

I look to Lark, who shoos me away, then follow Maddie out of the barn. She doesn't stop walking until we're clear of the barns entirely and she's leaning on her janky-ass sedan in the parking lot. It's wildly out of place in the sea of massive trucks that surrounds it, but Mads has loved that beater since she got it in high school, and nothing will talk her into driving anything else until the axles literally fall off the chassis.

And even then, she may try to propel it *Flintstones*-style.

"I would ask where you were all weekend, but I think the answer is obvious."

I raise a brow at her tone. "Do I have a backlog of concerned texts and calls I don't know about?"

Her face concedes the point, but she doesn't linger on the subject. "Promise me you'll be at dinner tomorrow, even if Lark cancels?"

"What's going on?"

"I don't know, and that's the problem." She frowns. "Dad's meeting with his old financial planner this morning."

"Shit." Mads has been all the financial planner we've needed the past couple years, so going back outside of the family is a sign of *something*, for sure. "Do you know why?"

"I'm not even supposed to know that much. He just left his phone in the kitchen and I saw the reminder notification come in yesterday."

"You're going to ask about it at dinner?" It's not that I don't think Maddie will ask—it's that I don't think she'll be able to wait that long.

"They have plans tonight, and I don't think this is a conversation I want to have here."

I nod, processing the information. I don't really know what to think; our parents aren't the type to sneak around, but this does feel odd. "And you're comfortable having Lark there for whatever it turns out to be?"

She returns my brow raise from earlier. "Would you un-invite her if I wasn't?"

The honest answer is: not willingly. But the *more* honest answer is that I won't put my sister in that position. "If you need me to, yes."

"The fact that I believe you is genuinely impressive. But

no, I meant what I said to her. If this is what I think it is, I'll be glad to have her at the table."

"I thought you don't know what's going on."

"I don't."

I try to stifle my exasperation. "Okay. What do you *think* is going on?"

"...I don't know." At my glare, she scowls. "It's not like I found a secret business plan, okay? I just have this feeling that whatever is happening is a big deal. And honestly, Lark knows as much about the industry as anyone, so her reaction will be useful."

On that, we can agree. "We'll be there."

I go to push off her car and return to the barn, but she stops me. "How are things with you two?" She's partly being nosy just to be nosy, but her voice is still careful. Like she's worried even the question is fragile.

"Honestly?" I think about the last few days, and the fact that Lark could have been rid of me, but chose not to be. She was on the brink of victory, but decided to keep playing. "We're good. Her walls aren't gone yet, but I think they're crumbling."

"I'm glad. I'm starting to think you're good for each other, when you're not being stupid assholes."

"Which is most of the time?"

She grins, relaxing for the first time since she arrived. "Your words, not mine."

"Well, this is just entirely too sweet of you, Lark. I can't remember the last time we had fresh flowers in this house!" My mother beams as Lark hands a small bouquet off to her as we step inside. I failed to hide my amusement when Lark showed up with the flowers in hand, realizing she felt retroactively guilty about not bringing something for my parents last week the way I did for hers. She can pretend all she wanted, but Lark is starting to care about more than just me.

"You're making me look bad, you know," my dad chastises, even as he pulls her into a one-armed hug. "Now I'm going to have to buy her flowers every week."

"Oh, please." Mom rolls her eyes. "Once a month will do."

She winks at Lark before she scurries off to the kitchen to find a vase, and Lark tucks herself against me as I guide her into the living room. Maddie's on the couch, staring at her e-reader with the expression of someone who hasn't actually read a single word on the screen, her hair still wet from a shower and piled onto her head in a loose bun. She looks up at our arrival with relief, practically tossing the device across the room. "Oh good, you're here. Did Bowen come with you?"

"Was Bowen supposed to come with us?"

"I invited him," she explains. "So I thought maybe he came with you."

I shake my head. "If either of you had bothered to tell me he was coming, maybe he would have."

Lark settles onto the couch next to Maddie, cutting off my attempt to follow with a pointed stare. I reluctantly settle into one of the armchairs instead of squeezing in next to her. "Does Bowen usually come?" she asks.

"No," answers the man himself as he steps into the room. He inclines his head in greeting and takes one of the other chairs, stretching his legs out in front of him. Either he didn't spend the day at a job site or he took time to shower and change before he arrived, because his Daffodil Builds shirt doesn't have a speck of drywall dust or paint on it. "But I show up every time I'm invited."

My best friend just volunteered an entire extra sentence to my girlfriend. He must really like her. "Maddie thinks a big conspiracy is going to unfurl tonight," I explain to both of them. "So she called in reinforcements."

"Hush!" Maddie glares at me. "Don't let them hear you. I have a whole strategy."

Both Lark and Bowen appear confused, though they wear it differently—Lark's eyes have gone wide at Maddie's lightly manic state, while Bowen merely tilts his head in curiosity. "Food is food," he says eventually, and my sister relaxes.

"Let's hope you still feel that way once you've tried the sauce," Dad declares, he and Mom stepping into the room with the rest of us. "I experimented tonight."

"That's comforting." I glower as Mom sits next to Lark, in the spot *I* wanted, but it doesn't take long to find myself a little overwhelmed at seeing the three most important women in my life—my mother, my twin, and my hard-won girlfriend—share space together. It's what I've wanted for so long, and the possibility I might not get to keep it is almost unbearable. Enough that I push to my feet, plastering a thin smile on my face. "I think I'm on table setting this week. I'll be back."

It's probably shitty of me to leave Lark there like that, alone with my family, but if she can handle a lifetime with her terrible parents, she can handle five minutes surrounded by people who adore her. Right now, *I* can't handle the uncertainty that exists between us, and I know that if I don't get my head right, I'm going to do something deeply stupid.

Like demand she fucking marry me when she hasn't even admitted she loves me yet.

Because that's my damn problem, and I know it: I'm constantly waiting for Lark to catch up to where I am. I'll do it happily, for the rest of my life, because she's worth every ounce of patience I have.

But I'm not sure if that's fair to her. And that's the part that is starting to eat me up inside. She said she wanted me to keep playing, that she's not ready for our game to end—but how can I expect her to take our relationship seriously when I'm the one who turned it into a game in the first place?

How can I fix what I've broken, without shattering it completely?

"Hey." Lark's voice is soft as she steps up behind me, looping her arms around my stomach and resting her cheek on my back. "You good?"

With the press of her body against mine, I exhale until the worst of my panic subsides. "Better now," I admit, squeezing her clasped hands in my own. "Sorry about that."

She tugs at me, loosening her arms just enough for me to turn to face her. I brush my fingers through her hair as she looks up at me. "Honestly, I'm glad you finally freaked out about something. I was starting to feel pretty alone on panic island."

I narrow my eyes at her. "How did you even know I freaked out? It really is my week to set the table."

"I mean, it's not like you to willingly let me out of your sight," she teases. "But also, your smile was too symmetrical to be real. You're not the only one who pays attention, Aladyne."

"Stay with me tonight?" I ask, not bothering to hide the begging tone in my voice. "So we can talk?"

Her grin settles into something gentler. "Just talk?"

"Yes. No. Maybe. I don't know."

She laughs, then pushes up on her toes to press a kiss against my cheek. "Okay."

After the way she avoided my apartment over the weekend, that one word has me practically floating through the entire meal. I keep an eye on Maddie, still unsure what this strategy of hers is, but I'm constantly stealing glances at Lark

—and counting all the glances she casts at me. I've got a good feeling about tonight.

Or, at least, I do until my twin shoves a forkful of green beans into her mouth and barely swallows before asking, "How was your meeting with Mr. McCloud, Dad?"

I should have known my sister's "strategy" would amount to "ask outright and hope for the best." Bowen catches my gaze with a questioning look, and I offer a small nod to confirm that this is, in fact, the main event.

He grabs two more rolls and starts buttering them, entirely unbothered.

Dad's pause is just long enough to reach the border of guilty. "How did you know about that?"

Maddie stares back at him, unperturbed. "I asked first."

"It went very well," Dad concedes. "Quite productive."

"Why did you need to meet with him in the first place?" Mads asks, a hint of hurt in her voice. "I've been doing his job for years now."

Across the table, Mom sighs. "Just tell them, Peter. It's clearly too late for it to be a secret anymore."

Lark reaches over to rest her hand on my thigh, lightly squeezing it as a show of support, and I'm quick to cover her hand with mine to keep her touch a little longer.

"Well, as it happens, I wanted to consult with him before I brought the discussion to you, just in case it wasn't possible at all. I didn't want to show up with a half-baked idea." Dad sets his fork down, his attention darting to Bowen and Lark. Lark's grip tightens, clearly remembering how her parents were so insistent on trying to keep me from being part of their conversations, but Peter Aladyne and Levi Reynolds are two very different men. "I'm glad you're both here, actually. Better to have the whole family in one place for this."

I watch Lark from the corner of my eye, trying to read her reaction to being lumped in as part of the family, but her expression is politely interested and nothing more. At least her hand is still under mine. I'll take it as a good sign.

"Your mother and I have been discussing a potential change of ownership at the farm."

"What?!" Maddie's shout is matched by my own stunned silence.

"Peter!" Mom's familiar exasperation sands the edges off my concern, but Maddie is too lost in her confusion and anger to register her tone. "It's like you're purposefully torturing them."

A slow, smug grin takes over Dad's face. "Maybe I am."

"I see where you get it," Lark whispers, and despite everything, I have to stifle a laugh. She's not wrong.

"Dad, I swear—"

"I know, I know." He cuts Maddie off, his expression settling back into sincerity. "We're not selling, Madison. You can relax."

Bowen snorts at the idea of Maddie relaxing. She swats his arm, but settles back down. "Okay, then what *are* you doing?"

"Nothing yet. We did intend to consult with you on this, and we still do. But we've been thinking it might be time to bring you and Mark on as official owners." My head snaps to attention at that revelation, a tightness filling my chest. I don't have to look at my sister to know she's torn between elation and number-crunching. "For a lot of reasons, including the fact that the two of you have been so instrumental in our recent success. But also because it will make things easier for you in the future should anything ever happen to us. Fewer things to sort out, legally speaking."

"That would be a big change," Mads muses. The gears are already spinning in her head, her teeth worrying over her bottom lip. "There are some financial ramifications, but I think there could be something to it."

Mom looks to me. "What do you think, Mark?"

I ignore the confusing discomfort I feel and give them what I hope is a confident nod. "I'm not sure I have an opinion. If the three of you think it's a good idea, then I'm fine with it."

My family all nod and accept that without hesitation. The conversation rolls on, with Maddie peppering our parents with questions about how it all would work, but I don't hear a bit of it because it's not my family or Bowen who have my attention.

It's Lark, who pulls her hand away. Who shifts in her seat, takes a sip of water. Who intentionally, pointedly, does not look at me.

The tightness in my chest becomes a fucking iron band around my lungs as I realize I may have just fucked everything up.

TWO YEARS AGO

LARK

"That was hot," Akiko commented when I returned to our booth, stupid expensive bottle of whiskey in hand.

"Don't remind me," I groaned. I twisted the bottle open, pouring a splash into one of the glasses the sweet bartender sent with me. She had no problem helping me spend Mark's money, which made me like her. Dicks wasn't my usual vibe, but maybe that would have to change. "I'm trying to pretend I'm not into his whole deal."

Akiko snorted, shaking her head when I offered to pour her some, too. "Don't tell me you're pining over someone, too."

"Okay, *thank* you!" I threw my hands up. "She's totally stuck on him, isn't she?"

Akiko and I were what I liked to call friends-in-law. She and Daphne became friends when they both lived in Chicago, and Daphne put us in contact when she heard that Akiko was going to be passing through the area. I'd probably never see the woman in person again after tonight, but she was fun to share a drink with.

"She never said a word about it, but it was obvious."

Akiko shook her head. "But she did train me to recognize deflection when I see it. Stay focused. Why are we resisting him?"

I threw back the whiskey and poured some more, because apparently we were doing this. I told her about what happened with my parents and Gabriel, and my secret plan to quit working at Landow soon to start my own business. How Mark wasn't just Mark, but Mark *Aladyne*, and how that was a significant distinction given that the whole point of what I'm doing is to prove I can do everything myself.

"Well," she said when I finished my rant, "I'm going to leave the hyper-independence and mommy and daddy issues for a professional to deal with. But I'm not sure why you can't just bang the man and get him out of your system."

"Can't." I slumped in the booth. "Our names rhyme."

"That only matters if you see a future with him."

I narrowed my eyes. "I *don't*."

"I think I understand how your friendship works now. Daphne's specialty is deflection, and yours is denial."

"I don't like you anymore."

She finished her beer, clearly amused. "I expect an invitation to the wedding."

I might have growled. It was hard to say. But I didn't get a chance to turn it into real words, because suddenly Mark slid into the booth next to me, trapping me between his body and the wall. "Is she planning to propose already?" he asked Akiko, as if I wasn't even there. "Make sure she knows I'll say yes."

"Do you have a preferred metal?" Akiko raised a brow, like this was a serious conversation and not literal torture.

"My girl picks out a ring, I'll wear it," he declared. "I'm not picky, so long as the world knows I'm hers."

I calculated whether it would be worth the embarrassment to slide under the table and crawl away while they laughed and exchanged introductions. But my impending escape was cut short when he grabbed the glass Akiko had refused and poured himself some of my precious whiskey.

"That's mine!"

"Hey, Elsie?" Mark raised his voice enough to call over to the bar. "Did you put this bottle on my tab?"

"Sure did, buddy," the bartender shouted back.

He inclined his head, his voice now quiet enough for just me to hear. "I guess you have to share."

"I think that's my cue." Akiko wore a mischievous grin, which told me Daphne would know every word of this exchange before I even got home. "It was great to meet you, Lark. If you're ever in Chicago, I'll return the favor."

"This shit ain't bad," Mark mused as he sipped the whiskey once Akiko left. I shoved at him, motioning to the seat she had just vacated, but his cocky-ass grin didn't waver as he held his position. "I think I'm good here."

His thigh pressed firmly against mine, and I debated between taking another shot or keeping my wits about me. Just as I was about to toss it back, his hand covered mine. "Not like that," he murmured, his eyes sparking with a challenge I already knew I was going to accept.

I licked my lips, the warmth of his skin on mine flooding my senses. "Then how?"

He raised his glass, taking a small sip of the liquid, then leaned down until his forehead pressed against mine. I debated. Hesitated. But I was desperate for a taste of him, and I had no true desire to resist.

I crashed my lips against his, letting myself be invaded by the whiskey and his tongue simultaneously. All the playfulness between us twisted into something more intense as we sank into the kiss, one of his hands gripping the nape of my neck with ferocious control. We were devouring each other, right here in this shitty dive bar, and the only reason I wasn't already straddling his lap was because the stupid fucking table was bolted to the stupid fucking wall.

How my hands ended up clawed into his shirt, I couldn't say. I didn't know when his other hand claimed my upper thigh. I couldn't have guessed how long we were lost to each other before he finally pulled away, his eyes glassy with undisguised need.

"Mark—"

"Go on a date with me."

I blinked as I tried to process that through my lust haze. "What?"

He kissed along my jaw, nibbled my earlobe, then repeated himself. "Go on a date with me."

It didn't make any more sense the second time. I made a half-hearted attempt to put some distance between us so I could *think*, but his fingers slid just under the hem of my cut-offs, teasing me like I teased him earlier, and my body instantly gave up the fight. "I told you—"

"Say you're not interested again, baby. Let me hear how it sounds when you lie."

The fact that he cut me off a second time was nearly as infuriating as the fact that he was right. "Just because my body wants you doesn't mean I do."

He grunted, the sound just shy of an acknowledgement. "Then what do you want?"

My mind was screaming at me to end this now. I had admitted too much to Akiko when I said our names were a problem, because it meant that I knew—I *knew*—this man was dangerous. Mark Aladyne was persistent and charming and hot as sin in the rolled sleeves of his button-up. My barbed-wire fences only seemed to pull him closer, rather than keep him out.

If I let this man into my life, I would be ruined.

But the taste of that whiskey and his kiss still lingered on my lips, telling me it was too late. I had already let him in. The only chance I had left was control.

"Sex only," I said. My voice was raspier than usual, the words fighting on their way out. "No strings. No small talk. No cuddling. *Definitely* no dates."

His lips curved into that smile that I hated to love. "You just want to use me for my body? Is that it?"

No, something dangerously close to my heart whispered, but I nodded anyway. *I want everything.* "That's all I can give you."

He thought it over, his eyes staring deep into mine. "All right, Lark. We'll play it your way." His lips caught mine again, the kiss thoroughly indecent and brimming with promises of pleasure yet to come. "Just know that I intend to change your mind."

I gave myself one fleeting moment to feel the hope that came with that vow.

And then, as he pulled me out of the booth and out the door, I locked the hope away like it never existed at all.

CHAPTER 17

LARK

"What was it, exactly?" Mark watches me warily. "I know when it happened, but I don't know why."

We're in Mark's barn apartment, a place I've fought entering for the entirety of the time we've known each other, and he's standing with his back against the door like I'm a flight risk. Which, honestly, I am. But I barely hear him, lost as I am to taking in the space around me, seeing this final piece of the man who refuses to let me go.

Most of it is about what I would expect from a guy like Mark: a little scattered, a little under-designed, a little generic. It's clear he took the space as it was when he moved in, and hasn't done much to change it since. The signs of life that are here are mostly functional. The worn and muddy shoes piled by the door, the smattering of coffee mugs and dishes settled in the drying rack next to the sink, the hoodie he probably hasn't touched since February tossed over the back of a chair.

And if it weren't for the damn library books, I might have made it through this moment unscathed. But there's a stack of three of them on the coffee table, one with a bookmark about halfway through. I don't know the titles or even the genres, and I'm not sure it really matters. It's not the books themselves that get me. It's the fact that this is something *new* about Mark, something I didn't know about him until this moment, that traps my breath in my throat.

Because I suddenly realize I want to know everything about him.

Because I love him.

The truth of it takes my trapped breath and knocks it away entirely. No equivocating or second-guessing. It just appears in front of me as a fully formed fact of the world. I'm in love with Mark Aladyne, and I have no idea if that's going to be enough to keep either of us from getting our hearts broken.

I love him.

I let the thought sit undisturbed for one last moment, then turn to face him, already knowing he'll be able to read it on my face the way he's always read everything else. And he does—everything about him softens when our eyes meet, but he doesn't relax. He knows there's more to this moment.

"What do you want from your life, Mark?"

He tilts his head, his eyes tracing over my face like I'm a puzzle he's desperate to solve. "Is that it? Am I not ambitious enough for you?"

"For fuck's sake." I yank my hair out of its ponytail only to put it right back, out of a frantic need to be doing something. "This isn't about me. What do *you* want?"

"You're pissed and you haven't touched me since dinner, so excuse me if it feels like it's about you at least a little bit."

The exasperated sound that tears out of my chest is entirely involuntary. "You went six months without touching me and you did just fine."

"Did I?" Mark pushes off the door and stalks toward me. He stops a full three feet away, but I feel the heat of him like his body is flush with mine. "Or did I spend every waking moment feeling like my heart had been yanked out of my chest even though I knew it was my own damn fault for giving it to you in the first place?"

"I *told* you—"

"I know!" He laughs, a thread of absurdity among the tension. "I know you fucking told me, Lark. That's half the problem, isn't it? I keep trying to convince you to love me, but maybe I should have just listened to you from the start."

The protest springs to my lips as quickly as it dies there. I want to say no, to assure him he was right to push. To tell him that I love him after all. That maybe I always did. But there's no point in saying it like this—not when the words would become a weapon the moment they appear. "Maybe you should have."

He flinches, and I work to hold my ground against the gravitational pull between us. The moment we touch, this fight will evaporate into a fog of desire, and there's too much left unsaid to let that happen. "Mark," I plea. "Answer the question."

"No." His voice is tight. "I asked first. Why did you shut down on me tonight?"

"Fine." I cross my arms to keep from settling his wild hair with my fingers. "You are a part of this place, Mark. Your damn name is on the sign. And the first opportunity you get to have it be *yours*, truly yours, you don't even have a single opinion to offer on the subject. You've spent the entire sale ignoring your crew to flirt with me just to win this stupid bet—"

This time, his laughter is drowning in hurt. "Is that what you really think I've been doing? Just *flirting* with you?"

"No," I admit. I can't pretend that's all it was, not even to score a point. "But that doesn't change the rest of it. You get the best damn farm in the city dropped in your lap and the best you can say is *I'm not sure I have an opinion?*"

He sighs, that puzzle-solving expression trying to crawl back onto his face. But I don't want him to figure it out. I don't want there to be a *solution*. I just want an answer to my question. "I pulled away because I don't understand why you are so determined not to care about something I would kill for. Your parents just handed you every single thing I ever wanted, everything that my parents took away from me, and you didn't *care*." My voice breaks. "There's your damn answer. Now it's your turn."

He takes a half-step toward me, my pain pulling him like a magnet, and my body can't decide if it wants to flinch away or collapse toward him. "Ask me again, Songbird."

I take a steadying breath, then do as he says. "What do you want, Mark?"

His fingers graze my jaw. "I'm going to risk breaking Daphne's rule and talk about what I don't want for a minute, okay? Because the truth is, I've never wanted to be the person poring over budget spreadsheets and breeding contracts. I don't want to be the one making decisions that affect someone else's salary and healthcare. I love this farm because I love my family, but I don't need to own it to be happy.

"And the truth is, the things that I do want have nothing to do with the land under our feet and everything to do with you. I want you to wake up with a fresh pot of coffee every morning, and I want to be the one who makes it. I want you to reach for your phone to call me only to have it already be ringing because I want to talk to you. I want you to find your place in this fucking industry, and I want to have your back while you do it, whether that's here or in Kentucky or in fucking Australia.

"I want to be part of the story of your life, Lark. If I have to settle for being a footnote, then so be it. But I'd rather be in every damn chapter."

"Mark." The word comes out as half-whisper, half-plea. I press my cheek against his palm, the simplicity of his touch my undoing. "I'm a person, not a prize."

His eyes flare with recognition as I give his old words back to him. "What does that mean to you, baby?"

"It means you can't build your life around wanting me."

"Nope." He shakes his head like he can't believe I've been wrong all this time. "It means you're not a *trophy*. It means I don't get to win you and show you off like an object. It means I can spend two years chasing you, and you can still tell me to fuck off. Because you're a *person*. You get to make your own damn choices. All I want is for you to choose to be *my* person, Lark."

My heart aches, desperate for everything he just said to be true and equally terrified that it's not. "You shouldn't want that."

"Why the hell not?"

"Because I'm not enough!"

Every part of him grows deadly still, except for his eyes. His eyes pierce a trail across my face, intent on breaking me open. And normally I'd try to hide, but I can't bring myself to hide from him anymore.

Side effect of being in love, I guess. My timing couldn't have been worse.

A look of horrified wonder crosses his face. "You honestly believe that."

"You heard my parents. What they said was shitty, but they were right. Odds are high I won't make it. And if I don't make it..." I trail off, unsure how to voice my uncertainty at my ability to pick up the pieces if this all falls apart around me. "You deserve better than that."

He still hasn't pulled his hand away, but now it slides

down to cup the back of my neck, his thumb against the base of my jaw. "And what about what you deserve, Lark?"

When I stare back at him in miserable, defiant silence, he uses his grip on my neck to crash my mouth against his. I whimper in relief, my fingers finally threading into his hair where they belong. My lips part of their own volition, begging for him to claim as much of me as he can. His tongue surges into the space I offer, and his other hand grips my waist with a ferocity that might leave bruises tomorrow.

I want the bruises. Hell, I want to fucking brand my skin with his touch so I bear the mark of him forever.

His forehead rests against mine, putting just enough space between our mouths for him to say, "I'm going to tell you what you deserve. I'm going to show you. As many times as it takes until you believe it."

I exhale a laugh, falling back on our old banter to hide the way my heart races at the promise he just made. "Then you better get started."

He pushes me backward until my back collides with a wall, and his body lands flush against mine. "Off," he demands, tugging at my shirt. When it hits the ground, I wrap my legs around him and we both groan as our hips rock into place. His lips trail down my neck, his hands teasing and exploring my breasts. "You're so fucking independent."

I barely hear him because my body is screaming for more. He unbuttons my jeans and I try to help him tear them off, but he doesn't give me what I want. Instead, he stares at me with an intensity that makes me clench my thighs—a move he doesn't miss, given that I'm still wrapped around him. "Always saying you don't need anyone. Let's see how far that gets you. Touch yourself for me, Songbird."

I don't know what lesson he's trying to teach me. It's not like I don't know how to get myself off. I trust Mark and the wall to hold me up as I glide my fingers into my undone jeans and under my already wet underwear. Mark's eyes grow dark as he watches, and I begin to touch myself in earnest.

It should be easy. I'm primed to explode already, my clit sensitive to every flick of my fingers. But each time I get close to the edge, it disappears before I can fall over. I start to rock against Mark, eager for more movement, more friction, just plain *more*, but he takes control, holding me firm against the wall. "If you want my help, all you have to do is ask. You don't have to do it alone, baby."

This fucker. To think I'm in love with him, of all people.

It's only a matter of time before my need to come overwhelms my need to be right. The moment I cry, "Mark, please," he replaces my fingers with his own, letting me grind and shift and ride his hand until I finally find the release that's been eluding me. I collapse forward, exhausted and embarrassed, and tuck my face into his neck.

"Listen to me, Lark." His words are a rumble against my skin as he carries me into his bedroom. He sets me on the bed with a care that borders on reverential, then peels my jeans and panties away. I divest myself of my bra, because the awe and hunger on Mark's face when he sees me naked gives me a sense of power I'm in desperate need of right now. He pulls his own shirt over his head and drops it in the pile of discarded clothes, and my hands itch to trace the contours of his stomach. "You deserve people who believe in you."

He tugs me closer to him before dropping to his knees. A light tap on each of my inner thighs has me spreading my legs wide for him, and I moan his name as his tongue takes a long, lazy path up the length of my slit. "You deserve to be worshipped," he murmurs.

And then he spends endless, luxurious minutes doing just that. He's in no hurry, his tongue and his fingers and even his goddamn teeth slowly, steadily luring me to the precipice once more. As he does, he never stops adding to the list.

"You deserve to be challenged."

"You deserve to be taken care of."

"You deserve to ask for help."

"You deserve room to change your mind."

Every sentence resonates with the weight of a benediction. I want to reject each one, to push his sincerity aside and stay safely tucked inside my own shattered cynicism. But his ministrations keep flooding my body with bliss so intense there's nothing I can do to fight it.

"You deserve to be wanted, because you've always been enough." His eyes lock onto mine, his fingers curving so deliciously inside that I grasp at the comforter like it can hold me down. "Say it, Lark. Tell me you're enough. Tell me you're worth wanting. You don't get to come until I hear you say it."

I mumble, whatever words I mange incoherent as they leave my throat. His scruff prickles my inner thigh as he shakes his head. "You can do better than that. You have to fucking mean it. Sing it loud, Songbird."

The part of me that wants to refuse out of sheer stubbornness isn't small. But I open my eyes to see Mark's already locked onto me, fierce and wild and so fucking *sure*, and in that moment, all I can do is believe him. The man has made a veritable mission out of wanting me. He's the expert here.

"I'm enough," I gasp out, my gaze never leaving his. "I'm worth wanting."

When I come, it's with my own voice ringing in my ears as I say it as many times as it takes for him to send me flying.

I don't know if it's a minute or a lifetime later that he crawls into the bed with me. He's stripped himself naked now, too, the heat of his skin meeting my own as he pulls me into his chest. His chin rests atop my head as I try to burrow myself into his body.

"I love you, Lark." He says the words like he's said them a million times and like it's the first time anyone has ever said them, all at once. Familiar and foreign in equal measure. "But I've never been a man with high ambitions. I'm not built to run this place, you know? I don't really care if we set records or win the Triple Crown. All I want is to make sure the people I care about are happy. And since the day we met, that's included you, too."

"You could have led with that, you dipshit."

"And miss out on the conclusion to that fight? No, thanks." He laughs, and I like the way it ripples through my body, too. "But I mean it, Lark. You've been doing the work of five people all on your own, but you don't have to do that anymore. Helping to lessen that load whenever I can makes me happy. Hell, I'd do it permanently, if you asked me to."

My heart aches at the image of him in the colors of Lark Sales the past week. The selfish part of me wants to take what he's offering, but the rest of me knows I could never ask him to leave Aladyne, regardless of what happens between us.

In my most secret dreams for the future, I'm not sure either of us are wearing robin's egg blue.

"I just..." Words fail me, and Mark waits patiently, his fingers tracing up and down the ridges of my spine with such gentle purpose that it makes me shiver. "I'm still scared of what happens when the shine wears off and you find something else to want."

"Some*thing* or some*one*?"

"Both."

He scoops his arm around me and rolls onto his back, settling me atop him. "I can't promise I'll never want something different for my life. Part of me still agrees with my six-year-old self that I'd be a pretty killer Jedi." I roll my eyes. Of course he's a damn nerd, too. "But I can promise that I know how to use my words. I swear I'll talk to you, if whatever I'm doing ever starts to feel like it's not enough."

"Is that what you did at dinner? Used your words?"

He takes the hit square on the chin and doesn't back down. "I'm running out of ways to explain that, so let me try this one: *you* are my priority now, baby. If my family thinks this is the right change to make, then I'll support it. But their opinions matter more than mine right now, because if I have my way, I'll be wherever you are."

Mark waits to see if I plan to argue, but for once, words have abandoned me. "As for the other part: if I could want someone—*any*one—else, I would have figured it out by now. You have consumed my fucking mind and body for two years, and you just keep digging deeper. Even if you don't ever love me back, I'll always want you. You're written into my damn soul, Songbird."

You're written into my damn soul.

It's melodramatic and cliche and cheesy and the worst part is, I know it's true. It's time for the game we've been playing to end, because this man—this handsome, infuriating, relentless man—deserves more than what I've been giving him. I slip off him without a word, retreating to the pile of clothes we've left on the floor. I dig around in his jeans, where I know he's been keeping condoms stashed just in case. Like he did a few nights ago, I toss them onto the bed.

But this time I keep one in hand.

I climb back over top of him, watching as some of the openness he had moments ago shutters itself away as he realizes what I intend to do. I wrap my fingers around his cock, and it doesn't take more than a few firm strokes for him to be fully hard. "Fuck, Lark," he exhales.

That's the plan, I nearly say aloud. Instead, I let the sound of the condom wrapper tearing open speak for me. I slide it down his length, then return to the position I was in moments ago. I can't resist grinding against him for a few torturous moments, but eventually I still. "Are you sure?" I ask him.

Are you sure about the promises you're making?

Are you sure about the future you're offering?

Are you sure about me?

He doesn't hide the pain in his eyes, as he waits for me to end this dance we've been doing, but the pain is outshined by a steady, unending confidence. "I'm sure, Songbird."

I lean down, caressing his face with my hands before taking his mouth for a slow-burn kiss that holds everything we've both thought and felt for the past two years. Eventually I pull away, positioning him at my entrance.

"I love you," I tell him, memorizing the awe that suffuses his face at my words as I grant him victory in a game I never should have made him play.

And then I sink myself down on his cock.

CHAPTER 18

MARK

No fucking words exist to describe the moment I feel Lark around me again. Or maybe there are too many fucking words for it. The profane: *she's so wet, so tight, her cunt milking my cock for all it's worth.* The sacred: *Lark is my goddess, her body is my altar.* The mundane: *it just feels so damn good.*

But none of them capture the reality of it, because none of them account for the words she just said.

I love you.

I thought I was prepared for what it would feel like to hear those words, but the sheer *relief* is more immense than I ever imagined. I wasn't making it up. I wasn't seeing only what I wanted to see.

Lark Reynolds loves me, too.

"Say it again," I plead. Her hips swivel in wicked circles as she rides me, her hands braced back against my thighs. I tease and roll her nipples for a moment before grabbing onto her hips again, just to feel the movement in as much of my body as possible. "Please."

"I love you, Mark." The words come out strained and gasping this time, but they're all the more precious for that.

"I love you, too, Songbird."

And then I flip us around, bringing her legs to rest over my shoulders, and we both lose the ability to talk as we make up for six months of separation and a week and a half of utter torture. I have a feeling we've both spent the whole time fantasizing about this moment, because we're desperate and wild and completely, entirely sure of what the other needs.

Her hips rock to meet my every thrust, her moans growing thick when I begin to tease her clit with my fingers again. Her hands wrap around my forearms, her fingers gripping tight, as if I plan to ever be anywhere but here. I'd spend the rest of my life buried inside her if I could.

"Come with me, baby." I change the pressure of my fingers, muscle memory telling me exactly what to do. She whimpers my name, her pussy clenching around me as her orgasm builds. I'm holding on for dear life, determined not to come without her, but there's only so long I can last after so long without her. "*Now*, Lark."

When her legs start to shake, I lose what little control I have left. I thrust into her with a groan, and both of us shudder our release over a few long, glorious seconds of shared bliss. I reluctantly pull away long enough to deal with the condom, then drop back onto the bed next to her. She snuggles up against me of her own free will, and I've never been happier.

"Let's not not do that for six months ever again," she murmurs when coherence finally starts to return to us both.

"I was thinking more in terms of minutes, not months," I counter. "We're already pushing my patience for starting round two."

She laughs, and it's easily the best sound I've ever heard—and that counts all her sexy little moans and cries. "That sounds like a you problem, Aladyne."

"Hate to say it, babe, but those don't exist anymore. It's *us* problems all the way down now."

"I take it all back," she groans. "I regret everything."

But she kisses me again anyway.

Sleep is scarce. By the time Lark's alarm goes off at four, we've been asleep for two, maybe three hours, after a night of sex interspersed with moments of basking.

Lots of basking.

I point her to the bathroom while I stumble to the kitchen to start the coffee. She's just stepping out of the shower when I bring her a mug, and she accepts with a quiet sleepy smile. She nudges the brand new toothbrush I left out for her, biting her lip for a moment before she looks at me. "Go through a lot of these, do you?"

"The jealousy is cute, but unnecessary." I lean forward and kiss her temple, warning my dick not to get any ideas from the brief contact. "That's been waiting for you."

"For how long?"

I shrug. "Long enough."

"Thank you."

"It's just a toothbrush."

"No." Her eyes hold mine. "It's not."

We end up running fifteen minutes behind schedule, but it's her fault, not mine.

It's the last moment of reprieve we get, because Lark's day goes to shit *fast*. One of the horses she sold Monday is still in the barn when we get there, even though the buyer was supposed to ship her out last night. Lark normally would have been here to supervise herself, but she coordinated with the sales company to handle it so she could make it to dinner with my family. She dashes up to the front office to find out what happened, but it's too early for anyone but Miss Betty to be in. For the moment, all Lark is able to get is a number for the owner that goes to a full voicemail inbox.

She curses each time she redials, and it only gets worse when she gets a call from her transportation team that her last three horses will be here within twenty minutes. "Fuck!" she cries when she hangs up. "I've got to find a stall. Somewhere. And figure out what to do with a horse that was never fucking mine in the first place."

I grab her arm and pull her with me into her feed stall. For maybe the first time, I do it without any intention of touching her. Not that I'd complain if the opportunity arose, now that we can finish what we start…

No. Focus. I snap myself out of the distraction. She's muttering to herself about how she doesn't have time for this, how she has to figure this out, but she doesn't try to leave. I rest my hand against her neck so I can make her look at me. "*We* are going to figure this out. Will you let me help you?"

I watch as she braces herself, her every instinct shouting at her to pull away. But instead, she presses into my hand, forcing a deep breath into her lungs. It takes her a moment to form the word, but she finally gets it out. "Please."

"Thank you." I kiss her forehead, then step away. "Focus on the rest of it. I'll find a place for the filly."

My first stop is the Aladyne side of the barn, hoping the solution will be that simple, but Javi just shrugs apologetically. With all of our stalls full, that means I get to make my own trip up to Miss Betty.

"Well, that's not your usual color at all." The older woman who's known me since I was in utero studies me with narrow eyes as I approach her counter. "And something tells me you're here for a favor."

"I'm helping Lark Reynolds out—"

"I bet you are."

"—and I was hoping you could find us a spare stall some-where on the premises. The new owners aren't answering, and she has three more horses arriving any minute." I purposefully ignore her brow-wagging innuendo, because there's not enough time to deal with Miss Betty's nosiness right now. She's already going to have more than enough gossip to spread by the end of this conversation. "We'll gladly take the worst stall you've got."

I'm prepared to personally walk this horse to the farm where she belongs if it comes to it, but a stall would be easier.

She huffs at the implication that any of the stalls are bad, even though I'm pretty sure she hasn't been in one of the barns in at least two decades, but she pulls up the records anyway. "Barn 41, stall 16, how's that sound?"

"Like a lifesaver. You're the best, Miss Betty."

"You can say that as loud and often as you want, darlin'." She slides a hard candy toward me. "Give this to your girl, and tell her that I'll need her signature to process the addi-tional scratches that were requested. That should solve the space issue soon enough, anyway."

I freeze. "What scratches?"

She taps away at the keyboard, not noticing my panic. "Hips 1210 and 1248. Their owner popped in right before close last night. I forgot to mention it to her just now because she was so stressed, the poor thing."

"So Lark doesn't know?"

Miss Betty blinks at me, finally picking up on the panicked elephant in the room.

It's me. I'm the panicked elephant.

"Well, I'm not her personal secretary, so I can't rightly say. Seems like something you could ask her yourself."

"You're right. Thanks again." I spin on my heel and start to make a quick exit, already terrified of the news I have to break to Lark. But I pause just before I reach the door. "Miss Betty," I say, turning around once more time. "Is there a deadline for when those scratches need to be filed? Hypothetically?"

"Hypothetically, I can still get them processed today if I get a signature by early afternoon. Especially if a mocha latte and some of those pastries from Brews happened to appear on my desk."

Guess Bowen will be making a stop on his way to the sale, then. A few hours is better than nothing. "And you wouldn't be able to share who those owners are, now would you?"

She eyes me again, like she's trying to decide how she wants to insult me, but my desperation must show through. "You plannin' to be rude to them?"

"Honestly?" She stares at me over her glasses, like I don't deserve an answer to such a useless question. No wonder Lark loves her. "If I need to be."

"Oh, you'll need to be. It was that Jack Nugent fella. Snapped at me while I was just doing my best to help him at the last minute. That's a man who needs to be put in his place."

"I'll do my best, Miss Betty."

"See that you do."

This time, I tear out the door like I'm being chased by an angry skunk. I don't know how I'm going to fix this for Lark, but I know I need to. She's already had one horse scratched—also by Nugent, if I remember correctly—and two more could destroy her financially. I don't know the nuances of her contracts, but even if she still earns her flat fee for managing the horses, she might lose the percentage of the sale price. A modest return on both horses could help pay her barn rental fees for next few months.

Even if this wasn't Lark's first dream, I refuse to let her lose it this way.

I hustle toward the barn, sending Bowen the order for Miss Betty on the way. There's a text from Maddie asking where I am, but I ignore that in favor of the update from Lark.

SONGBIRD

Shipper's here

ME

Got a stall. You're good

When I round the corner to our barn, I spot Maddie talking to Javi but see no sign of Lark or Alicia.

"There you are," Maddie says. "I need to talk to you."

"Not now." I look to Javi. "Did Lark leave already?"

"Couple minutes ago."

"Shit." It's going to take her a while to get the horses unloaded and settled—time we can't afford when there's a ticking clock on keeping two of them in the sale in the first place. "Have one of the crew take the filly in stall three up to barn 41, stall 16, will you?"

Javi gives me a curious look but doesn't argue. My sister, on the other hand, is gearing up for a fight. I don't give her a chance to start laying into me, too focused on the crisis at hand. "Have you seen Jack Nugent around?"

"No?" He's not someone either of us have ever had reason to ask about, so her confusion makes sense. He's one of those people we know *of* rather than actually knowing, though that's about to change. "Why?"

"He's fucking with Lark's sale," I say, already turning to leave. Mads grabs my arm, yanking me to a stop, and I glare at her. "Later, okay? I don't have time to talk to you right now."

"Make time. We got a bombshell dropped in our laps last night and you just disappeared without a word. It's bullshit."

"*Later*," I repeat. "I love you, Mads, but I have to find Nugent."

"What'd he do?"

I force a deep breath through my lungs. I adore my sister, but sometimes I wish she was less of a pain in my ass. "He plans to scratch two of her last three horses. I have to make this okay for her, but I don't have long."

Her expression softens. Even if she's mad at me, she doesn't want Lark to suffer. "Then let's find him. But you owe me a real conversation later."

"Deal." We split up, each taking a different part of the sales grounds. I'm starting to worry he isn't even here—it's not like he needs to drum up attention for his horses if he's scratched them—when I get a text from Maddie that she's got eyes on him. I find her leaning up against a wall by the front entrance, and she nods to a cluster of men chatting nearby. I'm glad she decided to help, because I'm not even sure I'd have recognized the man on my own. He's put on about twenty pounds of muscle since I last saw him.

Maddie smirks at my expression. "I don't recommend violence."

"Wasn't planning on it." I scowl. "But I'm really not planning on it anymore. Thanks, Mads."

"It's cute you think you can dismiss me. I'll sit here and watch from afar just in case I need to call an ambulance for you."

I attempt to roll my eyes and mostly fail because, honestly, I could probably use the backup. We drift closer, near enough I can pick out bits and pieces of the conversation, and watch Nugent hold court for a few minutes as I try to get a read on him. Aside from Miss Betty's commentary on his rudeness, I don't know much about the man. He's always just existed in the general vicinity, one of those people you take for granted.

But the fact that he's been around for so long and is using Lark as his consigner gives me pause. Not because she's not capable—she's a damn good choice—but because he should already have his contacts in place. He should have someone who's *not* scrambling to establish herself in his pocket already. The fact that he doesn't, and is now screwing with Lark?

I don't like it.

Most of the group's conversation is idle pleasantries that I let go in one ear and out the other, but I start paying attention when one of the other men asks, "Do you have any horses left in the sale?"

Nugent makes a show of looking disappointed. "Not anymore. I was supposed to have two, but I decided they aren't ready. Tried a new consignment, but—"

That's my cue if I've ever heard it. I'll be damned if he finishes that sentence. "Jack!" I call out, striding forward like I've been looking everywhere for the man. Which I have, to be fair. "Long time, man. Do you mind if I steal you away for just a minute?"

He looks at me in utter confusion as he tries to figure out who I am, but my approach is loud enough to send the rest of the crowd scattering, telling him they'll catch him later. "Have we met?"

His lack of recognition works in my favor, and he takes my offered hand on instinct. As we shake, I fight the urge to try to break his fingers. The fact that he could crush my entire body with a pinky is the only thing that keeps me from doing it.

"Name's Mark," I say, evading the question of whether we've met. "I wanted to talk to you about the scratches you entered yesterday."

There's a flash of panic on his face that he hides well—but not well enough for me to miss it entirely. "What questions could you possibly have? I thought that old lady was going to mess things up, so I probably shouldn't be surprised."

"Miss Betty has nothing to do with this," I snap. I was already prepared to hate this man, but accusing Miss Betty of being incompetent? That's an entirely different level of absurd. "I do, however, want to know if there's a reason you've now scratched three horses from this sale at the last minute."

"I fail to see what business that is of yours."

"See, I've come up with a few reasons. Could be you don't know what sales-ready looks like. Could be you're just flaky as hell. Or—and this is my favorite one—could be you're doing some back-room dealing to avoid honoring your contracts."

His face is slowly turning an interesting shade of red. "It's my business what I do with my horses."

"If you're trying to cut Lark Reynolds out of her commissions, it's not just your business, is it?"

"That bitch sent you, didn't she?" He tries to scoff, but there's no power in it. I've called his game out, and he's scrambling. "Should have guessed she can't even fight her own battles."

"Here's the thing, Jack. You don't know who I am, which means you don't know who you're fucking with. You have two choices here: rescind those scratches, or see how fast this community turns against you. I know which one I'd pick."

"I don't know what you think—"

"Aladyne!" Nugent's indignation is cut off by an interruption I couldn't have planned better. Domingo strolls up, lightly tapping my ass with his cane. "Almost didn't recognize you out of your reds, man."

"Morning, Domingo. Looking sharp, dude." Domingo raises a brow at the compliment, but it does the trick of drawing Nugent's attention to Domingo's Blue Moon Breeding polo, which marks him as a representative for one of the biggest breeding farms in Kentucky. The way the asshole's eyes nearly bug out as he processes my last name and my friendly connection with Domingo would be comedy gold if there weren't so much at stake.

"I was hoping to catch you. I've got some questions about the Night Walker filly."

A glance over my shoulder confirms that Maddie is still watching, undoubtedly wishing she had popcorn. "Jack and I are just finishing up our conversation, but my sister would have the answers you're looking for."

Domingo's gaze is shrewd, and I have no doubt he's rapidly recognizing that he didn't walk into a friendly conversation. His smirk tells me he fully intends to dig for dirt later as he nods. "Always content to talk with the better-looking twin, anyway."

I scowl at him, but he just laughs as he heads over to greet Maddie. Returning my attention to Nugent, I offer my coldest smile. "I see you've realized your misstep. If you're going to fuck with someone, make sure you know you're fucking with. Now, are you going to fix the mess you've made? Or am I?"

"I'll talk to the office," he grits out. "It was a misunderstanding."

"Honest mistakes, right?" He forces a small nod. "Swing by the office sooner than later. And be fucking polite to the staff, or we'll be having an entirely different conversation." I clap him on the shoulder, knowing that to all outside appearances, we're the image of two friends catching up. "Great to meet you, Jack. Let's not do it again."

I exhale as I walk away, adrenaline fading into relief.

When I return to the barn and see Lark leading one of the formerly scratched horses into the stall, a small voice inside urges me to tell her. But I push it aside, focusing instead on the satisfaction that she doesn't know how close she came to disaster. I'm not sure either one of us could have taken it today—let alone *us*, as a fresh, fragile unit.

I'll tell her when it's all over, when she can carry the extra weight.

But for today, she deserves to be free.

SEVEN MONTHS AGO

MARK

"Why do you keep saying no?" I risked interrupting the sated silence we had fallen into in the darkness of her bedroom. Maybe it wasn't fair of me to ask now, when she was clearly still reeling from her fight with her parents. But this was the longest she had ever let me linger after we had sex, and I couldn't help but feel like it meant something.

I still kept my arms wrapped tight around where she rested on my chest, just in case those instincts of hers kicked in and she tried to run.

"I told you when we started this. I can only give you so much. You want to fuck me, then that's fine, but you don't get my heart in the process."

"But *why*?"

"What are you, a toddler?"

"Let's hope not, for your sake." I drew circles with my thumb on her hip, doing my best not to smile in satisfaction when she exhaled and melted further into my skin. The moments she let herself truly relax around me were rare, and I cherished every one.

"Why are you so set on changing the rules?"

"Because for every part of yourself that you've shown me, I've only ever wanted to see more."

Her breath caught at my words, and I gave her time to feel the truth of them. I didn't know what made Lark so convinced keeping me at arm's length was safer. I had gathered some puzzle pieces here and there—slivers about a shitty ex, fragments about why she doesn't work for her parents anymore, snippets of her determination to prove she could succeed on her own—but I was still so far from seeing the full picture.

The pieces I did have were already beautiful. I could only imagine what the rest would show.

"What if I don't feel the same way about you?"

I tried and failed to hide my flinch; our bodies were too close for her to miss it. But maybe that was a good thing. Maybe she needed to know how viscerally I felt her words. "Then you should tell me, and I'll stop asking." I swallowed, bracing myself. "Is that how you feel?"

The silence lasted so long I would have thought she had fallen asleep, except that I could feel her fingers tracing the gentlest of lines against my chest as she thought over her answer.

"Yes."

"Yes?" I repeated the word with all the control I had, my heart already on the verge of shattering in my chest. The last thing I wanted in this world was to walk away from her, but I wouldn't break my promise, either. "That's how you feel?"

Another impossible pause, and then a whispered, "No." She snuggled her head closer to me, her lips pressing a sweet, affectionate kiss to my skin. "That was an answer to your other question. The one you keep asking."

"Yeah?" I couldn't stop the hope from leaking into my voice. "I need to hear the words, Songbird. Please."

"I'll go on a date with you, Mark." My grin was bright

enough to rival the sun, even when she sleepily added, "I just hope you don't hate me when it's over."

I promised her that would never happen, but it was too late.

For the first time since we met, she trusted me enough to fall asleep in my arms.

CHAPTER 19

LARK

By mid-morning, the explosive chaos of the early hours has settled into a more sustainable din. The new owners finally arrive to retrieve their filly, and they spend most of their time complaining that she isn't in my barn rather than apologizing for leaving her here an extra night without informing me. Mark and Alicia do a lot of glowering from the aisle, but at least they hold their commentary for after the buyers leave.

We have a steady stream of people wanting to look at the last three horses throughout the day, including a few scopes and vet checks, and as much as I hate to admit it, everything is just so much easier with Mark here. It's always been true—every time he's forced his way into my side of the barn, he's made my job simpler. But there's something about his help *today*, after everything that happened last night, that feels different.

Maybe it's as simple as the fact that I've finally let him in, finally decided to trust him. But whatever it is, I feel myself taking deeper breaths as the day progresses. As busy and stressful as the day is, I know we'll get through it. These last three horses are going to be the tipping point for me—if they sell well, or even at all, I'll be in good shape for the coming months. Good enough I can make it another year, if I so choose.

Good enough that maybe my parents will finally see that I'm not delusional about my own potential, even if I'm starting to wonder why I'm so desperate to prove myself to people whose opinions I no longer respect.

I don't know if I've ever been as grateful to see a sandwich as I am when Maddie and Bowen come wandering over with a bunch of subs. "Lunch has arrived!" Maddie declares. She plops down into one of our chairs, pointing at her brother. "You go fetch more seats."

Mark rolls his eyes. "Next sale, you're buying more chairs," he tells me, dropping a kiss on my head before nodding for Bowen to join him. I linger on the easy confidence with which he assumes there will be a next sale, half-listening as he confirms that Bowen ran some errand for him on the way here, but my attention gets called away by Maddie shoving a bag of chips into my hands.

"If your order is wrong, it's your boyfriend's fault."

"Noted." I drop down next to her, thanking Alicia as she hands me a bottle of water.

I regret the thanks when she immediately betrays me. "I think your brother finally found the orgasm button," she informs Maddie.

Maddie gags. "I can never un-hear those words now."

"Sorry," Alicia says, sounding less sorry than anyone ever has. "But she's finally stopped growling at him every time he touches the pitchfork."

I roll my eyes. "I don't growl."

"You don't *not* growl."

My eyes find Mark at the other end of the barn. A wave of affection washes over me as I watch him laugh with one of the Aladyne crew. I fought so hard to hold him at arm's length because deep down, I knew how easy it would be if I didn't. Even when I didn't want him to, he's always just made things better.

The way his muscles flex and shift as he lifts a couple chairs over his shoulder doesn't hurt, either.

"Trust me, he's always known where the orgasm button is." He looks up to catch me staring and breaks into that crooked grin of his. "I've just finally accepted that he's sticking around."

Maddie gags again, which makes Alicia laugh. "I'm glad," she says eventually. "We both know you're going to be lost without me when I ditch this popsicle stand."

I can't argue that, because it's true. I hired Alicia knowing she's going to leave—if I'm honest, I hired her *because* she's going to leave. It was supposed to make it easier to keep control of my business. But even with Mark's help, Alicia is the only reason this sale hasn't crumbled out from beneath me, and by this time next month, she'll be up in New York, saving someone else's ass. I'm starting to think I need to work on finding friends who don't abandon me for other states.

Which reminds me that Daphne is going to be *so* smug tonight. I feel a twinge of guilt at the fact that, for the first time, I almost want to break our standing date. Not because she's going to *I told you so* me to hell and back, though she will, but because both my heart and body grow a little restless at the idea of spending the time away from Mark. Which is exactly why I *won't* be canceling, but I'm already jonesing for the sale to be over so we can just exist together without all the added stress.

"Don't worry," Maddie says. "She's one of us now."

"That's not as reassuring as you think it is," Bowen snarks as he and Mark settle into the chairs they stole. I laugh, glad the quiet man feels comfortable enough to make jokes around us, but I realize that Maddie's not wrong. Ever since the sale started, Mark has gone out of his way to show me that he doesn't come to this relationship alone.

He comes with a complicated best friend and a nosy sister and parents who don't just throw their kids to the wolves.

I'm especially unsure of what to do with the latter, but my needy-ass inner child yearns to find out. Neither of my parents have called or texted to apologize yet, and I know that, even if they decide I can stay in the cottage, it's time for me to cut ties from Landow entirely.

Maybe they're right, and Gabriel will be a better manager than I could ever have been. Maybe there's no point in trying, and I'm doomed to fail.

Or maybe, I think as I look around at the people who have been showing up for me this entire sale, Mark's right and I've already succeeded.

Either way, I have to move on.

I'm halfway through my sandwich when a familiar figure clad in business attire rounds the corner and heads our way. Alicia and Mark both move to stand, but I wave them off and go greet her myself. "It's good to see you again, Evangeline. How's Marshmallow doing?"

She offers a smile that somehow manages to seem both practiced and genuine at the same time. "My barn manager has cursed me every day so far for buying a gray, but I'm pretty sure he also sneaks her extra treats."

"Sounds like an ideal fit." The hardest part of this job is not having any control over where the horses go once they're sold. Even back when I worked for my parents, I always breathed a little easier when we got updates from the new owners. It's not any better now, even if I've never owned the horses in the first place.

And I admit, I'm glad to know Evangeline has a barn

manager who seems to have a good head on his shoulders, given the reasons she's buying horses in the first place.

"You still shopping?" I ask. "We've got three that just shipped in this morning. All up on the last day."

"That's actually why I wanted to swing by." She glances around, then lowers her voice slightly. "I heard a conversation yesterday that worried me, but I got called away for a case so I couldn't follow up with you until now."

I frown. "What happened?"

"I was looking at a horse in another barn, and heard a conversation between three people. One of them was saying that he had a couple horses left in the sale, but if they came to an arrangement, he didn't mind scratching them to save on the consignment fee. I might not know horses, but I know contracts, and it sounded shady."

"Okay." That *is* shady, and I'd be pissed if I heard the conversation, too. "What does that have to do with me?"

"He mentioned your consignment by name."

I blink. "What did he look like?"

"About six foot, receding brown hair, muscle-bound in a try-hard way?"

"Jack Nugent," I sigh. "That dickface."

"I take it you know him."

"Unfortunately." I exhale slowly, then offer Evangeline the best smile I can muster. "I appreciate the heads up. I need to make a phone call, but Alicia can help you if you want to look at our last few head."

"I'll do that. And Lark?"

"Yeah?"

She hands me a business card. "If you ever need a lawyer, call me."

All I can offer to that is a grateful nod. She walks off to talk to Alicia, and I duck around to the side of the barn where it's relatively quiet. If what Evangeline said is true, then I could lose two of the three horses I have left in this sale just so their owner doesn't have to pay me the percentage I'm owed from their sales price. Would it destroy my business? No.

But would it make the next few months harder? Yes.

I debate my options, before deciding it's best if I start with Miss Betty. If I start with Jack, I'll be on the back foot from the beginning, and that's not going to help in the long run. But I barely get my phone out of my pocket before Mark is at my back, sliding his arms around me and pulling me close. He presses one of Miss Betty's candies into my palm, his voice a low murmur in my ear that makes me shiver despite the sticky heat around us. "Still love me, Songbird?"

I roll my head to press a kiss to his jaw. "For now," I say, trying to keep my voice light. I tuck the candy away for later, all too aware I might need the pick me up.

Mark sees through the facade. "Everything okay?"

"Evangeline just told me something..." I shake my head, not ready to say it out loud yet. "I need to make a call real quick."

He doesn't ask if he should leave, and I don't even try to make him. Personal growth, that.

It only takes a second to pull up the number to the front office. Mark's arms tighten around me when I ask for Miss Betty, but she answers the moment I'm transferred over, so I don't have time to overthink it. "You've reached Betty. How can I help you?"

"Hey, Miss Betty. It's Lark Reynolds."

"Lark, darling! You have perfect timing. I was just about to call and tell you the scratches have officially been canceled, no signatures required. You're all set to move forward as planned."

I freeze, my stomach instantly queasy. "What scratches?"

Behind me, Mark goes stiff. I close my eyes, like I can

keep the next moments from happening if I don't see them coming. "The ones Nugent requested yesterday. Your young man asked me to hold off a bit, and it paid off. He left here on quite the mission, you know."

I'm forced to turn in Mark's arms to look up at him, because he doesn't let me go. Like he's scared that if he does, he won't get me back. "Did he now?"

The pleading look on his face tells me more than enough about what happened—I might be lacking in details, but not imagination. On the phone, Miss Betty natters on, blissfully unaware of the turmoil she's caused. "Oh, darling, the two of you are the talk of the office! We're all so happy you're happy together."

I clear my throat, swallowing down the twin warmth and discomfort her words stir in my chest, and focus on the part that matters most. "The scratches have been voided, though? The horses are still in the sale?"

"Oh, yes, dear. You're all set. You know—"

"Thank you, Miss Betty." I cut her off and hang up on her. Right now, I can't bring myself to care about the rudeness.

"Lark." Mark's voice is gentle—the same one he uses when the yearlings are skittish. Calm and soft and so, *so* safe. "Will you let me explain?"

When I yank myself backwards, he lets me go. I feel the loss of his touch in my fucking bones, but there's no way I can have this conversation while tucked up against him all cozy. "Who was scratched?"

"Both of Jack Nugent's horses."

Shit. Fuck. Shit fuck damn. Evangeline was right. Nugent fully planned to fuck me over. Scratching the last two would be a nightmare. I've had a good sale, but I was banking on these last three at least getting to the sales ring. If two of them got scratched…

"But they're not scratched anymore," I say carefully.

"No. They're not." He doesn't hide from me, but wariness lines his eyes. It's smart of him to be concerned. It means he's not completely stupid. "I spoke to Nugent. He agreed to reinstate them."

"So let me get this straight." My voice is all ice. I'm speaking quietly so no one else can hear, but I have no doubt anyone who sees us will know this isn't a happy conversation. "You found out two of my horses were scratched, and instead of telling me, you tracked down my client and talked to him on my behalf. And then you spent the last few hours in my barn, *still not telling me*. I had to find out from a relative stranger instead. Does that sound right?"

A thousand excuses and justifications flicker across his face, but he doesn't settle for any of them. He nods once. "Yes."

I just finally accepted that he's sticking around. So much for the Lark from twenty minutes ago and the comfort she found in deciding she could let him in. Right now, all I can think is, *I should have known better.*

Known better than to rely on someone else.

Known better than to trust him.

Known better than to fall in love.

"Please leave." My voice is strained from my effort not to cry. "I can't do this right now."

The pain on his face nearly shatters my resolve. "Lark, don't shut me out."

"You did it first."

The words land with precisely the force I want them to. He takes a step back, his gaze leaping across every inch of my face—like he's trying to memorize something he might never see again. "I'm sorry, Songbird."

"Don't call me that," I snap. That nickname belongs to a different version of us. "Just leave."

"You don't have to do this," he whispers, his voice thick. "You said I could help. Just let me help."

The expression on my face must show him exactly how I feel about that, because he just hangs his head in defeat before he turns and walks away.

Leaving me.

Just like I told him to.

Just like I wanted.

CHAPTER 20

MARK

"Hey, buddy. I know, it's been a while." My breath whooshes out of me as Atlas shoves his head into my chest. Atlas might live in one of the paddocks next to my barn and I might be the one who feeds him every day, but I haven't spent any real time with him lately. Turns out, it's easy to neglect the things that matter, even when they're right in front of you. "Feel up for a trail ride?"

He shoves me again, which I take as a yes. I lead him inside and drop his lead rope, not bothering to secure him anywhere as I duck into the tack room for a grooming kit. He was young when he convinced himself the ground was holding him hostage anytime I let the rope go, and he's still perfectly content not to wander off two decades later.

It's perhaps the smartest and stupidest thing about him, all at once.

Atlas is a leopard appaloosa gelding who's been with me since I was a kid, when our parents got both me and Maddie five-year-old horses for our fifth birthdays. Maddie's horse, who she named Sonora after that movie she made me watch like six hundred times, was a bay quarter-horse mare who died while we were in high school, which about destroyed my sister. She still hasn't looked twice at a permanent riding horse for herself, and I can't say I blame her.

When Atlas's time comes, I'll be a wreck.

I settle into the familiar routine of getting ready for a ride. I take my time as I brush him, making sure to dig into all his favorite spots with the curry comb. Muscle memory takes over, guiding me through the motions of combing out his mane and tail, picking his feet, sweeping the soft brush over his coat until it shines.

Soon enough, the saddle is on his back and the bit is in his mouth. My phone buzzes for the hundredth time since I left the sale, and a glance tells me what I already know: it's not Lark. So I toss it into the grooming kit and haul myself up into the saddle, because there's no point bringing my phone with me when I know the only person I want to text me is the one person who won't.

Both Atlas and I take a minute to find our rhythm together as I point him toward the back acreage. I was never a competitive rider, which has always been fine by Atlas. We're both content to go for trail rides and just fuck around, especially now that he's a crotchety old man. I can already tell I'm gonna be sore as hell tomorrow, but it seems like the least I deserve.

The afternoon sun is oppressive, so we ride tucked close to the tree line until we reach the trail through the woods. Atlas knows the route by heart, so I let him take charge as we trek through the trees that ring the edges of our property. Someday, we might consider developing some of this land, but we've been pretty content to have it as a privacy buffer—there are farms east and west of us, but the northern side became a small subdivision a decade or so ago.

Picking our way down the trail is slow-going, but it's not like I've got anywhere else to be.

Not after how badly I messed up.

The look of betrayal she wore hasn't left my mind once since Lark told me to leave. Just last night, she handed me her trust. It was fragile and precious and worth the world to me.

And I shattered it, barely twelve hours later.

The moment I realized she was calling Miss Betty, I knew it was all over. Miss Betty had no reason to think the attempted scratches were a secret, because they shouldn't have been. Lark should have known about them the moment I did.

We ride for the better part of thirty minutes before I nudge Atlas back toward the fence line. I grunt as I lean down to open the gate I need, feeling far more precarious than I should, but Atlas is patient with me, even if we're back out in the sun. His coat is slick with sweat, despite us never going faster than a walk, but our destination isn't far now. A few more minutes of trudging our way through overgrown grass in one of our few empty fields, and we're able to step into the shade of a massive oak tree.

I swing off Atlas's back, taking time to loosen the girth and pull his bridle free so he can graze comfortably. I sneak him a mint from my pocket, which he chomps down happily, then let him be as I climb the ladder into the tree house.

The last time I was here was the last time I fucked everything up with Lark. I spent hours before that night making sure the treehouse was still safe and clean; it sat untouched for years prior, Maddie and I having outgrown the use of it once we found other places to hang out and have privacy. But there had been something about bringing Lark here that spoke to me.

I don't think I could have articulated it at the time, but I knew how much she wanted a place to belong. Sharing this secret spot seemed like a way to show her she could belong with *me*.

Maybe I should have known better. The February chill in the air had nothing on the frost coming from Lark after I told her I loved her. When she begged me to take her home, I knew I couldn't deny her.

But I also knew, deep down, that she was running scared. So I waited. I gave her time to think, time to miss me. Then I put myself back into her life. Got her to admit she's in love with me.

And then I fucked it all up.

Good work, asshole.

The air is swampy and stagnant, but I don't bother to reach for the battery-operated fan because I'm not sure I deserve to feel comfortable right now. The farm spreads out before me as I stare through the unfinished side of the structure, and I think about how frustrated Lark was last night with my reaction to potentially coming on as an official owner. She's right—utterly and completely so—that I take my position here for granted.

I took my first steps in the old foaling barn, at three in the morning when a tricky birth required all hands on deck, so my parents had to drag tiny me and tiny Maddie out of bed. The story goes that my parents almost missed it, because the foal finally emerged at the same moment that I decided to chase a barn cat in a more upright manner than usual.

My first kiss was after one of our employee barbecues, sneaking behind the loading ramp with one of the farm hand's daughters. It was the summer after middle school, and I didn't want to go to high school without checking that box off my to-do list. The kiss was wet and awkward and the best moment of my pathetic life up until that point.

I spent the first year Maddie went to college rebuilding every damn fence on the property because I didn't know what to do with myself without her by my side. I'm pretty sure I still have a splinter or twelve under my skin, but it was the only way I kept myself sane until she came home for summer break.

I've never needed to worry about my position here. My parents have made this a place that we're always welcome. Having met Lark's parents, I understand better now how lucky that makes me. I know how rare it is to have a home so safe you don't ever worry it will disappear.

I love this place. I do.

But I love Lark more. I'd give it all up for her in a heartbeat.

Hell, I'd give it all *to* her, if I could.

I startle when the trap door flies open. I'm not sure how long I've been sitting here, wallowing, but suddenly my sister's head pops up, and I'm not alone anymore. "Thought I'd find you here," she declares with smug satisfaction. She scrambles the rest of the way onto the platform, letting the door drop back down as she glances around the space. "Damn. This is cozy as shit. When'd you do that?"

"February."

"Ah." The math is easy enough for her to do. "Want company?"

"Is that an actual question?"

"No." She snags a blanket, rolling it up like a lumbar pillow, and leans back against the wall opposite me. "It was me or Bowen, and Bowen has an inspection this afternoon. So, you gonna tell me what you did?"

I stare at her. "Less than two weeks ago, you would have assumed it was her fault."

"Yeah, but then you did your weird bullshit and I got to know her." She frowns. "She tried to hide it, but she was sad after you left."

Fuck. That's as good as a dagger through my heart. "I

fucked up." It's basically my new mantra at this point, but admitting it aloud only makes it feel heavier. "I didn't tell her about the scratches Nugent tried to enter."

"Mark."

"I know."

"*Mark.*"

"I know!" If there was room for me to pace in this tree-house, I would be wearing a hole through the floor. "I should have told her."

"So why didn't you?"

I close my eyes and drop my head back against the wall. "Your guess is as good as mine."

"Bullshit." Maddie waits until I'm looking at her again to go on. "You don't get to do this to her, Mark."

"What am I doing, Mads?" Just as quick as my anger arrived, it dissipates, leaving me empty and exhausted. "Since you so clearly know."

"Let's review the tapes, shall we?" Maddie's voice is unamused. "You spent a year and a half as Lark's regular booty call. You hounded her relentlessly until she agreed to go out on a real date with you, and then when she did, you immediately told her you love her instead of giving her time to adjust. She sent you packing, but you're still you, so you figured out a way to make sure you'd be all up in her space at the sale. At a sale that could make or break her fledgling business, no less. *Then* you convinced her to take the worst bet I've ever heard in my entire life and did everything you could to fold her into your family and friends. Sound right so far?"

"God, I sound like a psychopath when you say it like that."

"Then I'm saying it right." My sister is unrepentant as she continues. "She *finally* decides she wants to keep you around, and for some reason you think that's the perfect time to really act like an asshole and lie to her."

"I didn't—"

"Not the point." She cuts me off again. "The point is, up until now, you've managed to convince yourself that you were the one in the right about this relationship. *You* wanted more than sex, *you* were in love with her, *you* needed her to give you a chance. And I'm not saying you were wrong to try, because her feelings for you are clear as day. But you don't get to push and shove your way into her heart, and then run away from your own shit at the first sign of trouble."

"I'm not running away."

"I literally found you hiding in a treehouse." She tosses my phone at me. "This was rattling around in a grooming kit. You're running away."

Sometimes arguing with my sister is the worst. Mostly because she tends to be right.

When I don't respond, she returns to where the lecture started. "Why didn't you tell her, Mark?"

I don't have to do any soul-searching to find the answer. Maddie's right. I was running away, because it was easier than confronting the truth. "Because I'm scared, Mads."

"Of what?"

"Of everything you just said being true. That she might not pick me if I'm not there to push her into it. That she doesn't need me the way I need her." I swallow against the lump in my throat as I remember watching Lark fight with every bit of her strength not to cry—just like that night in February, when she told me she could never love me. "And it turns out I was right."

"Are you? Or is she just hurt because you made a mistake?"

"It's the same thing."

Maddie grumbles under her breath about how I'm lucky to have lasted this long in life. "It's only the same thing if you let it be. *Talk to her.* Apologize. Figure out how not to do it again."

"She told me to leave."

"Jesus, and *now* you decide to listen to her? She was at work, trying to run a business she didn't even know had been threatened. Obviously she didn't want to deal with your groveling then and there. That doesn't mean you should just give the fuck up and never talk to her again. She clearly fell in love with your stalker ass, so you may as well see it through."

"I think I would have preferred Bowen," I grumble, even as a small flicker of hope reignites in my chest.

"Yeah, well, you owe me a conversation about the farm, too."

"I don't exactly have anywhere to be at the moment."

"Good. Turn the fan on and settle in. I have an idea."

TWO YEARS AGO

LARK

"What if I'm not interested in either one?"

It took Mark Aladyne less than five minutes to reappear at my side, that casually cocky grin back on his face. I was still eating my burger, content in my spot on the outskirts of the gathering where no one wanted to talk to me, but now I had to deal with a hot, needy asshole.

Someone likes you wants a night to brag about or a happy little wife, and I'm not either one. Honestly, I had been proud of that line. I hoped it would get the point across, but he seemed to be choosing the path of willful ignorance. "It doesn't really leave much else to choose from, so I guess you're screwed."

"Now, now, don't get ahead of yourself." I had never understood what it meant to say someone's eyes twinkled, but I was learning rapidly as I watched his face. "There's a whole third option you're forgetting."

Mark leaned back in his newly acquired seat, slinging an arm across the back of the empty chair next to him. The movement flashed just a sliver of skin at his hip before his shirt settled back into place, and I violently chastised my eyes for even noticing in the first place. The last thing this man needed was any sort of indication that he was as hot as he thought he was. Even though he was.

He really fucking was.

What I hated the most was that we both knew I was into his whole deal. The challenge and amusement in his eyes when I first saw him sitting with his friend. The way his worn boots suggested he was working before this party started, and would be working again after. The cling of his shirt across his chest, because he sized down on purpose and I couldn't even be mad at the results. The sexy-ass lean against the barn when he snuck up on me. The sheer anticipation in his expression right now as he waited for me to spar with him.

And fuck me if I didn't want to play. "And that is?"

"Whatever you actually are."

I snorted. "What I am, if you'll recall, is not interested."

If our names didn't rhyme, he might have stood a chance, despite all my better instincts. But that was a level of twee no amount of hotness could overcome.

"Mm." He rocked the chair onto its back legs as he eyed me up and down, and I found myself glad for the Florida heat. Any pink on my skin was from the sun, not from the impact of his gaze. "Fair enough. I'll leave you alone, then."

I startled when his chair dropped back to the grass. He was actually going to leave. "Wait. Really?"

A slow, satisfied grin crept across his face. "I thought you weren't interested."

Fuck me.

"I'm not." The protest sounded weak, but I blazed my way forward. "I'm just surprised you have listening comprehension skills. Most men don't."

He leaned forward at that, close enough for his body to impact the air around me but not close enough to touch. "Let me be clear, Lark. I don't mind a chase. But I'm not gonna chase someone who doesn't want to be caught. I'm a dick, not an asshole."

I wanted to tease out what, exactly, he thought the distinction between the two was, but the words that came out of my mouth were, "And what happens when the prize at the end of the hunt isn't want you wanted?"

His eyes bored into mine. "A person isn't a prize. You don't owe me shit. Hell, we might find out we hate each other." Some tiny thread inside of me rebelled at that idea, and I made a mental note to snip it away later before it could start to unravel my carefully woven facade. "But I'm willing to find out if you are."

He didn't wait for me to respond. The space around me felt empty as soon as he walked away, and I tried to go back to my quiet, peaceful lunch, but the burger had lost its warmth and I had too much going on in my head to be able to eat anyway.

Before Gabriel, I would probably have climbed this man like an arrogant tree before we got three complete sentences out between the two of us. I wasn't the type of girl who needed an emotional connection to have good sex. I had a pretty good success rate settling for an eager man who was open to direction. Something told me Mark Aladyne would be a quick study, if given the chance.

But I had new priorities now. I was meeting with my financial advisor next week to go over my business plan. If it was as solid as I thought it was—which it should be, for all the time I had spent on it—then I would start hustling for clients soon. Soon after *that*, I'd quit my job at the only place I'd ever known and start Lark Sales.

I wasn't chasing my dreams—I'd given up on ever getting to do that—but I could still prove to everyone I was good enough to stand on my own.

It all meant I couldn't afford to fuck around with

someone like Mark Aladyne. The risk to my reputation if he proved to be indiscreet and inflammatory was too high. And if we dated and it flamed out? That could prove even worse. The Aladyne name held a lot of power—all I had to do was look around the gathered guests here to see that the connections he had ranged wide and far. That wasn't a gamble I was willing to live with right now.

The afternoon wore on. I let my parents introduce me around with less resistance than I usually would, because I was going to need every ounce of familiarity I could get as I started networking. I found a few friendly acquaintances that I already knew, and chatted with them about their families and workplace drama. I ignored Mark, hoping that would be enough to bar our conversation from my mind entirely.

Or, at least, I tried. The man was suddenly everywhere, always existing just on the edges of my peripheral vision. It had to be intentional on his part. It had to be. I wasn't so easily distracted.

"Lark, right?" A voice at my side pulled my attention away from the conversation Mark was having with a few women around our age. One of them had her hand on his arm, and I shouted very loudly in my brain about how great that was for me because maybe it would make him chase her instead. It wasn't jealousy. It was simple practicality. "I'm Maddie."

So the woman who was being all chummy with Mark earlier had a name. And, it turned out, an oddly familiar expression on an oddly familiar face. "My brother insisted I come introduce myself. He also told me to refer to him as my brother as often as humanly possible so you'd get the point that I'm not a threat, but I try to do very little that he actually asks me to do, so that phrase won't leave my mouth for at least six weeks now that I've used twice."

His *sister*. I wasn't going to pretend there wasn't a little relief in that news, but the relief didn't matter. "Older or younger?"

"Older. Also the same age. First twin, and all that."

That explained the familiarity. It wasn't that I had Mark's face memorized, but I had a feeling the way it looked when he told me he only wanted to chase me if I wanted to be caught would be burned into my retinas for a good long while. "You can tell him the point has been taken," I assure her.

"I'm sure he'll be delighted," she said dryly. Then she softened, and I knew she was watching him charm the group he was with. "He's a good man, you know."

"I'm sure."

Her gaze refocused, her shrewd intelligence plain as day. "He's also stubborn and obnoxious and a nightmare to share popcorn with. But he's worth it."

"It's not like that," I said, both of us well aware of the fact that I was probably lying.

"Maybe not," she conceded. "Just do me a favor? Be careful with his heart, because he won't be."

I watched her go, glad she didn't seem to require a response. I had told him I wasn't interested, and it almost didn't matter if that was the truth or not. If we had a window at all, it was rapidly closing—my parents approached, both of them clearly ready to go. We started back toward the truck, my parents caught halfway there by someone they knew. I kept going. One more contact wouldn't make or break me today, and my ability to pretend everything was fine between me and my parents was at an all-time low.

I was reaching for the door handle when I realized I wasn't alone. Lean up against the bed of my parents' truck, Mark gave me one more slow, lingering appraisal. Lust sat thick in his eyes and in the bobbing of his throat, but it faded to something else. Curiosity, maybe, or hesitation.

"Were you just going to leave without saying goodbye?"

"Yes," I admitted. "Seemed safer that way."

"And here I thought I was approachable as hell. Am I really that dangerous?"

I considered the way my mouth was so tempted to curve into a smile, my body so tempted to fall against his. The flicker of disappointment I felt when our conversations ended. The heady promise of possibility that seemed to shimmer between us, even now.

"Yeah," I said. "I think you are."

His face cracked into a genuine grin as he pushed off the truck. "Then I guess I'll see you around, Lark Reynolds."

I watched him walk away, already knowing something had just begun.

I just hoped like hell I wouldn't live to regret it.

CHAPTER 21

LARK

"Oh, babe, I'm sorry." Daphne's tinny voice is full of empathy through the phone screen. "Are you okay?"

"What part of this looks okay?" I ask. I'm sitting on the floor in my living room, surrounded by all the junk food I could find at the convenience store on my way home. Which is a lot. But I haven't touched any of it, because I've just been staring off into space as I try to figure out where I went wrong.

She sighs, acknowledging the point. "I was really hoping tonight would be full of salacious details about your sex life."

I groan, dropping my head back to stare at the ceiling. "God, last night was so good, Daffy. It makes me physically angry now, it was that good."

"But?"

"But within hours, he was making decisions about my business without me. He didn't trust me enough to do it myself, and he knows that's something I hate. He was there this weekend when my parents said—"

I cut myself off, the pain of the memory too sharp, but

Daphne doesn't let me get away with it. Her voice goes flat and dark. "What did your parents say?"

"Short version is I'm destined to fail and they just want to save my from myself."

"Oh, fuck the hell out of that." Daphne's pacing now, the click-clack of dog toenails telling me Millicent is taking every step right along with her. Maybe I need a dog. Dog cuddles sound nice right about now. Maybe Gideon won't notice if I dognap Angus. "Please tell me Mark shut that shit down."

I glare, even though she's barely looking at the screen. "I'm perfectly capable of shutting it down myself."

She stops her pacing and focuses the entirety of her attention on me. "Are you? Because for years now, all of your stories about your parents end with you brushing it off and saying it doesn't matter."

Damn. My best friend didn't come to play tonight. The fact that she's right is a whole different problem. "He shut it down," I admit. "But he asked permission first."

The approval on her face would have been validating thirty-six hours ago, but now it just makes me want to punch something. "Good," she says, her voice gentling. "You deserve to have someone who fights for you, Lark."

That's too close to last night, to the way Mark kept murmuring promises of the kind of love I deserved against my skin. "He's not exactly fighting for me now," I counter. "I haven't heard a word from him since he left."

"Did he leave, or did you kick him out?"

Well. There's that. "Stop being on his side."

"For the hundredth time, I'm not on his side. But being Team Lark includes telling you when you're being a stubborn, self-defeating bitch." I glower, unable to argue because we've each said a variation of the same thing to the other many times over the years. "You're only going to get so far by blaming him for everything."

"What shouldn't I blame him for?" I demand. "Making decisions for me? Talking to my clients without me? *Lying* to me?"

"No, he deserves all of that. But I think he probably also deserves a chance to explain."

"There's nothing to explain!" I'm all but yelling now, and I'd feel bad if Daphne weren't being so willfully frustrating right now. I don't want to be *rational*. I want to be *mad*. "He knows more than anybody how important this is to me. He knows how scared I've been to fail and prove my parents right. There's no fucking excuse for cutting me out of my own business."

"Maybe not." Daphne takes my anger easily. "But Lark, that man is *obscenely* in love with you. And no matter what else you're feeling right now, you love him, too. Love is a lot of things, but sometimes it's just stupid. That doesn't mean you have to throw it all away."

"Right. Because you know so much about love."

It's a low fucking blow, and I wince the moment the words are out of my mouth, but Daphne doesn't waver. "I know more than you think."

"Daffy—"

"Tonight's not about me."

"Maybe it should be. Tell me more about the date you went on."

She rolls her eyes. "I'm not done with you yet, Reynolds. Lie of omission aside, why are you so mad that he helped you?"

"It's a hell of a thing to put aside," I grumble, before sighing. "I don't want to be saved from myself."

Daphne lets us sit with that admission in silence for a

long moment before she speaks again. "Have you ever topped off the water bucket of someone else's horse at the barn?"

I blink at her. "What?"

"Just answer the question."

"Yes?"

"And if you borrowed my car and it was low on gas, what would you do?"

"I'd pass out from shock that you were in the same city as me."

"Lark."

I sigh, not liking the direction she's guiding us in. "I'd refill your tank. Probably only partway, though. You make more money than I do."

She grins at that, because her having a stable career is still something of a novelty. "I do, and your stinginess is noted."

The joke almost coaxes a smile out of me, but I'm too determined to be grumpy. "Make your point, Daffy."

"Your parents have done a number on your understanding of what it means to be loved, babe. I can't talk, because fuck knows my family isn't much better, but they've trained you to assume accepting kindness is the same as admitting weakness, and that's bullshit. Taking care of someone doesn't always mean you don't think they're capable of taking care of themselves. The other owners would fill their horse's water bucket eventually. I can afford my own damn gas. But you would do it anyway, because you want to help."

"I take it back. I don't want to hear your point anymore."

"You don't have to like his reasons. You can break up with him if you think that's the right decision, and I'll figure out how to mail him a box of tiny glitter confetti dicks. Because I *am* on your side, no matter what. But I think you should at least talk to him before you decide. Let him explain how he got from Point A to Point Fuck Up."

I want to argue, but I know she's not entirely wrong. It's become painfully clear how much of my life is nothing more than a reaction to feeling overlooked by my parents. But there's a different issue eating at me now, one I can barely bring myself to say aloud to Daphne because of how small and pathetic it makes me feel. But she's already gotten the worst, most dramatic parts of me, so she may as well have this, too. "What if I fucked it up already, Daph?"

Beneath all my anger and hurt over what Mark did today lives a tiny, scared voice. The one that's worried that by sending him away, by not giving him the chance to explain, I've given him a way out. He's been chasing me for two years, and last night he finally got what he wanted. Maybe our fight today will show him that I wasn't worth the chase in the first place. Maybe winning the bet was enough for him, and he's already bored and ready to move on.

Maybe I've ruined my only chance at happiness, because I don't know how to let the man I love love me back.

"He hasn't texted or called," I whine to her. "He just left."

"Again, because you *told* him to. And you told him last week that Wednesdays are sacred best friend time. I might not know the man well, but I know he didn't just forget that information." She waits for me to acknowledge the possibility before continuing. "He's not hiding from you, Lark. He's waiting for permission."

Eventually I plead for a change in topic, not ready to acknowledge the full truth of her words, and she reluctantly distracts me with the story of her date this week. There's something hidden in the way she recounts the tale, the root of her ambivalence about what sounds like an objectively great date with an objectively great guy. I want to be the friend who pushes her to tell me what's going on, who sinks her claws into the admission about love she gave me earlier, and I promise myself I will be that friend, soon, but not tonight.

I don't have it in me to be anything but selfish tonight.

We're in the middle of shopping for a new shower curtain for her—apparently she fell and ripped hers during an incident I don't want details on—when her whole face brightens. "Thank fuck." Then, just as quickly, she puts on the worst, most pitiful face she can manage. "I'm suddenly very sick, Lark. I have to go."

"Wait, what?" It's not unlike Daphne to get up to nonsense, but this is particularly transparent, even for her. "You know I know you're not sick, right?"

She coughs weakly. "I think it's consumption. Like from the olden days. I've heard being on FaceTime only makes it worse. I have to hang up immediately but you should go check your front porch as soon as I do."

I don't get another protest out before she's ended the call. I'm still staring at my phone when it buzzes with a text.

DAPHNE

Check your porch NOW bitch

Deliveries aren't really a thing I get out here, so I'm wary as I approach my front door, half-expecting that she's ordered me a stripper as a distraction. It seems like the sort of thing she'd do. I take a deep breath and open the door, deflating when there's nothing—and no one—on the other side. But I lose track of that immediately, my gaze clinging to the vehicle parked next to mine.

A familiar truck. One that's not supposed to be here at all.

From the porch swing, I hear a voice. "Hey, Songbird."

I spin to look at him, and say the first words that come to mind. "You're not a stripper."

Bemusement crosses his face, both of us equally confused about that being my opening gambit. But his expression softens as his gaze tracks over me, undoubtedly taking in my current state of disaster. Ratty shorts, baggy t-shirt, tired eyes, dirty hair. "I could be, if that's what you need."

I just stare at him, at a loss for words. I had convinced myself that he wouldn't come. That me sending him away earlier would have irrevocably broken things between us.

But he's *here*, and that's more than I dared to hope for.

"Can we talk?" he asks, the most tentative smile I've ever seen from him on his face as he shifts his weight on the swing.

I lean against the doorframe, dragging my eyes over him. He looks as exhausted as I feel, which is something. "How long have you been here?"

"A while."

"You didn't knock."

"Wednesdays are Daphne time. I wasn't going to interrupt."

I tear my gaze away at that, mentally assigning a point in Daphne's column. It doesn't take much to deduce that her finding out he was here was what led to her kindergarten-level performance of a fake illness.

But if she was right about this, maybe she's right about the rest of it, too. So I force myself to face him properly and present him with my truth. "You hurt me, Mark. And I'm pissed about it."

"I know. I'm sorry."

His tortured expression bleeds the edge off my temper. There's no equivocation, no hiding from his choices. It's enough to make me step all the way outside, pulling the door shut behind me. It's not lost on me that we're back on my porch, back to the place we broke apart the night he first told me he loved me.

The place where he told me I'd regret not letting him in.

I eye the spot next to him on the swing for a moment,

considering, but settle for sitting with my back against the porch railing. He gives me the space I need to take a few steadying breaths before I ask for what I need. "Tell me what happened."

He does. He tells me about Miss Betty mentioning the scratches when he went to ask for a free stall, and how his desire to fix the situation took over his better judgement. "You weren't in the barn when I got back," he explains, "and it felt like there wasn't any time to wait. I know I should have, but Miss Betty had only given me a few hours, and waiting seemed like too big a risk."

The rest follows. How he and Maddie found Jack, the conversation they had, Domingo's unwitting help. Even Bowen was involved, delivering the bribe to Miss Betty. Apparently *everyone* knew except for me. "I wanted to fix it for you," he says when he finishes. "I wasn't trying to lie to you. I just…didn't want you to have another thing to worry about when I could make it go away."

"Have you ever heard a word I said?" My voice is sharp, and I don't attempt to blunt the edges. "You were sitting at the same damn table I was when my parents told me names are all that matter in this business. Did you really think I'd want to solve this problem by flaunting my connection to you?"

"No." He leans forward, the chains of the porch swing creaking as he rests his arms on his thighs. "I think your parents have you convinced it only counts as success if you're standing alone when you reach the finish line. But that's their baggage, Lark. It doesn't have to be yours."

I flinch, not liking the way that bit of commentary lands. It feels awfully close to a truth I don't know how to hold.

"You have no idea how impressive you've been the last two weeks," Mark continues, his admiration evident in the soft curve of his lips. "You've been doing the work of twelve people on any given day. Nothing and no one can take that away from you. But I can't change who I am any more than you can. I'm always going to be an Aladyne. People are always going to know your parents own Landow. Hiding from that is only going to hurt you in the long run."

"I hate that." My voice cracks, but I keep my eyes on him, because his presence is the only thing holding me down. "The whole point of leaving was to show them I was good enough to do it on my own."

"But you *can't* do it alone, baby. It's not physically possi-ble. Could you have survived this sale without Alicia? Without Gideon?" *Without me?* He doesn't speak the words, but I hear them loud and clear. "You're always going to need help. We all do. I know I fucked up today. I overstepped, and I made decisions I shouldn't have. But all I wanted was to help you. All I *want* is to help you."

"Did Jack say why?"

"Not in as many words." Mark rolls with the change in topic. I think he can tell I need time to process what he just said. "But I got the impression he was shopping for outside buyers and planning to cut you out of your sale commission."

I curse under my breath. My contracts are good—I have an extended window during which I get a percentage, so the sale itself isn't the only thing that matters. It's not uncommon for a horse to fail to meet its reserve, but to still end up sold within days to an interested buyer who was in the room. My terms protect for that. But that also means the terms clearly identify when that window ends, and a deter-mined asshole could use that to their advantage.

"It's not like it matters. My parents were the ones who introduced me to him, but I'm going to have to cut him as a client after this regardless."

"Good. Fuck that guy."

I chuff something approximating a laugh, and we lapse

into a moment of silence. I'm still angry, still not ready to forgive and forget, but the tension in the air has eased into something breathable. Mark carefully, quietly stands from the swing and lowers himself to sit next to me, just close enough for our shoulders to brush.

"I went to the treehouse today," he says. "To wallow, mainly. But then my sister found me, and we talked. Well, first she reamed my ass for what I did, and *then* we talked. And in the interest of full disclosure, you should know that she wants to offer you a job."

I startle. "What?"

"Javi is retiring soon, which puts us in a tough spot. He's been our sales manager for decades, and it's going to leave a hole. She thinks you'd be a good fit."

"I don't know what to do with that." I expect to feel a gut reaction to dismiss the idea out of hand—I have my own business now, and stepping into a role like that should feel like a demotion. But fuck if part of me doesn't want to revel in the idea of being good enough to take on a leadership role at a place like Aladyne.

It's all I ever wanted when I worked here at Landow. Not just the title or power, but the teamwork. The chance to guide the direction of a place that mattered to me. When the management job went to Gabriel instead, I told myself I'd find a different path, and I threw my entire self into building a consignment business.

I never once considered chasing that dream somewhere else.

Not until now.

"You don't have to do anything yet. I just wanted you to know it's coming."

I study his profile. "Where do you stand on that idea?"

"Honestly?" My deadpan expression makes him laugh, and I have to work to keep from smiling in return. "I told her that I wasn't sure you'd want to give up your business, but that we'd be stupid not to at least *try* to hire you." He smirks. "This is why Maddie should make the important decisions, though. I was going to start by trying to lease you half the stalls in my barn as a way to convince you to move in with me. Mine is much better as a back-up plan."

"You want me to move in with you?"

"Twenty-four hour Lark access? Hell yes, I want that."

My eyes drift to the door of my little cottage. My parents still haven't reached out, but I'm not optimistic enough to assume that means they've changed their minds.

I'm not sure I'm willing to stay, even if they do.

But am I ready to move in with Mark?

And, more importantly, what does it say about me if the answer is yes?

"It's not a trap," Mark says when it becomes clear I'm at a loss for words. "Maddie knows better than to ask until the sale is done, and even then, you'll have time to think it through. If you get the offer and turn it down, no one will think any less of you. I've just already been enough of an asshole by keeping things from you for one day, so I wanted put everything on the table."

"I thought you were a dick, not an asshole."

He grins at the reminder of the day we met. "I think that depends on if you can forgive me." He reaches for my hand, but stops himself. Keeps the ball in my court. "The last thing I want is to lose you, Lark, and I'm so fucking sorry I got so wrapped up in my own fear that I let you down."

"I don't want to lose you, either," I whisper. When this game started, I would have done anything to pretend our fight today didn't wreck me. But I can't bring myself to be anything but honest right now. "I might not survive it this time."

"*This* time?" he asks with a raised brow.

I shrug, not quite meeting his gaze. "I didn't like the last six months either, okay?"

"Careful, Songbird. You're gonna make me think you're in love with me."

"Fuck off." But I'm smiling, despite everything, and I don't let myself second-guess or hesitate.

I kiss him.

He freezes the moment our lips meet, like he was worried it would never happen again, but then he shudders with relief. My lips part, and I let him set the pace, content to just exist in this kiss forever.

Our head and our hearts get in the way all the damn time, but our bodies have always known the truth. We're better together than we are apart. As much as I want to believe that this is the moment when we fix all our problems and live life happily ever after, I know that's not how it's going to work.

What we have is going to take time. Patience. I probably need some therapy, and I'll make his well-adjusted ass go, too, just out of sheer spite. I'm going to shut him out again. He's going to overstep again. We're going to fuck this up.

And then we're going to figure out how to fix it.

Because I think maybe that's the whole point of being in love. It's not living happily ever after, but it's not accepting trampled boundaries and broken promises, either. It's something in between.

Something like hard conversations fading into heated kisses on a humid summer night, even when you don't know what the future holds.

CHAPTER 22

MARK

Lark's last horse of the sale is entering the ring, and I think I'm more nervous than she is. Nugent's first colt sold, but only just. His second has had the most interest the last two days—half of Lark's time was spent overseeing vet checks from interested buyers—but as an asshole to the bitter end, Nugent insisted on a frustratingly high reserve. Odds are, the colt will be going home and Lark will still be out of the commission, despite my ill-advised intervention the other day.

But Lark is at ease next to me as the auctioneer begins his patter. She's already informed Nugent that their contract will end after this sale, and I think part of her won't even be too disappointed if this final round of bidding doesn't go well. A few people have expressed interest in working with her in the future, including Domingo on behalf of Blue Moon Breeding. If she decides to go that route, it would make for a good pairing—Domingo would make sure she's paid well and treated fairly, and the operation being based out of Kentucky would keep them from micromanaging her.

It's a good reminder that she has a wealth of options

available to her, when she's ready for them. I'm trying not to put my finger on the scale too much; for all that I'd love to have her work more closely with Aladyne in some capacity, I want her to make the choice *she* wants more than anything.

But the job offer my family is putting together for her is going to be a damn good one, if I have anything to say about it.

I squeeze her hand as the first bids come in. So much of this sale is out of Lark's hands, but the parts she can control, she has knocked out of the park. Every single one of her horses has walked into that ring healthy, well-cared for, and groomed within an inch of their life.

If one or two of them decided to behave like chaos demons when faced with a new environment for the first time? That's between the Thoroughbreds and Satan.

As it should be.

Luckily, this final colt is representing Lark well—he's alert and spirited but well in-hand, with his dark bay coat gleaming even in the dingy lighting. The bids are steady, the price climbing at a comfortable clip. There's a brief delay a couple thousand shy of the reserve, and my tension must bleed through to Lark because this time, she's the one who squeezes *my* hand.

But the lull doesn't last long. Bidding resumes, with fewer interested parties but more intensity. It's not more than another minute before the gavel falls, even if it feels like a lifetime, and I exhale in relief at the final number.

Even with a near-irresponsible reserve price, the colt sold.

"Tonight, we celebrate," I declare, pressing a kiss to Lark's forehead. She beams up at me, pride mingling with relief and exhaustion on her face.

Because this was Lark's last horse of the sale, there's no rush for us to get back to the barn. Alicia nods to us as she grabs the colt on his way out of the ring, and I tag along with Lark as she heads to the cashier to find out who bought him.

"You've got to be fucking kidding me." Lark stops short, her attention laser-focused on the couple currently signing the purchase ticket.

Her parents.

"Do you want to leave?" I ask quietly. Technically, Lark doesn't *have* to speak with them right now. It might be common to check in with the buyer, but it's certainly not mandatory. I hesitate, unsure how my next words will be received. "I could…"

Lark offers a gentle smile when I trail off. "You could," she confirms, and I'm glad my implied offer of help didn't set off any leftover landmines between us. "But I need to get this over with."

I stay at her side as she approaches, fighting the impulse to fold her into my arms and pull her away. But Lark is steady as she nears her parents, no sign of the hurt they've caused her on display. "Mom, Dad," she greets them. "You bought the Third Rail colt?"

Levi nods sharply. "We did."

"Sight unseen? No vet checks? I'm surprised." She keeps her tone mild, but her mind has to be going a thousand miles an hour.

"Well, no," Levi replies, bristling slightly at being called out. "I had a long conversation with Jack a few days ago. He showed me the footage you sent and the latest scopes."

"Frankly," Jennifer cuts in, "we were surprised to get here today and find out Jack didn't scratch him."

I lurch forward, but Lark shifts her weight just enough to be in my way. The press of her shoulder into my chest keeps me from giving her parents another lecture.

"He was certainly considering it." Levi shrugs. "Might

have been more affordable for us had he followed through, but we'll make do."

Lark's fingers slide through mine, and I let her squeeze my hand for dear life as she fights to keep her cool. Lark's parents put her in contact with Nugent, but they still would have been perfectly content to let him cut her out of her commission.

"Besides, we get to show you our support this way." Jennifer's smile is brittle and false, undoubtedly designed to show anyone who might be listening to this conversation just how happy their little family is. "You don't have to take another horse home."

But Lark sees the lie for what it is. "We all know you would never have bought one of my horses unless you thought it was a good investment, so let's not make this a family bonding moment.

"He'll be ready to ship as soon as you can arrange it. Congratulations on your purchase." Lark nods, then pauses. "My lease ends in November. I'll vacate the cottage then, and not before. If that's not acceptable, I'll put you in touch with my lawyer."

I wait, hoping that her parents will get their respective heads out of their respective asses enough to change the trajectory they're on.

"If you insist on being stubborn," Levi sighs, "then I suppose we'll tell Gabriel he has to wait."

So much for that particular hope.

"I'll leave the keys on the counter when I move out." Lark offers a smile under glossy eyes. "If you're ever ready to apologize, you have my number."

When she turns away, she lets me wrap my arm around her. She tucks her face against my chest as we walk, vulnerable in a way that tugs at my heart. I find a quiet spot near the exit and pull her close, giving her a few moments to regain her composure. "You did good, baby," I murmur against her hair. "I'm so fucking proud of you."

"I hoped…"

She can't finish the sentence, her voice thick, but she doesn't have to. "I know. I did, too. But you aren't alone, Songbird. I won't ever let you be alone."

We stay there until she regains her composure. I'd wait with her forever, but it only take a few minutes.

My girl is strong as hell.

Maddie is lying in wait when we finally get back to the barn.

"Did he sell?" she calls from the Aladyne end.

"He sold," Lark confirms to a small cheer from the whole Aladyne team. She tries to hide her responding smile, but I see it.

I see *her*.

"Hell yeah." Maddie is careful as she comes down the barn aisle, doing her best not to disturb the newly raked dirt lest she invoke Javi's wrath. Once she reaches Lark's section—which is currently covered in footprints and hoofprints galore—she tosses her arms around my girlfriend in a congratulatory hug. When she steps back, she asks, "He told you already, didn't he?"

"Yup," I confirm, leaning back against the railing. Lark's gaze drifts over me with a smirk before pulling back to Maddie.

"He did."

"Good. I'll give you a week or so to recover, then you and I will have a chat. I'm fully prepared for you to say no, but I'm going to do what I can to make it hard on you."

Lark grins, and it's the most beautiful fucking thing. "See that you do."

We talk for a few more minutes, Lark relaxing more with every passing second, and make plans to drag the whole group—Gideon included—out to Dicks tonight to celebrate. We invite Alicia, but she begs off. Her move is approaching fast, so Lark assures her we can handle the breakdown and sends her home with a hug of her own and a promise to get drinks before she leaves town for good.

The next couple hours are an easy blur of dismantling Lark's side of the barn. The tent comes down—much easier than it went up, if my memory of watching Lark and Alicia fight with it is anything to go by—and the buckets and half-empty feed bags and grooming kits all get hauled off to her truck.

Only the colt her parents bought is left by the time we're mostly packed up. We're discussing how much hay to leave him with for the afternoon when a throat clears.

Gabriel.

His expression is hesitant but polite, a leather halter and shank in his hands. "I'm here for the Third Rail colt," he says, and I reluctantly give him credit for getting right to business.

I'm really not built for punching.

"Of course." Lark shifts into brisk efficiency. She ducks into the spare stall, returning with a sheaf of papers. "This is all the information I have on his feeding regimen and recent farrier and vet care. You'll have to coordinate with Nugent if there's anything missing."

"Appreciate that." Gabriel tucks the papers into his back pocket, following Lark to the stall. I keep my position, not wanting to interfere but needing to have an eye on the situation. It only takes a moment for Gabriel to have the colt in hand, but he pauses before exiting the stall. "Listen, Lark—"

"It's fine."

Despite Lark's abrupt cut off, Gabriel pushes on. "I just

wanted to say I didn't know you were being asked to move out. They made it seem like you had already decided to leave, so the house would be vacant. I'm fine in the barn apartment. Don't move on my account."

"Trust me, I'm not."

Gabriel opens his mouth again, but he takes in the expression on her face and seems to reconsider whatever he was about to say. "Good luck, Lark," he says instead, then leads the colt away.

I give Lark her space, focusing on removing the stall fans while letting her take down the hay bag and water bucket and clean out the final stall in peace. We make a small pile of the last pieces that we have to take out to her truck, and she slides the stall door into place with a fully body exhale. "It's done."

"You did it."

She smiles, but it pulls into something wry and knowing. "Yup. Just me. No one else."

I step up to her, bracing my arms on either side of her head. I don't miss the tick in her breathing when I press close to her, and I revel in the fact that these moments don't have an expiration date anymore. She's not pretending she doesn't care about me, not reminding me that all she promised was two weeks. She's mine, for as long as I can keep her.

I'm planning to start with forever, and see how things go from there.

"Take your credit, Songbird. Just accept the help when you need it, too."

"I'm working on it."

"I know." I kiss her, biting back a groan at the pleased gasp that fills her mouth when her lips meet mine. "Stay with me tonight?" I ask between kisses. "Start daydreaming how you want to redecorate when you move in?"

Her eyes sparkle as she squints at me. "I wasn't aware I had agreed to that."

"You haven't yet. But you will."

"Is that so?" Her fingers play with my hair. It's a little longer than I usually let it get, but if this is my reward for canceling my barber appointment for a bit more time with Lark, I'm going to be hard pressed to ever get it cut again. "You really think I'm gonna move in with you, Mark?"

"Yeah, Lark. I do."

She rolls her eyes as she always does at the reminder that our names rhyme, and I honestly can't wait to see that exact exasperation for the rest of our lives. "I'll think about it," she says eventually. "Maybe when my lease is up."

Three months. If I'm lucky, I can do it in two.

"I really am proud of you, you know." I repeat the words with one final kiss as a clattering noise nearby reminds us that we aren't alone, no matter how carried away we tend to get in this barn.

We both glance over as a ladder appears at the end of the aisle. One of the sales ground's maintenance team climbs up and starts removing the farm signs. We both watch as the Lark Sales sign comes off its hooks, and Lark accepts it from him with gentle thanks. I memorize every piece of the quiet moment, because I know watching this woman succeed will be the honor of my lifetime.

She walks back to me with her sign clutched tight in her arms and buries her face in my chest. "I love you."

"Really wish you had known that six months ago," I say with a mock-sigh, wrapping her in a tight hug.

"You're such a dick."

Her laughter is the only music I'll ever need. "I told you that day one, and you fell in love with me anyway. Sometimes I really question your judgement."

"Never mind. I'm breaking up with you."

"You can try," I tell her. "But we've already seen how well that works."

"Just say the words back, for fuck's sake."

"I love you, too, Songbird." I don't have to see the smile she hides in my chest to know it's there. "I love you, too."

EPILOGUE

LARK

"That's the last box." Mark slams his tailgate shut. "Need some time to say goodbye?"

I consider the question, staring at the cottage that I've lived in these last few years. I poke and prod at my feelings, unsure what to expect out of this moment. A sense of loss, perhaps, or even anger.

Instead, all I feel is a grounding sense of surety.

It's time to leave Landow for good.

I step inside long enough to set my keys on the counter, like I told my parents I would. We haven't talked since that encounter at the sale, and it's honestly been a relief. Without their snide comments and bitter critiques, I've found it far easier to listen to my own feelings.

For the first time, I can see that my parents were so desperate to stay locked in their past failure that they couldn't bear to see me succeed.

My therapist probably thinks he deserves some of the credit for that revelation, too, but I have to be careful not to inflate his ego too much. Can't have him getting complacent, especially with more big changes looming.

Mark is waiting when I step back onto the porch, and I walk straight into his arms after I pull the door closed. "We made some memories on this porch," he says, and I can't disagree.

"More good than bad, I think."

"All good, since they led us here."

I press up on my toes to kiss him, glad this will be our final memory here. The two of us, together.

Happy.

"Come on," I say before we can get too carried away. "Let's go home."

He grins. "I like the sound of that."

He would. It might have been his idea to have me move in, but for once, he didn't have to fight to convince me. I've slowly moved a lot of stuff over the last few weeks while we began to find our rhythm as a real couple without the relentless gauntlet of the sale to worry about. Today, we're taking everything else: a few pieces of furniture, boxes of clothes and pictures and kitchen supplies, and my mattress, because it's objectively better than Mark's.

It isn't much—we managed to fit it into a horse trailer and the back of Mark's truck—but I don't quite know where we're going to put it all. That will be our next project.

Bowen, Gideon, and Maddie are all waiting when we make it back to Aladyne, and between the five of us, it takes less than an hour to get everything unloaded. Some of the furniture gets stashed downstairs in an empty stall for now, but all the boxes make it up to the land of climate control.

"You're staying, right?" I ask Gideon when we finish up. "It's been ages since I've seen you."

The man has been hustling since the sale, picking up small one-off gigs from other farriers while he decides how he wants to replace the client he lost. I feel a twinge of guilt, knowing he and I might have to have a conversation about that soon, too, but I mostly just want him to take a break for once.

He chuckles as he stretches his back, clearly sore from the week. "I wasn't aware leaving was even an option."

"Because it's not." His dog, Angus, trundles over and drops himself down on my feet. "See? Now we're both stuck."

Except I don't get to use the pup as an excuse for long. Once the twins and Bowen come back downstairs from the apartment, we all trek across the farm to the main house. Diane and Peter insisted on feeding us lunch to celebrate my move; their kindness still catches me off guard sometimes, but you'll never see me turning down one of their home-cooked meals. Turns out, cooking is not a skill that either Mark or I have bothered to foster. I can assemble a basic lasagna, and he can grill a decent steak, but we leave it up to the professionals—or his parents—when we can.

I take a moment to check my phone as we walk, finding a text from Evangeline. We've exchanged a couple of messages since the last sale, and I took her up on her offer and had her look over my contracts, just to make sure everything was solid after the Nugent debacle. We might not be all the way to friend status yet, but I'm trying to leave the door open because I get the impression she needs good people on this side of her life.

EVANGELINE

Do you have any farrier recommendations? I need to find a new one ASAP.

I frown, worried about what that might mean, and make my way over to Gideon. "Have you decided you're ready to take on a new full-time client yet?"

He shrugs. "Why? You got one for me?"

"Maybe." I show him the text, noticing the same concern on his face that I felt when I read it. "She bought Marshmallow from me at the August sale. Not sure she's your type, but I know she's got a decent barnful."

"What does *not my type* mean? I'm looking for a client, not a date."

I cringe, knowing I'm about to ruin my sales pitch. "She's the type of client you hate. Rich girl looking to 'diversify her portfolio.'"

He eyes me. "But?"

"But she's the one who told me about Nugent, so I owe her. And I think she actually does care, even if she's an amateur. I think you'd be good for her."

"I'm not a damn mentor," he grumbles. "But fine. Send me her info. I'll call her when I leave."

"You're the best!" He shakes me off, and I text Eva back.

ME

> With my farrier now. I'll give him your info, and he'll call you when he's done here.

EVANGELINE

> Thank you so much. You're a lifesaver.

A few minutes later, we're all gathered on the back deck, Angus pleased to have lizards to chase. The temperature has a ways to go before we get to revel in our sixteen-ish hours of Florida fall, but it's far more tolerable than it was a month ago. We settle into a cluster of wooden chairs, Mark close enough to tuck his hand under my hair, his fingers gently massaging my neck, and we take advantage of the opportunity to all just hang out for the first time in a couple weeks.

Bowen grumbles as Maddie admits that her car broke down again the other day—both parts of which I've learned happen with frequency, because Maddie's car is a disaster waiting to happen and the boys hate it—and Gideon tells us about the cougar who came out to the barn in lingerie in an attempt to seduce him last month.

I'm wiping tears of laughter out of my eyes when Mark waggles his brows. "Maybe she'd have suggestions for some sexy little outfits you can wear for me when we go to Seattle."

"I think I'd rather be naked."

Maddie gags, as she does whenever our sex life comes up, but the joke catches Gideon's attention. "What's in Seattle?"

Mark winces, and for a moment, I consider dancing around the truth. It would be easy enough to do, and far simpler, given current company. But I remember the way Bowen reacted to the knowledge that Daphne was in Vancouver, and think maybe he'd want to know, even if it hurts. "Daphne's finally moving back to the States. She made me promise to go out to visit her once she gets settled in Seattle."

"Please. She invited *me*," Mark corrects, his voice light even as he carefully watches his best friend's reaction. "But I'll let you go with me."

"How magnanimous of you," I drawl.

Bowen doesn't give anything away, but when he says he needs to take a call a few minutes later, we let him escape.

"He'll be okay," Mark murmurs into my ear.

"At least he doesn't have to worry about seeing her. Nothing short of us getting married will bring her back to this town." Frankly, I'm not even sure that will be enough.

"Don't put ideas in my head, Songbird. Not unless you're ready for the consequences."

Outwardly, I roll my eyes, but inwardly, my little bunny has never been happier. I'm not ready for that yet—not when the truck engine is still warm from me moving in with him— but the idea doesn't scare me much, either.

So long as I don't kill him along the way, we'll get there.

Bowen eventually returns, helping Mark's parents bring out plates of food. I join Maddie in setting the table, and task Gideon with fetching drinks so he doesn't have to stand there looking helpless and awkward. The moment everyone is settled at the table, Diane raises a glass. "Congratulations to Mark and Lark—"

"Malarky," Maddie coughs into her hand.

Her dad hides a smile, while her mother cuts a good-natured glare in her direction before shrugging. "Congratulations to Malarky on moving in together." This time *I* glare at Maddie. The only thing worse than our names rhyming will be if that stupid portmanteau catches on. "And congratulations as well to the newest member of the Aladyne team."

Everyone clanks our glasses together, and I do my best to embrace all the emotions that come with the moment. Just as the twins warned would happen, Maddie came to me shortly after the sale with a job offer on behalf of the Aladynes. A good one, at that—one that was awfully close to that dream I once had for my future at Landow. But it was also one that meant I would once again be putting all my eggs—job, boyfriend, even housing, now—in one basket.

I called a therapist the next day.

After countless hours of conversation and negotiation, I decided that a version of Mark's so-called back-up plan made the most sense. When my barn lease ends in December, I'll move the handful of horses I have for the February sale over to Aladyne. In the meantime, I'll begin shadowing Javier in a part-time capacity as he starts to transition toward retirement.

It's the best of both worlds: I get to run another sale under my own name to see how it feels when I'm not trying simply to spite my parents, and I get to be part of a crew on a farm I respect while learning from a man with a lot to teach.

When the February sale is over, I'll decide whether to take the sales manager position here at Aladyne or to commit to making Lark Sales a recognizable name.

Mark has promised—threatened, more like—that I'm stuck with him either way.

That night, I trudge up the stairs to Mark's apartment—*our* apartment, I correct myself with a smile—eager for a shower to wash off the day's dirt and grime. For all that Mark whined about us taking the rest of the day off to properly christen the apartment, we both had plenty of real work to do today.

I missed him, though. It's still a novelty, letting myself acknowledge how much I love him, even when he's a pain in my ass.

Like when my body aches from hauling hay bales, my stomach rumbles eagerly for dinner, and I open the door to find him waiting for me in the apartment.

Naked.

Naked and leaning against the kitchen doorframe.

Still a menace to society.

"Welcome home, baby."

"Absolutely not." The words sound more convincing than they feel. I scowl, even as my tired, greedy eyes track the lines of his lean muscle down to his cock, which is rapidly thickening under my attention. "I need a shower and food before I deal with your horny ass."

"Then I have the perfect plan," he declares, that crooked grin turning heated. "I'll help you shower, make sure you get all soaped up and squeaky clean, and then I can feed you—"

"If you end that sentence with any variation of the phrase 'my dick,' I'm moving back out."

He laughs, making my heart squeeze, then turns around and walks toward the shower. "Fine, we can wait for dessert until after dinner, like the mature adults we are." He pauses in the doorway, holding out a hand. "You coming, Songbird?"

"Yeah." For once, I don't put up a fight. I take his hand, and let him pull me into our future. "I'm coming."

ACKNOWLEDGMENTS

Getting this book off my computer and into the world took the support and indulgence of far too many people. If I fail to name you here, please feel welcome to take some inspiration from Maddie and throw something soft at my head next time you see me.

I owe an immense debt to Mariko, who has read this book in every form and at every stage and talked me through countless questions and quibbles. Someday I'll learn what a plot is, I promise.

To the Planeteers—Becky, Cassie, Kendi, and Rebecca—who haven't read a bit of this book but still watched vlog after vlog of me talking about it. (Bonus points to Becky for coining 'Malarky.') To steal a line from some random band you've probably never heard of: I was born to love you.

I also owe thanks to: Emily, for being an enthusiastic reader of a rough first draft; Mary, for all the dog pictures; my beloved book club crew, especially Rebekah, Hilary, and Kelly; the rest of my grad school family, including Alyssa, Rafael, Jill, Asmaa, and Kate; and my wonderful coworkers.

Finally, this book—and, indeed, the entire series—wouldn't exist without my family and the years I spent surrounded by horses. And even though they can't read, I should probably thank my dogs Archer and Mollymauk, who each served as laptop desks on more than one occasion as I wrote. Ergonomic? No. Efficient? Definitely not. Worth it? Yeah, I think it was.

ABOUT THE AUTHOR

Gemma Brooks is a contemporary romance writer who drafts each of her books surrounded by two very nosy, very large dogs. She grew up on horse farms in Florida and still misses foaling season every spring. She now spends her working hours as an English professor in South Carolina, where she gets to read romance novels in the name of research. You can find her on social media and at Gemma BrooksBooks.com.

www.ingramcontent.com/pod-product-compliance
Lightning Source LLC
Chambersburg PA
CBHW031140160726
47991CB00004B/1505